The
Cincinnati
Red Stalkings

TROY SOOS

KENSINGTON BOOKS
Kensington Publishing Corp.

http://www.kensingtonbooks.com

KENSINGTON BOOKS are published by

Kensington Publishing Corp.
850 Third Avenue
New York, NY 10022

First Kensington Hardcover Printing: May, 1998
First Kensington Paperback Printing: May, 1999
10 9 8 7 6 5 4 3 2 1

Printed in the United States of America

Acknowledgments

I am deeply grateful to the many people who helped with this book.

I'd like to thank Kate Duffy, my editor, for her encouragement and guidance; Sara and Bob Schwager for their fine copyediting; Meredith Bernstein and Elizabeth Cavanaugh, my agents, for their continuing efforts on my behalf.

I am indebted to Darryl Brock for information on the 1869 Red Stockings, Jeffrey Marks for answering my many questions about Cincinnati, and Dave Collins for researching artifacts at the Baseball Hall of Fame. Also providing valuable research assistance were Detective Richard Gross and Specialist Cathy Boone, Cincinnati Police Department; Patricia Van Skaik and Rick Ryan, Public Library of Cincinnati and Hamilton County; Anne Shepherd, Cincinnati Historical Society Library; Debbie Mize, Seminole County Library; Jean Chapman, Society for American Baseball Research; Cindy Haigh; Greg Rhodes; Steve Cummings; Nat Rosenberg; Kate Buker; Leigh Shaheen; Naomi Diesendruck; and the staff of the Ohio Historical Society. I am grateful to all of these individuals and institutions for so generously sharing their time and expertise.

Chapter One

○ ○ ○

The old horsehide had a patina, dark amber in color, like the tint of an antique photograph. Appropriate, I thought, for this baseball was also a window to a bygone world. More than that—it was *part* of history, a relic from the days when baseball players were "ballists" and the game they played was just starting to be proclaimed "the national pastime." And it was right in front of me, inviting my touch, offering me a chance to make physical contact with another era.

I couldn't resist the invitation. I reached out . . . and as soon as the ball was in my grip, I felt myself being tugged backward in time. More than half a century dissolved, as I slipped—willingly, eagerly—back to the summer of 1869.

The sensation was familiar to me; I'd made these journeys before. I wasn't sure what it is about baseball that makes such a phenomenon possible, however. Perhaps it's because the essence of the game has changed so little over the years; boys playing ball on paved city streets do much the same as their grandfathers did when those streets were village cow paths. Or maybe because baseball history is more a collective memory than a sequence of events; stories told by old-timers, personal experiences at the ballpark, and yesterday's box scores all mingle together in one vast pool of shared experience. You can dip your foot in any part of it, stir up the mixture, and wade right into the past.

I cupped the baseball in my palm and gently ran the tip of my thumb over the scarlet stitches. Neatly lettered on the ball in dark red paint was:

Cin'ti BB Club
July 2, '69

The first all-professional team in baseball history: the Cincinnati Red Stockings of 1869. Lead by the legendary Wright brothers, manager Harry and shortstop George, that pioneering ball club traveled from coast to coast, taking on the top teams in the country and never suffering a single defeat. Their winning streak captured the fancy of the nation and helped popularize the young game. As a result, Cincinnati became to professional baseball what Kitty Hawk and those other Wright brothers were to aviation.

I turned the ball slowly, studying the discolored leather. The stains could have been sweat from the hands of George Wright himself . . . particles of earth and grass from the fabled Union Grounds . . . maybe a shot or two of tobacco juice from pitcher Asa Brainard. It was as if a foul ball batted fifty-two years ago had just come down into my hands. I imagined myself sitting in the grandstand, watching the Red Stockings take their positions on the field—

"Don't touch anything!"

The anxious yell jerked me back into the present. Once again I was in a second-floor office above the main entrance to Redland Field, home of the Queen City's current professional baseball team, the 1921 Cincinnati Reds.

"Sorry." I put the ball back down on the table, between a stack of scuffed baseball cards and a mangled catcher's mask. "Just wanted to touch it. I didn't hurt it none."

A chubby fellow of about forty-five stepped quickly into the office, swabbing his high forehead with a wadded handkerchief. He slowed down as he drew nearer, and the worried frown that crinkled his round face softened. "That's okay," he sighed. "Didn't realize it was from the discard table." His brow was already dotted with sweat again, and thinning brown hair was matted to his scalp. He reached around to mop the back of his thick neck with one hand and extended the other. "Oliver Perriman. Everybody calls me 'Ollie.' "

I returned his damp grip. "Mickey Rawlings."

"Oh yes. You're the . . ."

"Utility infielder." Over the years, I'd learned to say it with pride.

"Yes, of course." Perriman hitched his shoulders uncomfortably, then started to peel off the jacket of his tan sack suit. "Warm in here."

It was a glaring understatement. I'd been in steam baths that were cooler. Despite the sweltering summer hot spell, the office's two windows were barely cracked open. The postgame sounds from Findlay Street drifted in—vendors hawking peanuts and lemonade, trolleys squeaking their way south on Dalton, automobiles bleating their horns to disperse slow-moving pedestrians—but little air came through. A single ceiling fan was motionless, probably a precaution lest anything in the room be disturbed by the breeze that it might generate.

Perriman carried the jacket toward a massive oak desk

in the corner of the office and carefully draped it over a straight-backed chair that didn't match the desk. The two pieces of furniture were about the only standard office furnishings in the spacious room. Bookcases and tables of various woods and styles lined the walls; they held hundreds of baseballs, dozens of bats, folded uniforms, gloves, caps, catcher's gear, magazines, score books, and newspapers, all neatly arranged. Wherever shelving didn't cover the walls, team photographs and player portraits hung in close formation. One long table in the center of the room was piled less neatly; it was there that I'd found the old ball.

Perriman turned back to me. Dark crescents were visible under the arms of his blue shirt, and his yellow butterfly bow tie was wilted. "Now, then." He looked at me with big eyes that sagged at the corners like a basset hound's. "Something I can help you with?"

I thought he already knew why I'd come. "Lloyd Tinsley said you wanted a player to appear at the opening of your museum here."

"He did?" The creases in his forehead deepened. "He asked *you?*"

"Yes. Well, he asked all of us. He came into the clubhouse after the game, told us you were putting together some kind of exhibit, and said if any of us were interested, to come up and talk to you about it." Tinsley, the club's business manager, usually spoke to the players only about travel arrangements or contracts; his announcement about the museum was the first intriguing thing I'd ever heard him say.

"I thought he was going to ask Edd Roush," Perriman said with obvious disappointment. "Or Heinie Groh . . ."

I didn't feel offended; if I was in Perriman's position, I'd have preferred to have one of the team's stars, too.

"Maybe Eppa Rixey or Greasy Neale," he went on. "Larry Kopf even . . ."

Okay, now I was insulted. Before he named the bat boy, I said, "I'll see if I can talk one of them into coming," and took a couple of steps toward the door.

"No, no!" I turned back to see Perriman shake his head. "I'm sorry. Been under a lot of pressure lately." He dabbed at his throat with the handkerchief. "Lloyd Tinsley's been a bad influence on me I think—always pushing the business angle, and saying how we need publicity. Excuse me. Please. I'm really glad to have you here."

"S'okay." I returned to where Perriman was standing. "But you know, I don't think you need a player to attract a crowd. It's the history that'll draw folks in. Just looking at these photos and the uniforms . . ." I picked up a pillbox-style cap with horizontal red-and-white stripes that probably dated from the 1890s. "Brings back the stories I heard when I was a kid listening to my uncle and grandfather talk about the old days. You know, there's games I never saw myself, but I feel like I remember them better than some of the ones I played in!"

Perriman smiled broadly, and he shook my hand again. "I must say I'm delighted to meet someone else who understands!" He beamed at me for the better part of a minute, then asked, "Did Tinsley tell you what the exhibit is for?"

"Tribute to the '69 Red Stockings, he said." I gestured toward the walls. "But most of this has nothing to do with the old Red Stockings." When I'd first come into the office I'd had time to explore the room and examine some of the materials. Most were of recent vintage, and a few had little or no relation to Cincinnati baseball at all.

"Yes, I know," Perriman said. "A couple of reasons for

that. First off, even if I could acquire everything that club ever had, it wouldn't amount to as much as you might think. They didn't use gloves back then, and there were no such things as shin guards or chest protectors or even catcher's masks." He paused, then recited like a schoolboy:

> *"We used no mattress on our hands,*
> *no cage upon our face;*
> *we stood right up and caught the ball*
> *with courage and with grace.*

"That's from 'The Reds of Sixty-nine' by Harry Ellard," he explained. "Lovely poem. Been thinking I might have it printed up and give it to everyone who comes in." He touched my elbow and led me to the desk. "Now, let me show you"—his voice dropped to a conspiratorial hush— "the *treasures.*"

Several artifacts were carefully arranged on the scarred desk top. Perriman picked up a filthy lump of gum rubber. "This little mouthpiece is all the protection Doug Allison used behind the plate."

It looked disgusting enough that I might have preferred broken teeth to putting that thing in my mouth. "Nice," I said.

"This is where I keep everything from the '69 team," he said proudly. "Got some of their equipment, the score books, a few trophy balls . . ." He handed me a dingy white cap that was hard with age. "This was Asa Brainard's." It was shaped more like a golf cap, with a flatter crown and shorter visor than a modern baseball cap.

Mounted above the desk, like a rifle on a gun rack, was

a willow bat, thick and long, without much of a taper. "Whose was that?" I asked.

"Charlie Gould's." He hesitated, then offered, "Go ahead. Take a swing."

I lifted the bat from the brackets that held it, and took a couple of easy swings. As I pictured myself playing for the old Red Stockings, Perriman went on, "Only native Cincinnatian on the team, Gould was. Biggest fellow on the club, too—over six foot tall, and strong." I could tell that by the weight of his bat. "Good-fielding first baseman; called him 'the bushel basket'—and remember, there were no gloves, so it took some guts to catch a hard throw." He took the bat from me and gently put it back on its mount. "Came back in '76 to manage the club when Cincinnati was one of the charter franchises in the National League. Weren't called 'Red Stockings' anymore, though. The new name was 'Porkopolitans.' Dreadful thing to call a baseball team, but the club's owner was a meat packer who wanted to advertise his product. Well, maybe it fit—the players turned out to be as bad as the name. Finished in last place, with only nine wins on the season. Charlie Gould retired the next year and became a streetcar conductor running a trolley on the ballpark line."

I pointed to an odd metal device shaped like a large pencil sharpener. "And that?"

"Cigar cutter," he answered, handing me the object. *Red Stockings Cigars* was barely visible painted on the side, and the figure of a baseball player adorned the top. "Fred Waterman—team's third baseman—he opened a cigar store during the '69 season. Waterman was one of five paid players on the 1868 club, before the team went completely professional. Had a great throwing arm and was a solid hitter—he won the Clipper Prize that year as the best batsman in the country at his position. Speaking of the *Clipper* . . ." He directed my attention to a framed page from the *New York Clipper* hanging on the wall. Formal portraits of the Red Stockings nine were arranged in a montage. "Here they all are. And this is Waterman." He pointed to a man with a receding hairline and droopy, guileless eyes. "Called him 'Innocent Fred' because of the way he looked." It occurred to me that there was a similar innocence to Perriman's features. "Anyway, did pretty well for himself with the cigar store, stayed in business for several years."

A glass display case was on a small table next to the desk. There were four ancient baseballs in it, with dates, teams, and scores marked on them in faded paint. "And these?"

"Ah, the trophies. In those days, one baseball had to last an entire game, and the winning team got to keep the ball." I read the scores: 85–7, 63–4, 103–8, and a 40–0 shutout. "I wish I could have found more of them," Perriman said wistfully.

"What about that ball I was looking at—why isn't it with these?"

"Because it's a fake."

"Fake!" A sense of betrayal jolted me. "How do you know?"

"I'll show you." He led the way back to the center table and picked up the ball I'd been holding so reverently a short time ago. "The stitches, for one thing. They're all red."

I'd noticed the unusual color—I was accustomed to the alternating red-and-black stitching of National League balls and the red-and-blue pattern used in the American League—but assumed it had been adopted to go along with the team name. "What's wrong with that?"

"The Red Stockings used the Ellard ball, made right here in Cincinnati. It was sewn with black thread." Perriman pulled a magnifying glass from his vest pocket and unfolded the lens from its case. "And that got me to looking a little closer." He handed me the glass and pointed to a spot on the ball. "See here?"

It took a moment, but I was able to make out the faint trace of a baseball-shaped trademark stamped on the leather with the word *Spalding* on it. "It's a Spalding ball," I said.

"Yes, and Spalding didn't start making baseballs until 1876. And once he did, he used black stitches, too, up until about ten years ago. My guess is this ball was probably just used by kids, and they restitched it after the cover came off."

"A fake . . ."

Perriman shrugged. "Got to expect some chaff with the wheat, I suppose." He put the ball back on the table. "See, the other reason it was tough to acquire Red Stocking relics was because the club got rid of them all after the team broke up. Once the winning streak ended in 1870, people stopped going to the games. Two years later, the club was bankrupt and had to auction off everything from the balls to the bleacher seats—even the groundskeepers' scythes and shovels. No record of who bought what. So I cast a wide net and offered a lot of money—too much, according to my wife and Tinsley." He paced around the center table, looking over the walls packed with memorabilia. "Some took advantage. A lot of this is just old junk that people unloaded on me after clearing out their drawers and attics. I figured I'd keep some of the better material and expand the museum later. The rest I'm going to try to sell back. Kept an account of everything I bought."

"How much did this ball cost you?"

He answered promptly. "Not a penny. It was donated. By Ambrose Whitaker. I'm happy to say that some of the more civic-minded citizens, like Mr. Whitaker, preferred to share what they had rather than try to make a buck off it."

"You gonna give the ball back?" I asked.

He shook his head. "Don't want to offend him. Mr. Whitaker seemed to think it was an important item. He was the bookkeeper for the '69 club, so I had my hopes up that he'd be a good source for material."

"But he wasn't?"

"For the most part he was. Gave me some letters written by Harry Wright, and a marvelous photograph of the Red Stockings on the Forest City grounds in Cleveland—only photo I know of that shows the team on a playing field. Those were all real. But not the ball." Perriman swabbed his throat with the handkerchief. "At least that was an honest mistake. There was one fellow tried to sell me shin guards he swore were worn by Doug Allison—I told him that must have been some trick since they weren't invented till thirty years later." He chuckled at the recollection.

"When did you start collecting all this?" I asked.

"Two years ago. It was the fiftieth anniversary of the old team, and I wanted to make a display to honor them. That's when I found out everything they had was long gone."

"Well, you did a great job getting it together again. This room is going to be packed with visitors."

"Oh, this is just for storage until I get everything sorted out. Then we'll set it up in one of the concession stands downstairs. I wanted the exhibit in the library or someplace— a public area where anyone could see it. But Tinsley insisted that it be inside the park so folks will have to buy a ticket for a game. Never misses a chance to make a dime, that man."

"That's why he's the club's business manager, I expect."

"I suppose. But it's frustrating to deal with him sometimes. To me, these things are part of our heritage; to him, they're merely an attraction to get people through the turnstiles." He turned to me and smiled. "Not everybody feels the way you and I do about baseball's history."

"Yeah, I know." There were even some people who didn't care about baseball at all, past or present.

Perriman waved his hand at the discard table. "Say, these things that I'm getting rid of . . . They're nothing special— mostly duplicates of standard publications. Would you like some of them?"

"Sure!"

"Just give me a minute to mark them down." While he went to the desk I looked over the pile. It was a treasure trove of old baseball cards, programs, guides, and magazines.

He came back with a small green ledger. From under the table, he pulled out an empty wooden crate stamped *Hauck's Lager* and started filling it from the pile, periodically making notations in the ledger.

When it was filled almost to the top, Perriman said, "Here you go," and handed me the box.

"Thanks!"

He then tossed in the ball that had first caught my attention. "Might as well take this, too. I'd only be throwing it away."

I thanked him again, shifted the box under one arm to shake his hand, and started toward the door. "Oh, when is the opening going to be?"

"Not sure. I was shooting for the Fourth of July, but with

all the fuss about"—his voice faded to a whisper—"you know, the scandal ..." Back at normal volume, he concluded, "I might wait till that's all settled. And I do hope you'll be there."

"I wouldn't miss it," I said.

As I walked downstairs to the exit gate, I was thinking that it was a relief to have something to look forward to again. Recent events in baseball had been totally disheartening. The "scandal" that Perriman couldn't voice aloud had been the subject of heated debate in barbershops and hotel lobbies and Pullman cars for months. And the arguments were about to intensify: Shoeless Joe Jackson and seven of his White Sox teammates were scheduled to go on trial tomorrow in Chicago. The formal charge was conspiracy to defraud the public. What they were accused of doing was selling out to gamblers during the 1919 World Series and giving Cincinnati a tainted championship.

Some baseball people thought the trial would be healthy for the game—the accusations and evidence would all be aired in open court, and a jury would evaluate the case against the players and determine their guilt or innocence. The owners were hoping that a verdict would remove the dark cloud that hung over the game.

Myself, I wasn't so optimistic.

Chapter Two
○ ○ ○

By the time I'd trudged the three blocks south from Redland Field to Liberty Street, I was sweating more than Ollie Perriman. Cincinnati, like the rest of the Midwest, was suffering through a stubborn heat wave that showed no sign of ever lifting. My Palm Beach suit was getting damp, and the trousers starting to bind. The straw boater tilted low over my face kept the late-afternoon sun out of my eyes, but salty rivulets escaped the sweatband and trickled down my cheeks.

At Liberty, I set the crate on the ground while I waited for the next streetcar. Itching from the heat, I dug a finger behind my celluloid collar, tried to pull it a little looser, and promised myself that one of these days I would make the switch to soft-collar shirts.

In a matter of minutes, an eastbound trolley pulled up, and I paid the nickel fare. Fortunately, there were few other passengers; I was able to take a double seat for me and my load of baseball treasures.

A ruddy-faced man with a gray walrus mustache leaned

toward me, and whispered, "What I wouldn't do for a drink of that."

"Me, too," I answered, tilting the *Hauck's Lager* box enough so that he could see there were no bottles in it. Prohibition had been in effect for more than two years, and the only beer available was either home brew, bootleg, or near beer.

"Ah, that's a shame," the man said sadly, settling back in his seat. "Had my hopes up for a minute there."

I returned an apologetic smile. The thought of a cold brew stayed with me, and I soon developed an intense thirst. There's simply nothing better than a beer on a hot summer day after a ballgame. And near beer was no substitute—in my opinion, whoever gave it that name was a poor judge of distance.

I tried not to think about how parched I was, and settled back for the mile and a half journey home. Liberty Street ran all the way from Cincinnati's West End, where Redland Field was located, to Mount Adams in the East. The homes along the street ranged from neat row houses of brick and stucco to spacious wood-frame dwellings painted quiet hues of blue and yellow. Interspersed among them were modest churches and a few grocery stores and clothing shops.

Above the broad avenue, it looked as if a colossal game of cat's cradle was being played with electric wires as twine. Cincinnati had more trolley wires stretched over its streets than any city I'd ever seen. I knew that it was partly due to the Queen City's historic fondness for that mode of transportation; there were streetcars everywhere, with routes to just about any destination worth visiting. Also, someone explained to me, the trolley companies had to string double lines because residents wouldn't let the rails be used as electrical grounds—they feared electricity would contaminate the water supply.

The squealing wheels of the trolley carried us into the predominantly German community known as Over-the-Rhine, so dubbed because the area was north of where the Miami Canal used to flow. A few years ago, the canal was drained; now, some sections of it were filled in and other sections excavated, as city politicians battled over whether to construct a subway or a highway in its place. Also gone, killed by Prohibition, were the beer gardens and saloons for which the neighborhood was famous. The breweries remained, but they now produced only unpalatable near beer and kits for making home brew.

After passing through Over-the-Rhine, we reached Liberty Hill, a quiet area between Mount Adams and Mount Auburn, overlooking downtown. I hopped off the trolley at Highland Avenue and began walking in the welcome shade of the maples and locust trees that grew on the hillside. Two blocks from Liberty was home. And Margie.

Five months ago, we'd been living in Detroit with the expectation that I'd be playing another season with the Tigers. Then came the telegram informing me that I'd been traded to the Cincinnati Reds for a forty-year-old pitcher with bad knees and a dead arm—I took some consolation in the fact that there had once been a minor-league player traded for a twenty-pound turkey, so mine wasn't the least valuable trade on record. While I reported to the Reds spring-training camp in Cisco, Texas, Margie went on to Cincinnati to set up a home for us.

The narrow, two-story house she'd selected, made of red brick like most of the others in the city, came into view. As did Margie, playing hopscotch on the sidewalk with a dozen or so children from the neighborhood.

Despite the heat, and a hip injury from her days as a moving-picture serial queen, Margie was the most active participant. She threw the stone, then hopped over the chalked squares, her white middy blouse billowing and navy skirt fluttering. Her long chestnut hair, never kept under control in the best of circumstances, cascaded about her face and shoulders. There was laughter in her dark eyes and a broad smile on her tawny face.

Margie halted the game when she saw me. "Okay," she panted. "That's enough for today."

There were a few disappointed groans from the children, then all but a couple of them capered off. The two who lingered were Erin and Patrick Kelly, sister and brother twins who lived next door. They were twelve years old, and the past three of those years had been tough ones for them. Their father had been killed in the battle of St. Mihiel during the Great War, and their mother died shortly thereafter, a victim of the influenza epidemic. They now lived with a spinster aunt who worked in Procter & Gamble's Ivorydale plant during the week and liked to have her weekends undisturbed by the presence of children. So they spent much of their time with Margie, who delighted in their company.

"You win?" Margie asked. She kissed me, delaying the answer.

"No. Lost, 6–4."

"Did you . . . ?"

I shook my head. No, I hadn't played.

Patrick asked, "Whatcha got in the box?" His voice soared into a falsetto on "box," and he flushed with embarrassment.

"A whole slew of stuff—books, magazines, baseball cards . . ."

"Baseball cards! Can I see 'em?"

"Sure." I moved to set the box on the front porch.

"Let's go inside," said Margie. "There's lemonade in the refrigerator. And cookies—if Mickey's left any." She gave me her crooked little half smile to show she was only teasing.

As we walked through the door, Patrick said plaintively, "I used to have baseball cards, but my mother threw them out."

○ ○ ○

The furnishings were of Margie's choosing, too. At the front end of the long room that served as both parlor and dining room, she'd put together something like a study for me: a white oak rolltop desk, a bookcase for my baseball guides and Mark Twain collection, and a Morris chair covered in a fake leather called Marokene. In the middle of the room, was the parlor section: a plush sofa, a pair of armchairs, and a mahogany Victrola that I'd given Margie for her last birthday. Over the fireplace were photographs, knickknacks, and a bronze mantel clock. Near the kitchen was a small round dining table covered with a lace tablecloth.

As I spread the contents of the crate on the table, I asked Erin, "Would you like to see these, too?" The coltish girl shook her blond head no. I knew she wasn't a baseball fan, but she was a good kid anyway, so I wanted to make the offer.

Margie brought in three lemonades and a ginger ale for me. "Where'd you get all this?" she asked.

"There's a fellow at the ballpark putting together some

kind of exhibit about the 1869 Red Stockings. He was going to throw these out, but he gave 'em to me instead." I took a long swallow of the soda pop.

"Can we look at the scrapbook?" Erin asked Margie.

"Of course. You know where it is."

The two of them settled onto the sofa with the leather-bound scrapbook that documented Margie's years as a movie actress. It was fuller than any book I could put together on my baseball career. As Marguerite Turner, she'd made dozens of action serials, most of them involving wild animals and impossibly dangerous situations. Although a fall from a camel put an end to her movie acting, she went on to perform in vaudeville for a few years, and remained so popular that photographs of her were still advertised in the back of *Photoplay* magazine.

As the two of them went through the scrapbook, Patrick and I started exploring the materials Ollie Perriman had given me.

Besides the red-stitched baseball, there were a couple of books—one of them a slim blue volume titled *Base Ball in Cincinnati* by Harry Ellard—and dozens of programs, guides, and magazines. Perriman had also thrown in some other mementos: felt pennants, pins, and a paper fan with *I'm a Reds Fan* printed on it.

But it was the cards that caught Patrick's attention. "Are there any of the '69 Reds?" he asked.

"Don't think they had baseball cards back then." I quickly sorted through the pile; there were at least a hundred of them. "This looks like the oldest," I said, pointing to a faded pasteboard image of Tony Mullane. The card advertised Old Judge cigarettes, and had a copyright date of 1888.

"Who was he?"

A pitcher for Cincinnati, according to the caption, which I repeated to Patrick. "That's when the Reds were in the American Association, not the National League," I added. "The Association was a major league in the eighties."

"Did you play against him?"

I laughed. "I'm not *that* old. I wasn't born until 1891." I looked closer at the photo of the pitcher and some memories started to flicker. Maybe from stories my uncle told me when I was a boy, or tales spun by old coaches around the clubhouse stove, or from articles I'd read in *Baseball Magazine*. "I'm glad I *didn't* have to face him," I said. "Tony Mullane was the reason they put in the rule giving a hit batter first base. He was always plunking batters—and he enjoyed doing it." Mullane was an ornery cuss, from all I'd heard, the Ty Cobb of his day. A few more tidbits came to mind. "He could pitch with either arm. Sometimes he'd change from one batter to the next. Oh—and he was supposed to be the best-looking player in the game. Cincinnati held the first Ladies Day because Mullane had so many female admirers."

"This I have to see," said Margie. She came over and took a look at the darkly handsome man pictured on the card. Wrinkling her nose, she said, "Not my type. Mustaches tickle. Oh! I forgot the cookies."

She went to the kitchen, and I pulled out a couple more cards. "I knew *him,*" I said, pointing to a Mayo's Cut Plug Tobacco card of Arlie Latham. "He was a coach when I played for the Giants." The card showed him as a player, probably in the late 1890s. "There was a song written about him called *'The Freshest Man on Earth.'* Don't ask me why." I knew how the uninhibited Latham had earned that title, but it wasn't something I wanted to explain to a twelve-year-old. So I proceeded to another card from the same series.

"Buck Ewing here was one of the best ballplayers ever. A catcher mostly, but he could play anywhere. Good manager, too."

Margie looked at the pictures of Latham and Ewing as she put a plate of oatmeal cookies on the table. "Aren't you glad you don't have to wear a tie when you play?" The Cincinnati uniforms shown on the cards included bulky neckties and long collars.

"Sure am," I said. I would never wear the things at all, if it wasn't for the fact that a major league ballplayer has to maintain a certain image.

She returned to the sofa with a second plate of cookies for her and Erin. Patrick and I moved on to the new century, looking at cards of former Cincinnati stars like Hans Lobert and Clark Griffith, as well as those of my current teammates Edd Roush, Heinie Groh, Eppa Rixey, and Greasy Neale.

I shared much of what I knew or believed with the boy. On a number of points, I wasn't entirely certain what was history and what was myth, but in baseball, it's often impossible to distinguish between fact and fable—and there's usually no reason to do so. As my uncle used to say when I'd questioned the veracity of one of his yarns, "Well, if it didn't happen exactly that way, it should have."

The bogus 1869 baseball Perriman had given me caught my eye. Suddenly I didn't feel cheated anymore. It wasn't the inherent value of relics that mattered, but their ability to kindle memories.

I slid the entire pile of cards over to Patrick. "You can keep these," I said. "And I'll see if I can get any more for you."

"Thanks!" He squirmed in his chair like an excited puppy.

There were a million boys whose mother had thrown out their baseball cards, but few ever got them replaced.

As Patrick shuffled through his new collection, I looked through some of the other materials. I came to a single page from *Frank Leslie's Illustrated Newspaper* dated July 17, 1869. "Here's some pictures of the Red Stockings," I said. They were drawings, actually, an array of individual cameo portraits.

The man in the center was identified as *Henry Wright.* "His name was really 'Harry,' " I said to Patrick. "He was the manager. And centerfielder."

"Looks old," said the boy. The elder Wright brother's side whiskers and solemn expression did give him a mature appearance.

I pointed to the clean-shaven George Wright. "This was his brother. Best shortstop of his day. He was the star of the team."

I went around the circle of portraits, relating to Patrick the things I'd heard or read about the first professional baseball team. There was pitcher Asa Brainard, with muttonchops even bushier than Harry Wright's; catcher Doug Allison; slugging right fielder Cal McVey . . . I d gone through the team nine, and realized for the first time that there were actually ten pictures. The tenth was a drawing of a dark-haired man with a thin mustache; he was identified as *Hurley (substitute).*

"Who's he?" Patrick asked.

I struggled to remember if I'd heard anything about him. "His first name was Dick, I think. Yeah, Dick Hurley."

"What position he play?"

"Substitute. Guess he played any position they needed." Like me.

"What happened to him?"

"I don't know . . ." Did he ever play in the major leagues?

Manage? Umpire? I finally remembered what I'd been told about Hurley—or had I read it? "He disappeared," I said. "In the middle of the season."

"Where'd he disappear *to?*"

I'd never thought of that. "Disappeared" had always struck me as pretty much final. Where did things go when they disappeared? I stifled a laugh as I imagined a dark cavern deep in the earth that served as a repository for stray socks, lost marbles, and washed-up utility baseball players.

Patrick repeated the question.

Dick Hurley had been the first professional utility player. I'd often wondered what would become of *me* when my playing days were over, but never thought to find out what became of those benchwarmers who'd come before.

"What happened to him?" the boy asked once more.

I wanted the answer to that question, too. "I'll try to find out," I said.

I stepped out of the third-base dugout onto the soft green turf of Redland Field with a greater appreciation of its history than I'd ever had before.

I already knew that Redland had opened in 1912, just a week before two of the other parks I'd called home, Fenway in Boston and Detroit's Navin Field. After a late-night reading through some of the books Ollie Perriman had given me, I now also knew that this corner of Western and Findlay, once a brickyard, was the oldest continuous site of major-league baseball.

It dated back to 1884, when the Reds were an American Association club and their roster included bespectacled pitcher Will White, who three times won more than forty games a season; Bid McPhee, the finest second baseman of the last century, who played his entire eighteen-year career with Cincinnati and refused to wear a glove for more than a decade after it had come into common use; and first baseman Long John Reilly, a local boy from the city's East End, who was one of the league's most fearsome sluggers.

In 1902, with the Reds a National League team featuring such players as speedy center fielder Dummy Hoy, first baseman "Eagle Eye" Jake Beckley, and ace southpaw Noodles Hahn, the "Palace of the Fans" was unveiled. The new park included a concrete-and-iron grandstand that looked like a cross between a Greek temple and a bank building, with Corinthian columns and a host of other classical embellishments. The concrete crumbled in less than ten years, though, and the "palace" was replaced by Redland Field.

"Now or never, Rawlings!"

The yell came from Rube Marquard, once a teammate of mine on the Giants, who was pitching batting practice. Last fall, Marquard had been pitching for the Brooklyn Dodgers in the World Series against the Indians. But the Dodgers dumped him after he was arrested for trying to scalp tickets to a Cleveland police officer. So here he was, having gone from the league champions to a seventh-place ball club struggling to stay out of the cellar.

I grabbed a bat and strode up to the plate. Marquard served me a fat one right down the middle, and I hit it half a mile to left field. Even though I got all of it, the ball didn't come close to reaching the fence. Redland boasted the biggest playing field in baseball. Other parks might be deeper in one direction—like center field in the Polo Grounds—but overall nowhere were the fences farther away than in Redland: 360 feet down the left-field line, 420 to center, and 400 feet to right. The park was now in its tenth year, and it was only a week ago that our left fielder, Pat Duncan, hit the first home run to clear the wall.

Marquard kept throwing soft pitches to me, and I hit them

hard, first batting right-handed, then lefty. It felt good to be hitting a baseball again. I hadn't had a chance to do so in a game for more than a week.

I was the last one in the batting cage. After I took my licks and tossed the bat aside, groundskeeper Matty Schwab moved in to lime the batters' boxes. I watched for a few minutes as he did his magic, creating razor-sharp lines that looked like they came right off an architect's blueprint.

Schwab's handiwork was a major part of Redland's appeal. The man was an artist, using the diamond for his canvas. The edge of the outfield grass didn't make a continuous arc from first base to third; instead, Schwab had landscaped it into a scallop pattern. Sometimes he did the same with the pitcher's mound, once shaping its border like the ace of spades. He gave the outfield a distinctive touch, too, creating what he called a "terrace," an embankment that started fifteen feet in front of the fences and rose to a height of four feet at the walls. His skills went beyond what he could do with a rake and shovel; the scoreboard in left-center was of his own design and was the first in baseball to give the players' names and positions, the ball-strike count, and the scores of other games.

The beautiful grounds made a striking contrast with the neighboring factories and warehouses. Past the outfield walls, smokestacks, water tanks, and stark signs dominated the horizon. Across York Street, beyond left field, was a sign reading *The Standard Electric Tool Co.* On Western Avenue was *Jantz & Leist Electric*, and next to it, behind the right-field bleachers, was the largest building, Hulbert Hall, with a sign above it that read:

THE OLIVER SCHLEMMER CO.
Plumbing, Heating & Power Work

I considered myself fortunate that I got to play on Matty Schwab's ball field instead of working in one of those buildings.

I looked over toward the dugout. Starting pitcher Eppa Rixey, a towering lefty who'd starred in college basketball, was warming up with catcher Bubbles Hargrave. Near them, the infielders were starting a game of pepper. I grabbed my mitt and ran to join in.

Veteran first baseman Jake Daubert batted, rapping sharp grounders that we scooped up and pitched back to him for the next swing. The three players with me were a talented bunch, but not terribly solid—which gave me a fair amount of playing time. Heinie Groh had given me the chance to play regularly during the early part of the season, when he tried to set a record for the longest holdout by a National League third baseman. Shortstop Larry Kopf was barely batting .200 and had slowed down considerably in the field. Cocky young rookie Curt Stram had the talent to be one of the best second basemen in the league, but his fondness for the nightlife often left him unable to play the next day.

After the pepper, I was about to head into the dugout when I spotted Dave Claxton hitting fungoes to the outfielders. The wiry old coach was an institution in Cincinnati baseball, having played or coached here since the 1880s.

I walked up to him as he hit a fly to Rube Bressler. "Say, Clax," I said, "You go back a ways, right?"

"Am I old?" he snapped. "Is that what you're asking, if I'm old? Take a look at me, boy—the answer's yes. So what of it?"

I'd caught him in one of his better moods. "I was wondering if you knew another fellow played for Cincinnati some years back. Dick Hurley—was with the '69 Red Stockings."

Claxton grunted as he hit one to Greasy Neale. "Ain't *that* damn old. Wasn't but a boy in '69."

"I was just curious if you ever heard what happened to him."

He handed me the bat. "Here. You hit 'em a few." With a dour smile, he added, "At my age, I got to save my strength, you know." I took the fungo bat and hit a pop-up to Bressler. The coach went on, "Don't think I ever heard what become of Hurley. I remember when he disappeared there was some talk, but I don't know where he ended up."

"What kind of talk?"

"Well, I was about eleven at the time, and like most boys that summer I followed the Red Stockings pretty close. None of us could ever understand why Hurley left the club in mid-season. He was with the most famous team in baseball— why would he give that up?" Claxton took the throw from Bressler and flipped me the ball. "Anyway, the story going around was that it had to do with a girl."

I hit another that Edd Roush and Neale let drop between them. "What girl?"

"Hell, I dunno if there even *was* a girl. Maybe it was just some way to make sense of him leaving like he did. There a reason you want to know?"

"Not really. Saw a picture of him yesterday and got to wondering is all."

Roush complained loudly about making him run too far on the next hit, and Claxton took over again. I didn't get another chance to hit for the rest of the day.

O O O

The door to Oliver Perriman's office was half-open. I was one step inside when I saw that Perriman already had a visitor— and it wasn't a friendly one.

"How long you going to drag this out, Ollie?" Lloyd Tinsley demanded. "Figure out how you want to display this crap, and do it!" He slammed his palm on the center table, causing a bat to roll off onto the floor. Perriman quickly bent and scooped up the bat, cradling it like a baby that had fallen from its crib.

I started to retreat from the doorway when the Reds' business manager spotted me. "Rawlings," Tinsley said. "Come in. We're just having a little discussion about scheduling."

Tinsley was about fifty years old, with short salt-and-pepper hair that was mostly salt. His face matched descriptions that I'd read of Piltdown man—an otherwise normal head, but with an apelike jaw and large prominent teeth. His quiet pin-striped business suit covered a physique as powerful as his jaw.

While Tinsley appeared impervious to the sweltering atmosphere in the room, Perriman wasn't faring so well. Sweat beaded his forehead and ran down his cheeks. His jacket was off, and his shirt stuck to his broad body in several places. He smiled at me, looking relieved that his "discussion" with Tinsley had been interrupted.

I'd stopped in to see if I could get a few more cards for Patrick Kelly, but didn't want to ask in front of Tinsley. "I, uh, I just came by to see if there was any word on when the opening was going to be."

"That's what we were discussing," Tinsley said, turning to Perriman. "It's going to be *soon,* right Oliver?"

Perriman pulled a crumpled handkerchief from his trouser pocket and ran it over his face. "Yes, Lloyd. Just give me a few more days, and we'll set a date."

"Give me a firm date by tomorrow afternoon. Or I'll set it myself."

Perriman nodded weakly. "I'll work through the night."

Tinsley smiled—which was a frightening sight with those teeth. "Good. We understand each other then." He checked his gold pocket watch and snapped it shut. "Well, I have to go—giving a speech to an Elks lodge." He then straightened the perfectly straight knot of his burgundy silk tie and stepped past me toward the door. "Fine game today, Rawlings."

"Thank you." I'd had nothing to do with our 3–1 win, but perhaps Tinsley didn't know that; I had the feeling he spent more time with accounting books than box scores.

Perriman's face visibly relaxed when Tinsley's footsteps faded down the hall.

"Sorry," I said. "Guess I came at a bad time."

"No, not at all. It was like Mr. Tinsley said, just a business discussion."

"He sounded pretty peeved."

Perriman gave me a broad wink. "You should have been here at the start of the discussion. That's when *I* was peeved." He reached for a copy of the *Enquirer* that was on the table. "Look at what he put in the paper." The newspaper was folded back to an item in the Amusements section: *Baseball Museum to Open Soon.*

"Isn't that good?" I asked. "Don't you want publicity?"

He sighed. "Not when I'm not ready for it. There's too much material that still has to be sorted and authenticated.

And I have to figure out *how* it should be displayed. Can't just pile it all on a table—the exhibit has to be arranged properly, and I have to write up cards explaining each piece."

I had the impression that Perriman might have grown a little too fond of his collection and simply didn't want to relinquish it to public view.

"Oh! Come look!" He started toward the desk, beckoning me to follow. "Got a couple new items I think you'll appreciate."

On the wall next to the desk hung a neatly pressed white flannel jersey with a crimson old English "C" on the front. "Is this—?"

"Yes," Perriman said, beaming. He took the hanger that held the shirt down from its peg. "And I know it's authentic. Cal McVey sent it to me himself."

"He's still alive?"

"Living in San Francisco, a night watchman in a lumberyard. He was the youngest on the club, only eighteen. Came over from the Indianapolis Actives to play right field." He ran a finger over the "C" on the shirt. "My, but I'm glad to have this. You know, if I wasn't worried about tearing it, I'd have tried it on!"

"It's wonderful," I said. The old uniform looked too stiff to move around in, but I thought that might have been because of age; from the scores the Red Stockings ran up, they must have been able to run around just fine.

He hung the jersey back up, then reached to the wall under the Charlie Gould bat, and took down a small walnut frame that held two large medals pinned to a piece of green velvet. "These are both solid gold. Came today on loan from George Wright—he's the only other one of the Red Stockings still alive."

Perriman pointed to the one on the left, a fairly plain disk attached to a red ribbon. "This was given to Harry Wright by the Union Cricket Club in '66, before the club took up baseball. He was champion bowler and instructor." The other medal, with a striped ribbon, had a starburst pattern that reminded me of a French Croix de Guerre that I'd seen during the war, but with crossed bats instead of swords. "This is the Clipper Prize awarded to George Wright in 1868—he was playing in New York that year, with the Morrisanias." He put the display back on the wall. "Well, I better get to work. Especially since Tinsley doubled the amount I have to do."

"Doubled?"

"Yes. He doesn't want the exhibit to honor only the 1869 club, he's insisting that I put together something to commemorate the 1919 championship. Says the White Sox shouldn't be getting all the publicity. We should let people know about the team that *won* the championship."

"Sounds like a good idea to me." The Reds were sometimes scorned as having been "given" the World Series. I thought they deserved to be treated as champions. Especially since it didn't look likely that the city would have another championship anytime soon; the Reds had dropped to third place last year, and this season only the Philadelphia Phillies were below us in the standings.

"Oh, I have no quarrel with the idea, just the work that's involved."

"Why do you have to put everything out at once? Why not make a nice display of the '69 team to start with, then later you can add things or change things around? That way people will keep coming back to see the new displays."

"Huh." Perriman looked thoughtful. "You know, that's

not a bad idea. I'm surprised Tinsley didn't think of it—he always has some gimmick or another to boost business."

"Isn't that what he's supposed to do?" Overall, I'd had few dealings with Tinsley. His job as the team's business manager was to take care of the routine operations, like arranging our road trips and publicizing our home games. As far as I could tell, Tinsley was good at his job; the team stayed in decent hotels, paychecks were issued on time, and everything at Redland Field seemed to function smoothly.

"Yes, yes, of course. I probably need his skills. Lord knows I haven't any business sense of my own. If I did, I wouldn't have put so much money into something like this." He ran the handkerchief over his sweating upper lip. "I've had offers to sell the collection, but I can't bear to do it. I was lucky that Tinsley decided to become my partner in this. Now I better just hope that he can really bring people in to see the exhibit. Only way I might get some of the money back."

"You're going to charge admission?"

"I'd have preferred not to. I never wanted this to be a money-making venture—all I wanted to do was honor the old Red Stockings. Tinsley convinced me that a nominal admission fee wouldn't be inappropiate, however."

I wondered how much of that fee would end up in Tinsley's pocket.

"Well, I suppose I'm going to have another late night here," Perriman said. "Better call my wife and let her know. You married, Rawlings?"

"No, but I have a . . ." The common expression for Margie's and my living arrangement was "light housekeeping," but I didn't care for that term. "It's almost like . . . Well, we're keeping company . . ."

Perriman's droopy eyes perked up. "Yes, I understand."
"And I guess I better be getting home to her," I said.

○ ○ ○

It wasn't until I was on the trolley home that I realized I'd forgotten to ask Perriman for more baseball cards. My thoughts were occupied with Margie and the status of our . . . whatever it was called.

We'd been sharing a home for less than a year, a situation frowned upon by proper society but not unusual for ballplayers or people in show business. Although living together felt comfortable and natural to Margie and me, it also seemed transient. Neither of us talked about whether or not we'd be together next year.

Perhaps it was in our backgrounds. Both of us had been on our own since an early age, and we both ended up in careers where uncertainty was the only constant. Margie never knew where her next movie would be shot, or how long a vaudeville run would last in a given town. I never knew what team I'd be playing with next. Even while we'd been together, there was an unsettled quality to our lives; I'd been away at spring training while Margie set up house in Cincinnati, and now that the season was under way I spent half of it on road trips.

Be nice if things could be more permanent, I thought . . . and it would sure make it easier to answer questions like the one Ollie Perriman had asked me.

When I entered the house, I was greeted by a familiar aroma: burgoo. The spicy stew was especially popular across the river in Kentucky. Margie had discovered it in the spring, and ever since then she'd been cooking batches of it, varying the meats and vegetables like a chemist developing a new soap at Procter & Gamble.

"Smells good!" I hollered toward the kitchen.

"You hear the news?" she called back.

I crossed the dining area and saw Margie stirring a large black kettle; her hair was pasted onto her forehead with sweat. "No, what news?"

"The trial's been postponed. It's in the afternoon paper."

I grunted and looked down into the pot. "What did you put in it this time?" The trial of the White Sox players wasn't something I wanted to hear about. It was an aftermath, as far as I was concerned. The case was settled for me when Joe Jackson confessed to a grand jury last September that he had accepted $5,000 from gamblers to throw the World Series.

"It's a surprise," Margie answered.

I then set the table, poured the ginger ales, and cut a loaf of rye bread. By the time we sat down to eat, I was ravenous.

"This is good," I said, after the first mouthful. "There's no possum in it, is there?" That was the main ingredient of her last batch.

"No, mutton mostly." She smiled. "And a dash of squirrel."

At least she hadn't tried eye-of-newt yet. "Did you have the kids over today?" I asked.

"Took them to see *Peck's Bad Boy* again at the Orpheum. You know, you made quite an impression on Patrick. He brought those baseball cards along and repeated the stories you told him about the players. Sounded like he memorized every word you said."

"Really? I thought I might have talked too much and

started boring him." That reminded me—I'd also forgotten to ask Perriman if he knew what happened to Dick Hurley.

Margie shook her head. "Not at all. He was thrilled." After swallowing a bite of stew, she added, "And you should have seen *your* face when you were talking with him. I could tell you really liked it. You'd be a good teacher."

It had been fun sharing what I knew with the boy. "My uncle used to tell me stories like those all the time," I said. "And he always seemed to enjoy the telling as much as I enjoyed the listening. He took satisfaction in it, like he was passing on a family heritage or something." I put my fork down. "I don't know what it is about baseball, and history . . . But it was always something my uncle and I could talk about, no matter what else happened."

"You ever think about having a boy of your own?" Margie asked.

No quick answer came to mind, so I went for another piece of mutton, which I chewed until it was almost liquid. "Someday, I suppose."

After a minute's silence, Margie said, "Well, speaking about teaching . . . you remember I took the kids to the zoo last week?"

"When the sea lion spit up on Erin?"

She laughed. "Yes. I don't think she'll be going near the sea-lion basin again! Anyway, when we were there, I talked to one of the trainers who handles the big cats. He remembered me from my pictures. And today I got a call from Sol Stephan—he's the zoo superintendent. He offered me a job."

"Doing what?"

"Giving talks about the animals, mostly to children. Mr. Stephan said he thought it would attract some publicity by having a former movie actress there, especially since most of my pictures involved animals."

My first reaction was that it would be good for her to get a job here, because she might feel more settled and more likely to stay. "It sounds like fun," I said. "Are you going to take it?"

"I already told him yes. I start after the Fourth of July."

"You'll do great," I said. Then I began to worry that she might find she really wanted to perform again. What if she decided to go back to vaudeville or making movies?

I didn't detect much flavor in the rest of the meal.

Chapter Four

○ ○ ○

"**R**awlings!" Pat Moran barked. "Yer up for Stram."

I bolted from the bench and grabbed my bat from where it lay in front of the dugout.

It was bottom of the ninth inning, tie score, runner on first, one out. And the manager was calling on *me* to do the job.

Curt Stram didn't like being pulled from the game. As I passed him on my way to the plate, he muttered, "Reckon old Whiskey Face is givin' up on this one."

"Watch and learn, busher," I said.

I approached the batter's box, my attention shifting from Stram to Phillies' pitcher Specs Meadows. It was disconcerting to face a hurler wearing thick eyeglasses—what if he couldn't see the difference between the catcher's mitt and my head?—but I dug in my spikes and choked up on the bat. I felt no extra pressure at being called on to pinch-hit; actually it gave me added confidence knowing that Moran thought he could count on me to come through for him. I looked to the third-base coach for the sign, though I already knew what it would be. Meadows knew, too. Hell, every one of the twenty-some thousand fans who'd come to Redland Field for the final game against Philadelphia must have known what was coming.

Greasy Neale took a cautious lead off first base. Meadows went into his motion and served up a fastball, high and tight. He wasn't going to make it easy for me. I laid off the pitch for ball one. His second delivery was a sharp curve, low and away; again I held back. Two balls, no strikes. Meadows couldn't risk walking me, so I figured the next pitch would be in the strike zone.

Fastball, right down the middle. I slid my right hand up the barrel of the bat and squared around, dropping a perfect bunt toward third base. It was a sacrifice, intended only to move Neale into scoring position, but I sprinted for first base with all the energy my legs could muster. Never know—a bobble fielding the ball, a throw in the dirt, and maybe I could beat it out.

Two steps from the base, I knew the throw wasn't headed for the dirt. I felt the baseball bang into my right shoulder blade, then saw it from the corner of my eye as it rolled into foul territory.

Both base coaches were yelling, "Go! Go!" and Neale and I kept running. By the time the Phillies' first baseman retrieved the ball, Neale was on third base and I was safely on second. As far as I was concerned, that bunt was as good as a home run—better, in a way, because it was the right strategy for the situation, and I'd executed the play as well as anyone could.

Most of the fans were on their feet when Edd Roush calmly stepped up to bat. Specs Meadows tried to avoid giving Roush anything hittable, throwing three straight balls nowhere near the strike zone. Then he put one a little too close to the plate, and the two-time batting champion reached out and smacked a line drive that dropped into center field. Greasy Neale scored the winning run, and I trotted off to join my cheering teammates in front of the dugout.

Pat Moran clapped me on the back. "Way to go, Mick."

A smirking Curt Stram needled me, "You run pretty good for an old codger."

I tried to hold back a laugh; it was only a few years ago that I thought a player pushing thirty years old was a "codger," too. "Beat you around the basepaths anytime you want to take me on," I said.

A uniformed usher with white hair worked his way through the ballplayers and stepped in front of me. "Mr. Rawlings," he said. "Some gentlemen want to speak with you." He nodded toward the box seats next to the dugout.

The Reds' president, Garry Herrmann, was there, along with two police officers standing straight and stiff. From their expressions, I was pretty sure they weren't there to compliment me on my bunting skills.

"What happened?" I asked.

The usher hesitated, perhaps unsure if he was supposed to tell me. "There's been a death," he said.

"Who?"

He put his fist in front of his mouth as if covering up a cough. "That fellow who was putting together the museum. Oliver Perriman."

OOO

I wasn't allowed time to change out of my uniform, so I was still wearing my white flannels and holding my spikes in my hands to avoid marring the floors of Redland's administrative offices. I padded along the hallway in my red-stocking feet, escorted by Herrmann and the patrolmen.

The club president said nothing to me directly. He repeatedly muttered to himself, "Terrible thing. Terrible." I knew that the fun-loving Herrmann, for whom every day was Oktoberfest, didn't like problems.

When we reached Perriman's office, I was relieved to see that his corpse wasn't in the room. There were four more uniformed police officers and two other men: Lloyd Tinsley and a tall man in a wrinkled suit who was questioning the business manager and writing in a little black notebook. From his manner, I had no doubt that he was also with the police department.

The two officers who'd accompanied me joined the other four standing idly by the windows. They were wide-open, and the ceiling fan was turning at full speed. There was no longer much worry about anything being disturbed by the breeze. Although the shelves and tables were still overflowing with Perriman's relics, there was no longer an order to them; bats and balls were scattered on the floor, and the neat stacks of guides and magazines had been toppled. I wondered if an intruder had made the mess or if the police had been searching for evidence.

I looked over toward Perriman's desk. The drawers were open, and his chair was turned around to face the middle of the room.

Then my gaze dropped, and what I saw on the floor next to the chair made my stomach lurch. A reddish brown splotch, about the size of a pancake, darkened the beige carpet. It was as if Ollie Perriman had melted away into a little puddle, and that crust of dried blood was the only remaining evidence of his existence.

The plainclothes officer finished with Tinsley and came to where I was waiting. His suit was a shade of drab between tan and gray, and the complexion of his stolid, thin face was almost a perfect match. "I'm Detective Forsch," he said. A lit cigarette dangled precariously on his lip.

"Mickey Rawlings." I reflexively stuck out my hand.

"I know." He turned to a new page in his notebook, ignoring the offered handshake. There was a bored look in his pale eyes.

I moved my hand and pointed to the stain on the rug. "Is that . . . ?"

"Yes. Tell me—"

"What happened?"

"That's what we're here to find out." Forsch gave me a pointed look. "I have some questions for you now, if you don't mind answering."

Right. I was here to answer questions, not ask them. "Uh, sure. But I don't know what I can tell you."

"For starters, Mr. Tinsley tells me you were in here yesterday afternoon."

I shot a glance at Tinsley. It felt like he'd ratted on me, though I knew it was perfectly reasonable for him to tell the police I'd been in the office. "Yes, after the game. Not for long, though. I was home by six, and I stayed there all night."

Forsch stopped writing and his eyes fixed on mine for a moment. "Is there some reason you feel you need an alibi?"

"No, I— It's just—" Don't get defensive, I told myself. Just because I'd had a few bad experiences with law enforcement in the past, there was no reason to assume the worst about this cop. "I only wanted to say that I didn't see Perriman at all after I left here about five-thirty."

"What did the two of you talk about?"

"Well, when I first came in, Mr. Tinsley was here, too. Him and Mr. Perriman were talking about the opening of the museum." I briefly wondered if I should mention that it had sounded like more of an argument than a discussion, but decided not to. "Then he left, and I asked Perriman how the exhibit was coming—I'm supposed to be there when they have the grand opening."

"Why?"

"Why what?"

"Why are you supposed to be at the opening? Were you a friend of Perriman's?"

"Not really. Well, maybe we'd have become friends—I think we would have—but I only met him twice before he . . ." My attention strayed to the bloodstain on the floor.

"So why were you going to be at the opening?" Forsch prodded.

"Oh. Mr. Tinsley wanted somebody from the team to be there. For publicity."

"And they picked *you?*"

I ignored the note of incredulity in Forsch's question. "I volunteered. Mr. Tinsley asked for players who might be interested. Guess I was the only one."

We were interrupted by two more cops, one of them with sergeant's stripes, entering the office. Forsch stepped aside to talk with them. There were enough officers in the room to fend off an invasion, but they didn't seem to be doing much in the way of investigating.

I turned to look at Tinsley and Herrmann. They stood huddled together near the desk but standing well clear of the blood spot on the rug. The two were an odd match. Garry Herrmann, his short, portly body a testament to his patronage of Cincinnati's sausage makers and breweries, wore a bright green-checked suit, and diamond rings glittered from the fingers of both hands. He was visibly agitated, and Lloyd Tinsley, more sober in both appearance and manner, appeared to be trying to calm him.

Having finished with the officers, Forsch directed his attention back to me. "Let's see, where were we ..." He made a quick check of his notes. "When you spoke with Perriman yesterday, did you notice anything unusual?"

"Like what?"

"Did he say anything about being in danger? Did he seem scared, nervous?"

"Only about getting the exhibit open soon. Said he was going to work late and try to get things in order."

"Did he say how much the collection was worth?"

"Not specifically. Told me he spent more money than he should have for some of this stuff, but didn't say exactly how much. Mr. Tinsley would probably know that better than me. Or Mrs. Perriman. He said his wife wasn't happy about how much he was spending."

"Did he say if any items had been lost or stolen in the past?"

"No ... but you can check his book. He had a list of everything in the collection."

"Yes, Mr. Tinsley has been reviewing that for us."

Forsch then took my home address and phone number in case he had additional questions later.

When he flicked his notebook closed, I pointed again at the bloodstain. "How did—?"

With a heavy sigh to show that he didn't really have to

answer any questions of mine, the detective said, "Shot. Bullet to the head."

"But *why?*"

"Well, I'm just making a wild guess here," Forsch said facetiously, "but this is a museum . . . a lot of valuable items . . . the shooting happened around midnight . . . In my professional judgment, I'd say he was likely killed in an attempted robbery."

"So you think—"

"Thanks for coming in. If I have any more questions for you, I'll be in touch."

I was dismissed. But instead of leaving the office directly, I went over to Herrmann and Tinsley. "The detective says he's finished with me. Anything you need me for?"

Herrmann shook his head. "No, no, you go shower now."

I hesitated a moment, unable to keep from staring down at the carpet again. Yesterday, Ollie Perriman had been standing here, alive, enthusiastic about his latest treasures. And now he was dead, killed on almost the exact spot where I'd last seen him.

As for those treasures, I saw that Charlie Gould's bat was still on its rack above the desk, and the trophy balls were in their case. Cal McVey's uniform jersey was on the wall—but I noticed that the bottom of it had been scorched; there was a burn mark on it about the size of my hand. If Perriman was killed in a robbery, why had those things been left at all— surely they were among the most valuable in the collection.

I turned to go, then shot a quick glance at the wall below Gould's bat. Harry and George Wright's gold medals were still there. Helluva thief, I thought, who'd pass those up.

Chapter Five

ooo

I fanned myself with an unused 1913 Cincinnati Reds score-card, trying to stir up the warm, humid air that hovered in the parlor. The resulting breeze was too weak to prevent sweat from trickling down my face and splashing onto the pages of the *Baseball Magazine* I was leafing through.

It was an hour or two after midnight, and I was alone, seated at my desk, where I'd stacked the publications Ollie Perriman had given me. I was in my summer underwear—a sleeveless nainsook shirt and knee-length drawers—but neither the light clothing nor the open windows could alleviate the oppressive heat. I found the quiet of the night peaceful and calming though. The only sound was the sporadic thwack of a moth bumping into the window screen; it was attracted by the glow from the brass lamp on the desk's top shelf.

A light footstep fell behind me, and I swiveled around in my chair to see Margie coming down the stairs, tying the sash of her red floral kimono. Her tread was somewhat unsteady, and her eyes were puffy.

"Can't sleep?" she asked in a drowsy voice.

"Can't stop thinking about Ollie Perriman getting killed." I shifted in my chair, carefully peeling my posterior off the leather cushion as I moved.

"It's awful what happened," Margie said soothingly, "but staying up and fretting won't change things. Come back to bed, get some sleep, you'll feel better in the morning."

"Something about it doesn't feel right," I said. "I don't think this was a simple robbery gone bad."

Margie let out a long breath, then sat down on the sofa and tucked her legs under her. "Why not?"

"Because there were valuable things left behind." I stuck the scorecard in the magazine to mark my place and set it down. "A couple of big gold medals were hanging on the wall right above Perriman's desk. No thief could have missed seeing them. So why didn't he take them?"

"Maybe he thought they'd be too easy to trace?"

"Could melt them down and sell them for the gold."

"Well . . ." The muscles in Margie's neck strained as she stifled a yawn. "Maybe he got scared after the shooting and ran out."

"Could be. But I don't think it happened like that. The blood on the floor was by the desk—in a corner away from the door. So I don't think Perriman walked in and surprised the robber. And if the killer walked in and shot Perriman where he sat, why rummage through the shelves and drawers afterward, but not take the medals?"

"I don't know," she answered with a note of finality. "But I do know that reading all night isn't going to help anything. How about if I get you some warm milk and cookies and then you try to go back to sleep?"

"I'm not reading. I'm looking."

"For what?"

"Not sure . . ." I'd been trying to imagine what the man who killed Ollie Perriman could possibly have been after. "It seems to me like the thief was looking for something specific, not just something he could fence for a few bucks. And from what I saw, it didn't appear that much, if anything, had been taken. So . . . I got to wondering: what if he was after something Perriman had given me? What if it's here?"

"Oh!" Margie sat up a little straighter and her eyes opened a notch wider. "But that's just a pile of . . . What could be valuable in there?"

"I can't imagine." These things were interesting to me, and they were rich with memories and history, but were they valuable in the sense of being worth stealing—worth killing somebody over? "But I want to see."

"And if you find something?"

"I'll turn it over to the police. Maybe they can figure out who would have wanted it badly enough to kill for."

"Good. Let the police handle it." Margie relaxed a bit. "You know . . . it could be that the robber did find what he was looking for in the office. Maybe it just wasn't one of the things *you* thought were valuable. Never know what's important to someone else."

"You could be right."

"Good. Coming to bed then?"

"No, I'm going to go through the rest of this stuff."

Margie began to point out how stubborn I was, then she emitted a yawn that could have sounded the way for a barge on the Ohio River. "Well, I have to go to the zoo tomorrow to talk to Mr. Stephan about that job. I'm going back to sleep." She pulled herself up from the sofa and stretched. When she finished, her kimono was partly open.

I had a brief notion to put off going through the rest of

the items until morning. No, it would nag at me all night. As Margie started for the staircase, I reached for the *Baseball Magazine*.

She paused on the second step. "You're *not* going to get involved in this, right?"

"No, I promise."

○ ○ ○

Detective Forsch stubbed out his cigarette, adding the butt to an already full ashtray. "Thank you for coming in, Mr. Rawlings."

"Glad to," I said, although I really wasn't. I'd finally gone to bed shortly before dawn, having found nothing of value in the materials Ollie Perriman had given me. A few hours later, I was awakened by Forsch's phone call. He asked me to meet with him at police headquarters, and since I could think of no way to refuse, I was soon on a streetcar headed downtown.

City hall, a towering stone block structure that took up the entire block of Plum Street from Eighth to Ninth, looked more like a cathedral than a municipal building. There were even stained-glass windows depicting scenes of early Cincinnati. Inside, stunning murals covered the lobby walls, and the flooring was of decorative tiles. The opulence didn't extend to the offices of the Crime Bureau, however. Detective Forsch and I sat in a windowless interview room on the building's east side, with a plain pine table between us.

On the table were a green ledger book that I recognized as Ollie Perriman's, a pack of Murads, and the ashtray, which was made from a brass artillery-shell casing. Forsch pulled a fresh cigarette from the pack, and methodically lit up. The detective was either wearing the same clothes he'd had on in Perriman's office or an identical suit in the identical shade of drab, perhaps a plainclothes version of a uniform. Standing inside the doorway of the room was a beefy young man in the more recognizable uniform of navy blue flannel and brass buttons.

Forsch said nothing while enjoying the first few drags on the cigarette. I thought he might be trying to unnerve me by taking so long. He probably didn't know that this wasn't my first time in a police interview. "Got to be at the park for batting practice in an hour," I said.

The detective's gray eyes glittered momentarily, as if getting me to speak first was some kind of victory for him. "Wouldn't want the team to be without your talents," he said.

I tried to remember what I might have done to get on this man's bad side; if I had done anything, it eluded me.

He opened the ledger. "Mr. Tinsley has completed an inventory of the collection, comparing everything in the office to Perriman's entries in this book—and it turns out a number of items are missing."

Huh. So it *was* a robbery. I found myself disappointed that Forsch had been right.

The detective turned the book to me and pointed to one of the lines. "And every item that's missing has your name written next to it."

I read one of the entries: *Ellard's BB in Cin.*, acquired from *Anon*. who'd donated it. Written in the margin was *Rawlings*. There were similar entries for the guides and other materials now in my parlor. "Perriman gave me these things," I explained. "He kept a record of everything in the collection, and I guess he wanted to keep track of where they went."

"*Gave* them to you?"

"Yes. They weren't worth anything. Mostly duplicates of things he already had, and he was going to throw them out otherwise. I can show you the stuff if you want."

"That won't be necessary. Mr. Tinsley has already confirmed that the missing items weren't of any value."

I was thinking to myself that this meant all the mementos in Perriman's collection were accounted for—they were either still at the ballpark or at my house. So the killer didn't find what he was looking for.

Forsch exhaled a stream of smoke. "You didn't by any chance tell anybody about what was in the office, did you?"

"I probably did. There wasn't any secret about it. Hell, Lloyd Tinsley was already starting to publicize what was going to be in the exhibit."

"Yes, I know. Might have led somebody to think there was something valuable in there."

I recalled the announcement that had appeared in the paper the day before Perriman was killed. "Long-lost treasures" was one of the phrases that had been used to describe the collection. "I suppose it might have."

"Somebody who knew his way around the ballpark," Forsch said.

"What do you mean?"

"No sign of a break-in. How'd the killer get in? And how'd he know where the things were kept?"

"Well . . ."

"Unless it was somebody who'd been there before. Or somebody who'd been told where to go."

That's what Forsch was getting at: that I was in cahoots with somebody to steal the collection. "As far as getting into a ballpark," I answered, "just about any ten-year-old kid can find a way to sneak in. And it happened the night after a game; anybody in the park that day could have hidden inside and waited until nighttime. As far as the robber knowing to go to the office, where else would things like that be stored but somewhere in the administrative area? And both times I went to Perriman's office, the door was open—maybe he kept it unlocked when he was working there."

"So you knew the door was kept open." Implying that I could have relayed that piece of information to an accomplice, too.

"Yeah, I did. But you know, if I told somebody what was in the room to help them steal it, they'd have taken it."

Forsch stubbed out his cigarette. From the look on his face, whatever half-baked theory he might have been entertaining about me being involved was also extinguished.

Judging by his questioning of me, his investigation wasn't amounting to much, and I didn't have a lot of confidence that it ever would. But in case it could turn out to be of some help, I said, "There's something I noticed when I went to the office to talk to you yesterday."

"And what's that?"

"One of the uniforms was partly burned. Maybe whoever killed Perriman tried to set the place on fire to cover it up."

Forsch grunted. "You been reading the papers too much."

The front pages of the last few days had been filled with stories and photographs of a massacre in Mayfield, Kentucky—a family of eleven had been murdered and their house burned down to try to cover up the killings. "Yeah, I read the papers. But I also know what I saw. The day before he was killed, Perriman showed me a uniform jersey he'd just gotten. It was from Cal McVey, who wore it when he was with the '69 Red Stockings. I *know* there weren't any burn marks when Perriman showed it to me. But when I saw it yesterday, it was burned."

Forsch reached for the Murads. "Maybe it was an accident. You should hear how the wife yells at me about holes in my clothes." He then stuck another cigarette in his mouth and lit up.

"It wasn't a cigarette hole," I said. "Anyway, just thought you might want to consider it."

"Consider it?" Forsch's eyes narrowed. "I got to answer to Lloyd Tinsley, I'm getting pressure from Garry Herrmann's pals upstairs, and now I got a goddamn ballplayer—and a lousy one at that—telling me how to do an investigation?"

At least now I knew why Forsch had been so hostile to me: my bosses were giving him a hard time, so he was going to give some of it back to one of their employees. I said calmly, "It was just something I noticed, and I thought I should report it to you."

"Fine, fine. Never mind." As a peace offering he asked, "Cigarette?"

"No, thanks."

"Well, I appreciate you coming in, and I assure you: we are doing everything we can. Today we're rounding up anybody with a record for burglary or armed robbery, and they're all gonna get a *thorough* questioning. It ain't like this is a case of a couple roustabouts on the docks killing each other over a bad batch of hooch. There's important people interested in it getting solved. And if I wasn't doing a good job, Garry Herrmann would have me walking a beat with Jimmy there."

Like a dog, the uniformed cop perked up at the sound of his name.

"Herrmann could do that?" I asked.

The cigarette in Forsch's lips jiggled as he let out a laugh. He tilted back in his chair and took a long drag. "You're new to the city, aren't you?"

"Only been here a few months."

"Ever hear of Boss Cox?"

"Of course." Cox had been one of the most notorious political bosses in the country. "He pretty much ran Cincinnati. Died a few years ago, though, didn't he?"

"Ran all of Hamilton County. For thirty years. And yes, he's dead—but not his organization." Forsch's chair clacked on the floor as he let the front legs down. "You know how Garry Herrmann became president of the Reds?"

"Bought the team?" I ventured.

Forsch shook his head. "Herrmann was one of Cox's lieutenants." He took another drag and let the smoke out slowly. "In 1902, John Brush was the owner of the Reds. He opened a new ballpark—the Palace of the Fans—and it was a big hit with the folks around here. Boss Cox took such a liking to it that he decided to buy the team. When Brush refused to sell, Cox threatened to run a street right through the middle of his nice new park—and he would have, too. Brush changed his mind and Cox, Herrmann, and Max and Julius Fleischmann—of the yeast and gin family—took over the club. And they appointed Garry Herrmann president."

"Jeez." I knew that most owners were of the robber-baron mold, but I'd never heard of tactics as outrageous as this.

"So I can assure you Mr. Herrmann will be very pleased with our efforts to solve this case."

With that assurance, I left for the ballpark.

Before I got to Redland Field, though, I wasn't so certain that Forsch's primary interest was in solving the case. His efforts seemed intended more for show than for results—

there'd been all those cops standing around the office yesterday, and he was planning mass roundups for today. I had the feeling it was a higher priority for Forsch to impress Garry Herrmann and his political cronies than to get justice for Oliver Perriman.

Beautiful day for a funeral, I thought.

The sky was high and clear, the air drier and cooler than it had been in weeks, and the scent of fresh-mown grass wafted about Redland Field making it smell like a garden. Red-white-and-blue bunting dripped from the front-row railings of the grandstand and streamers of the same colors ran along the top of the outfield fence. In left-center, the American flag billowed freely, no longer in the grip of the oppressive humidity that had been smothering the city.

This was Saturday, July 2, the start of the Independence Day weekend. The Reds players were lined up along the third-base foul line, and on the first-base side were Wilbert Robinson and his Brooklyn Dodgers, reigning National League champions.

The ballpark was packed to overflowing. Some fans took standing-room spots in the right-field bleachers; others were on the field itself, seated on the left-field terrace behind a rope barricade. Across the street, the Western Avenue Irregulars had gathered on the roof of the Jantz & Leist Electric Company for a free view of the activities.

There was more than a ball game to entertain them today. A brass band in the right-field bleachers was playing John Sousa marches, and a fireworks display was scheduled for after the game. And preceding it all, was a memorial service for Oliver Perriman.

His actual funeral had been yesterday, but the team was holding a special "tribute" to him today. It was now under way, with Lloyd Tinsley speaking into a large megaphone set up on the pitcher's mound. Behind him were Garry Herrmann and a group of dignitaries—the sort of men who like to be seen at such events and get their names in the next day's newspapers. Tinsley began by introducing the others. Among those present were Louis Kahn of Kahn's Meats; Maynard Kimber, the sausage king; and the heads of the Moerlein, Hudepohl, and Wiedemann breweries. The guests had no connection to baseball that I knew of, and appeared to have been invited solely because of Herrmann's fondness for their products. At least none of them were called upon to say anything; they simply puffed up and waved when their names were announced. Garry Herrmann himself was quietly beaming—things weren't so terrible anymore.

"We are here today," Tinsley said, his voice echoing like thunder, "to honor Oliver Perriman. Mr. Perriman wasn't a player or an owner or even an umpire. He was more important than any of those: he was a *fan.*" As I'm sure he expected, a solid round of applause greeted this declaration. After pausing to milk the ovation for all he could, Tinsley went on, "Oliver Perriman—'Ollie' to those of us fortunate enough to be his friend—worked hard to preserve our history, to document the achievements of our city's ballplayers"—another pause for effect—"and to show the baseball world that Cincinnati *is* the city of champions." The cheers were loud and long.

I thought a championship every fifty years hardly justified a claim to being "the city of champions." I also thought that a baseball diamond was for playing ball, not for self-serving speeches. I started scratching the earth with my cleats, mixing the lime of the foul line into the clay.

As Tinsley continued to speak, I noticed that he never explicitly mentioned that Oliver Perriman was dead. Instead, the emphasis was on Perriman's achievement in putting together "such a magnificent collection"—and on how Cincinnatians were sure to enjoy seeing the exhibit.

It had been pretty much the same way in the newspapers: Perriman's death had garnered little attention. Initially, there were a few brief reports on the inside pages that he had been killed during an attempted robbery "by person or persons unknown." But the front pages had been taken up by coverage of other events: President Harding's appointment of a former president, Cincinnati's own William Howard Taft, to be Chief Justice of the U.S. Supreme Court; the controversy over a woman being seated on a jury in Cleveland; and the upcoming boxing match between heavyweight champion Jack Dempsey and challenger Georges Carpentier. A few days later, a couple of follow-up pieces described the "exhaustive" investigation by the Cincinnati Police Department and reported their conclusion that the would-be robber and murderer had left town.

". . . and now, to make a very special presentation, I am happy to introduce Mr. Nathaniel Bonner, president of the Queen City Lumber Company."

Bonner, a lean man who must have been six and a half feet tall, took Tinsley's place at the megaphone, bending over to bring his mouth down to its level. He coughed and cleared his throat a few times. "It is my understanding," he finally began, "that there was one relic in particular that Oliver Perriman most wanted to retrieve from the dust of history—but could never find. That object was a bat, a twenty-seven-foot baseball bat inscribed with the names of the 1869 Red Stockings." There were some murmurs from the crowd at the notion of such an enormous bat. "It was fifty-two years ago yesterday, that my father, Josiah Bonner, presented that grand bat to Red Stockings president Aaron Champion on behalf of the Queen City Lumber Company. Unfortunately, my father is a bit under the weather today, so I'm pinch-hitting for him, as it were . . ." He'd started to stand upright and his voice began to fade. Leaning closer to the megaphone again, he continued, "As I said, that original bat has never been found. But"—he gestured toward a group of people standing behind home plate—"it gives me great pleasure to present a new bat, inscribed with the name of Oliver Perri-man, to his wife Katie."

Team captain Jake Daubert led a short woman dressed in black toward the mound. She was wearing a veil, so I couldn't tell much about her appearance other than that her figure was on the stout side, the kind that had been popular in the nineties.

As the crowd gave her a respectful ovation, a small flatbed truck came out of the left-field corner, pulling something shaped like a telegraph pole covered by a red cloth. The truck stopped between home plate and the pitcher's mound, and Nathaniel Bonner went over to it. He grabbed a corner of the cloth and tried to whisk it off with a magician-like flourish, but it snagged, maybe on a splinter. Bonner tugged and yanked at the covering until it tore away to reveal a magnificent bat supported on blocks. The varnished wood shimmered in the sunlight, and painted in red along one side was *Oliver Perriman*.

Katie Perriman said a barely audible "Thank you" into the megaphone, then Lloyd Tinsley led her to the bat. She ran a hand over her husband's name, almost caressing it. Then she reached under her veil and wiped her eyes, exposing a pale face framed by mousy brown hair.

Curt Stram, standing to my right, nudged me with his elbow. "You know," he said, "she don't look like much in the daylight, but at night, with the lights out, she don't *feel* a day over eighteen."

"Who?"

"Katie Perriman. I tell you, she's a wild one all right. Get a couple glasses of wine in her and—"

I couldn't believe he was talking about Ollie Perriman's widow that way. After I recovered from the shock, I warned him, "You say anything like that again, and you'll be tasting my cleats."

"Sorry. Didn't know you were a milk-and-water—"

This boy didn't know when to shut up. I dug an elbow into his ribs, hard, and he finally closed his mouth.

Lloyd Tinsley took over at the megaphone again. He mentioned in closing that the "setback"—again avoiding the word "death"—would delay the opening of the exhibit somewhat, but that it would be worth the wait. And he added that the bat Bonner had just donated would be part of the display.

The truck circled around the infield. When it turned, I saw that on the other side of the bat, in larger print than Perriman's name, was painted *Queen City Lumber Company*.

I didn't like the way people were cashing in on the exhibit that Perriman had planned. It was supposed to be a tribute, a way to pass history along to another generation, not a commercial venture.

As the dignitaries left the field, and the bat was carted off, I was thinking about Perriman. His death was more than a "setback," and his life had been more than the collection. There was a personal side to him that I knew little about.

O O O

In most homes these days, about the only wine you could hope for was made from a kit. In a clever way of circumventing the Volstead Act, vintners sold grape bricks, solid blocks of concentrated grape juice that came with detailed instructions on exactly what you should *not* do with their product or you would end up with wine—and that would be illegal.

Katie Perriman was serving the real stuff, though, bottled before Prohibition. I'd have preferred beer, or a sweeter wine, but the dry white I was sipping wasn't bad. In fact, it was the most enjoyable aspect of the gathering.

This wasn't the way I'd planned to spend Saturday evening. But after our 2–1 victory over the Dodgers, Lloyd Tinsley came into the clubhouse and announced that Mrs. Perriman had invited the entire team to her house as a thank-you for the "tribute" to her husband at the ballpark.

I felt obligated to go, and Margie agreed to come with me; we figured we'd put in enough time to be polite, then leave for a late dinner and dancing.

The Perriman home was a rambling three-story Victorian that would have been considered a mansion in most parts of the city. Situated on fashionable Price Hill, however, it was one of the more ordinary residences.

Inside what the butler called the "drawing room" half the Reds team stood awkwardly around a lavishly stocked buffet table. The antique furniture, Oriental rugs, and gilt-framed paintings that filled the high-ceilinged room made for an intimidating atmosphere, and it seemed that the main goal of every ballplayer there was to avoid coming into contact with anything breakable.

While Katie Perriman sat on a daybed at the far end of the room with several other women to keep her company, her guests stayed near the food and drinks, exchanging few words. The lack of conversation among the players wasn't unique to this occasion, however. Although the club could play well enough together on the diamond, there was little social interaction once the games were over. Some preferred to keep to themselves, like Jake Daubert, who had the personality of a blank lineup card, and my road roommate Bubbles Hargrave, who had a stuttering problem—he'd been given his nickname because of his trouble saying B's. And there were those who were avoided by others, like the arrogant youngster Curt Stram, and temperamental pitcher Dolf Luque, "The Pride of Havana," who sometimes challenged his teammates to duels. Absorbed in the refreshments were manager Pat Moran, who was gulping wine at a pace to make it the alcoholic equivalent of whiskey, and bony old coach Dave Claxton, who kept stuffing down shrimp and crackers.

Completely absent were Garry Herrmann, Lloyd Tinsley, and the businessmen who'd been at the game; this wasn't a public event, and they wouldn't get their names in the papers for coming, so why bother.

I was the only one who'd brought a date, so at least I had Margie to talk to. But since I was also the only one as far as I knew who'd even met Ollie Perriman, I felt I should be the first to pay my respects to his widow. I excused myself from Margie and approached our hostess.

Katie Perriman was still in mourning attire, but without the hat and veil. Her round face was heavily powdered and her drab brown hair was in a chignon. By far, her most attractive feature was her vivid green eyes.

"Mrs. Perriman," I said, "my name is Mickey Rawlings. I met your husband a couple of times, and . . . and I just want you to know that I'm sorry for your loss."

"Thank you, Mr. Rawlings. My Ollie was a sweet man." She raised a lacy handkerchief and dabbed at her eyes— although they didn't appear wet. "I don't know what I'm going to do without him."

The other women immediately dispersed, probably grateful to be temporarily relieved of their duty to stay with the bereaved.

That meant I was going to be stuck with her for a while. "I, uh, I was going to be at the opening of your husband's museum. He showed me the things he'd collected. Sure did a wonderful job getting them together."

"Well, he certainly spent enough time and money on his hobby. I admit I wasn't too happy about it at the time, but thinking back I realize a lot of husbands do a lot worse things to entertain themselves."

It was a long, awkward moment until I could come up with another question. "What did he do for work?"

"He didn't." She smiled sadly. "Oh, he tried his hand at business a few times—a sporting goods store, a couple of hotels in Covington, even a dance studio once—but it never worked out. I finally told him to stop trying."

I looked around at the expensive furnishings. "Then

how—?" I caught myself; it was none of my concern how they could afford to live here.

She answered anyway. "I have enough resources to live quite comfortably, Mr. Rawlings, and I was happy to support my husband as well. You see, my family used to make Catawba wine. Our vineyards were on Mount Adams. By the time the black rot wiped them out, we'd invested in other ventures. So my Ollie didn't have to work." She sighed. "The poor man simply had no head for business. It was such a relief to both of us when Mr. Tinsley became his partner in the museum. Ollie needed someone with business sense to take charge of matters."

I caught the eye of one of the women who'd been with Katie Perriman. With raised eyebrows, I silently pleaded with her to come and relieve me, but she turned away. I was stuck. "There were other people interested in the collection," I said. "Your husband told me he had offers to buy it."

"Yes, well, from what I know, those offers were all from the same man."

"Lloyd Tinsley?"

"Oh no, the calls continued after Mr. Tinsley bought a half interest in Ollie's exhibit."

I heard somebody step near us and thought I was about to be relieved. It was Curt Stram, a smirk on his baby face and mischief in his eyes. His suit was too flashy for this occasion and, as usual, his appearance was careless. He laid a hand on her shoulder. "Everything will be fine, Katie, I'm sure."

She flinched at his touch and shot him a look of admonishment. His gesture was far too familiar and totally inappropriate. He let his hand linger a few moments before withdrawing it.

I was briefly tempted to use Stram's arrival as an excuse for me to leave. But Katie Perriman didn't look like she wanted him there. Her chin began to tremble. Stram then sidled away.

She turned back to me. Now her eyes were wet.

Not knowing what to say, I proceeded as if Stram had never come by. "Will you keep the collection?" I asked.

After dabbing her eyes she quickly composed herself. "I don't believe I have anything to say in the matter. My understanding of their arrangement is that Ollie's share in the business goes to his partner—Mr. Tinsley."

"Oh, I see."

Another of the women came a little too close to us. Instead of relying on silent gestures, I said "Hello," forcing her to come over for introductions. She took a seat next to the widow, and I started to make my escape.

Mrs. Perriman thanked me for coming, then added, "I thought the most senseless thing in the world was for Ollie to spend all that time and money on a collection of old baseball mementos. Now I think the only thing more senseless was for someone to kill him over it. Who would do such a thing?" Her eyes pleaded with me for an answer.

I couldn't think of any. "I don't know, ma'am. Again, I'm very sorry for what happened."

Fortified with a fresh glass of wine, I went to join Margie and found her speaking to Dolf Luque in Spanish. Another talent that I wasn't aware she had.

I then drifted over to where Heinie Groh and Greasy Neale were talking together. They were quite a contrast in physiques. Groh, who was about my height, was sometimes called "tiny Heinie" in the press; his hands were so small that he used a "bottle bat" with a thick barrel and an exceptionally narrow handle. The burly Neale was big enough that he played professional football in the off-season.

"We're talking about Mac," Groh said to me. "You played for him, right?"

"Three years," I said. "Mac" was New York Giants manager John McGraw; I'd been on his roster from 1914 through 1916, my longest tenure with a single club.

"I'd never play for that old cuss," said Neale.

"Wouldn't want him for a father-in-law," I said. "But if you want to learn baseball, you can't beat having him for a manager."

Neale snorted and stepped away. "Think I'll see what they have to eat here."

"He's outvoted." Groh chuckled. "I was telling him I wished to hell I could play for McGraw again."

Groh had started his career with the Giants a couple of years before I joined the club, and was now in his ninth season with the Reds. He'd held out for two months this spring, hoping to be traded to New York; the trade finally went through, but the new baseball commissioner, Judge Kenesaw Mountain Landis, vetoed the deal and forced Groh to stay with the Reds.

"You'll get to New York again," I said. "If McGraw wants you, he'll get you—never mind what Landis says."

"Dunno. That Landis seems like a tough cookie."

"So's McGraw." And there was another fellow who appeared to be a tough cookie that I was curious about. "Say, Heinie, was Lloyd Tinsley involved in making the deal with New York?"

He shook his head. "Nah, Bancroft got it started, then Herrmann took over the negotiations."

"What do you think of Tinsley?"

"He's no Frank Bancroft. Bancroft was a *baseball* man. Tinsley's a glorified bookkeeper."

Frank Bancroft had managed seven major league teams—including the 1884 world champion Providence Grays—before becoming business manager of the Reds. When he died a week before opening day this spring, he was starting his thirtieth year in that role. "Did they get Tinsley after Bancroft died?" I asked.

"No, a few years ago. Tinsley was running a ball club in the Western League—Wichita, I think. Then during the war, the minors shut down. Bancroft was already getting sick, so he hired Tinsley to help him out. But I guess after all them years, you don't give up your responsibilities easy. Bancroft never let Tinsley be anything more than his assistant."

I felt a touch in the small of my back and twisted my head to see Margie standing almost on my heels. "Bubbles Hargrave just left," she said. "So if we go, too, we wouldn't be the first ones."

"Good thinking," said Groh. "You two go ahead. Then I'll follow."

After saying good-byes to Katie Perriman, Margie and I left and caught a Warsaw Avenue trolley.

Once we were seated, I asked, "Where'd you learn to speak Spanish?"

"California. I only know a little."

"I didn't know you could talk it at all."

"You don't know everything about me. If you did, you might get bored."

There were times when we did seem to run out of things to say at dinner. But I never felt bored with Margie. "Not with you," I said. "Ever."

She smiled. "Some men know how to talk to a lady. Not

like Curt Stram. You can give your teammate Stram some lessons on what to say. And maybe on what *not* to say."

"Why? Was he rude to you?"

"Not to me. I overheard him talking to Dave Claxton. He made it clear he'd had an affair with Katie Perriman. He was *gloating* about it—and while she's mourning her dead husband."

I agreed with her that Stram had a lot of learning to do in the manners department.

But after we got off the car at Haberstumpf's for dinner and dancing, I forgot all about Stram and the Perrimans and concentrated on our own affair.

I should have been sound asleep already, like Margie, who was snoring lightly next to me. She'd given me more exercise on the dance floor this evening than the Reds had given me on the baseball diamond all week, and we didn't get home until well after midnight.

But I did little better than doze, my thoughts on Ollie Perriman and why he might have been killed. When I'd first met him, I thought he was harmless, obsessed with an innocent hobby that many people might find childish. And since his death, I hadn't been able to imagine why anyone would want to hurt someone who was so absorbed in preserving the past—it was like killing a librarian.

The more I thought about it now, though, the more I realized I hadn't given him proper credit. His wasn't a childish hobby, it was a passion. Ollie Perriman had something in his life that he loved, and he gave himself to it wholeheartedly.

From what I'd heard today, he'd also had an unfaithful wife who didn't care for his hobby, and a pushy partner who now owned the entire business.

And I started wondering if maybe the reason nothing was

stolen from Perriman's collection was because theft wasn"
the intent of the crime. Maybe the "robbery" was to cover
up a murder. But who would gain from such an act?

Lloyd Tinsley? According to Katie Perriman, he stood to
inherit the collection. But why would he kill Perriman *before*
the opening of the exhibit? Tinsley had been pressing for i
to be opened soon, and Perriman's death was only going to
delay that. And why wouldn't Tinsley wait to find out if people
wanted to see the collection first—what if it was a bust? Big
risk killing somebody when you don't know what it gains
you.

If it wasn't to gain something, maybe it was to get rid of
something: an unwanted husband. Was Katie Perriman tired
of supporting Ollie financially? Or did she want him out of
the way so that she would be free to take up with Curt Stram?
She could have simply divorced him, though, instead of
resorting to something as rash as murder.

Rash. That practically defined Curt Stram. He certainly
had no discretion in his personal behavior, but I didn't think
he was stupid or calculating enough to murder a man.
Besides, could he really care about Katie Perriman to talk
about her the way he did? What *was* going on between the
two of them, anyway?

I'd start to nod off, but every time I did, a new scenario
would intrude and demand attention. Finally, I decided that
putting something in my stomach might help me fall asleep.

Careful not to wake Margie, I slid my shoulder out from
under her head, replaced it with a pillow, then gradually
eased myself out of bed.

In my bare feet, I padded downstairs, through the dining
area, and into the kitchen. I was about to hit the light switch
when I heard a rustle behind me.

Then my skull exploded.

The blast sent fireballs from the back of my head through to the front, where they flashed before my eyes. I felt my knees start to melt and sensed the kitchen floor coming up to meet my chin.

The lights in my head sputtered, replaced by a calm darkness. I was vaguely aware that the pain was fading. So was consciousness.

○ ○ ○

The pain came back, pounding and intense.

Margie, wearing only a chemise, was bent over me. Her hands gripped my shoulders and she was shaking me as if trying to wake me from a sound sleep. "Are you all right?" she asked.

"Think so." She continued the shaking until I added, "I'm awake. Please stop."

"Oh, sorry. What happened?"

"Somebody hit me." I slowly raised myself on my elbows and lifted a hand to feel the back of my head. It was tender to the touch but there wasn't much of a lump. "Came up from behind me; must have been in the parlor." I held my fingertips close to my bleary eyes to check for blood; there was none. On the whole, this was no worse than a nasty beanball—except I wasn't going to be awarded first base. "How long have I been out?"

"Not long. I heard the door slam—that's what woke me. You weren't in bed, so I came down to see if you'd gone outside for some reason."

"No, I wanted cookies."

She stifled a laugh, and I realized how silly that sounded.

I stood up carefully, my knees feeling like they were going to buckle again. My head didn't want to stay up either; it felt like the dull pounding in the back of my skull was trying to knock it forward onto my chest.

I struggled to get vertical, then walked to the front door.

"Shouldn't we call the police?" Margie suggested.

"Good idea. Go 'head." I opened the door and peered outside. Of course, the burglar would have been long gone, but I felt compelled to check. Everything was quiet and calm, not even a passing automobile.

While Margie placed the phone call, I looked around the parlor. Everything of obvious value—Victrola, mantel clock, silver candlesticks—were still there and looked untouched. My desk appeared to be the only thing in the room that had been disturbed. The stacks of guides and magazines were in disorder and the desk drawers were open. But from what I could tell, nothing had been taken.

While waiting for the police to arrive, Margie checked the kitchen, and I looked around upstairs. She then put on a pot of coffee.

A disheveled young officer eventually arrived in a patrol car. He looked like he'd been asleep not long before. "You called about a break-in?" he asked.

"Yes," Margie and I answered in one voice. I then gave him the story in all its brevity.

"Well, let me take a look-see."

Margie offered him a cup of coffee, which he accepted and sipped as he walked around the house, checking the front and back doors and the windows. "Doesn't look like a forced entry. You keep your door locked?"

Who locks their doors? "Not when we're home."

"Could have walked right in then. What all was taken?"

"Nothing. I don't think." I pointed to the messy desk. "He went through that, though. Probably looking for something."

"Probably," he repeated. The officer scribbled in a notebook, muttering to himself, "No forced entry. Nothing taken." He gulped the last of his coffee. "Well, I'll file a report, and we'll keep our eyes open."

"That's it?" I wasn't sure what I expected, but I assumed the police could do more than this.

"For now."

I touched the back of my head, where a lump had started to bloom. "He knocked me out."

The cop grunted. "But you're all better now?"

"Uh, yeah."

"Good." He wrote some more in the book, reciting aloud, "Assaulted resident. Minor injury." He then thanked Margie for the coffee and advised us to lock the door from now on. "Good neighborhood, but you never can tell," he said.

After he left, we followed his advice, locking the doors and windows. Then we went back upstairs to try and get some rest. I lay on my side to keep my bruised head from touching the pillow, but I never did get to sleep.

○○○

By eight-thirty, with Margie still asleep, I'd taken a hot bath and eaten breakfast—the cookies I'd wanted last night. I was on my fourth cup of coffee and holding the second bag of ice to my throbbing head. This was one of the rare times I was hoping not to play; my head and eyes were in no shape to pick up a fastball.

I was thinking about the break-in, and was struck by the similarities with the one at Ollie Perriman's office. Detective

Forsch had never talked to me again after I'd met with him at police headquarters. Maybe I should contact him.

I phoned the Crime Bureau and was put through to Forsch. "Glad you're there," I said after identifying myself. "Wasn't sure if you worked Sundays."

"They don't give us weekends off," he replied. "Fridays and Saturdays are the big crime nights. Matter of fact, I got a stabbing on Front Street I need to look into. So what's on your mind?" I heard him take a drag on a cigarette.

I told him of our intruder.

"So what do you want from me?" the detective asked. "You reported it, the local cops looked into it, end of story. Who knows—maybe they'll find him. Did you give a description?"

"Never saw the guy. Just felt whatever he hit me with."

Forsch's grunt was as unsympathetic as the patrolman's.

I went on, "The reason I'm calling you, is because he was interested in the things Ollie Perriman gave me—those are the only things he touched. So I figure it was probably the same guy who broke into Redland Field and killed Perriman."

"Well, that may be what *you* figure, but *I* don't see that there's any connection. You know how many burglaries we have in a week? Dozens. You're just one of the statistics. As for the Perriman case, we did a thorough search. Whoever killed him must have left town."

I thought I knew why Forsch was being stubborn: he'd put on enough of a show to satisfy Garry Herrmann, and opening things up again wouldn't do him any good. "They *have* to be connected," I said. "Why would—"

"I *have* to be going. If you have any more trouble, contact your local district." With that, he hung up. I had the feeling that to him my little break-in was in the same category as a couple of roustabouts fighting over a bad batch of liquor.

I sat down at the desk. I was sure nothing had been taken. Same as in Perriman's office. Was the robber really looking for something, though? Or was it a cover, a way to maintain the pretense that robbery was the motive behind the break-in at Redland Field? But if the police were no longer pushing the Perriman investigation anyway, why take the risk of breaking in here?

Oh, jeez. This wasn't all that Perriman had given me. There were also the cards that I'd given to Patrick Kelly. Could those little pieces of pasteboard have been what he was looking for? What if the killer goes after them? I thought hard, and when I was sure that I hadn't told anyone about giving the boy the cards, I felt some sense of relief.

But I felt no more at ease about what had happened here. It was more than a bump on the head. I felt violated. I'd had apartments and houses before, and lived in hotel rooms on the road, but this place was different. Margie was living here with me. This was the first time I'd shared a place with a woman, and that made it a home.

What if Margie had been the one to come downstairs last night? Perriman had been killed; the same could have happened to her.

Then it occurred to me that with nothing missing, either from Perriman's office or from my desk, the robber—killer— might be coming back for another search. And judging from Detective Forsch's attitude, I sure wasn't going to be able to depend on the Cincinnati Police Department for help if he did.

Chapter Eight
ooo

The *Island Queen* pulled away from the Public Landing, her bells clanging and whistles shrieking. As the elegant steamboat started up the Ohio River, Margie and I maneuvered our way through the crowd, ushering Erin and Patrick Kelly along with us. Margie had offered to take the children to the big Fourth of July fireworks show, and their aunt had given her ready consent.

Like most of the others on board, we were dressed up for the occasion. Margie looked stunning in a teal silk skirt and embroidered white shirtwaist. The children's clothes were styled a bit too young for them, Erin wearing a frilly white organdy dress and Patrick in a serge knickerbocker suit. I wore blue seersucker and a crimson necktie with blue-and-white polka dots. That same color scheme was all about us; the steamboat's railings were swathed in patriotic bunting, and many of the passengers were waving small American flags.

All five decks of the vessel were packed with holiday revelers, but we managed to work our way to the front of the middle deck, where we had a marvelous view of the river stretching ahead of us.

The side-wheeler's smokestack was tilted back to prevent it from being shorn off by the bridges we passed under, first the Central, then the L. & N. To our left was Mount Adams with the chimneys of Rookwood Pottery visible on top of the hill. To our right was Newport, Kentucky, then Bellevue and Dayton.

Music from the *Island Queen*'s calliope attracted those on land to the grassy riverbanks; they waved to the passengers and we returned the greetings. It reminded me of when I was a kid in New Jersey, waving to the engineers of passing trains, who'd blast their whistles in reply. Boats were my least favorite mode of transportation, but even I was having fun.

Altogether, it had been a good day so far. Thanks to Larry Kopf twisting an ankle, I spelled him at shortstop in the afternoon game, going 3-for-4 in another win over the Dodgers; and Margie and the children were on hand to witness my performance. My head felt good enough to play; the only lingering effect from the attack Saturday night was that I required a slightly larger cap to accommodate the bump.

It took almost an hour for the steamboat to complete the eight-mile journey, during which Erin and Patrick took turns asking if we were there yet. Margie had answered "Almost" for the twentieth time, when the splashing of the paddle wheel diminished and the boat pulled up to a landing in front of an entrance arch with a sign that read *CONEY ISLAND*.

The site was originally "Ohio Grove, the Coney Island of the West," but soon became known simply as "Coney

Island"—no Cincinnatian was going to mistake it for the one in Brooklyn. For me, though, the name brought back memories of the original Coney. I'd first met Margie in Brooklyn, when I got a bit part in one of her moving pictures, and the amusement park had been the site of some of our earliest dates.

With Erin and Patrick in tow, Margie and I filed down the gangplank with the rest of the crowd, and through the park entrance. There was a small group of people in the sheltered pavilion waiting to take the steamboat back to the city, but most were staying for the evening festivities.

This Coney Island was noted as much for its beautifully landscaped grounds as for its amusements, and was a favorite place for picnicking. Many of those pouring into the park with us were carrying wicker baskets and would be heading for the picnic areas.

We hadn't brought our own food, so we made the concession stands our first stop. Erin and Patrick had eaten enough molasses popcorn at Redland Field to feed the entire Cincinnati team, but they were ready for more.

After buying weinerwursts and soda pop, we found an empty table and sat down to eat.

The children and I had finished, and Margie was on her last couple of bites, when Patrick turned to me. "Miss Turner said you wanted me to bring them baseball cards."

"Yes. Do you have them?"

He eyed me warily. "You gonna take 'em back?"

"No, I'd just like to see them." I wanted to reassure myself that they weren't anything a burglar could have been after. And I hadn't wanted Patrick to bring them to our house—I was probably being overly cautious, but preferred to err on the side of safety.

Patrick didn't look totally reassured that he was going to get the cards back, but he reached into his jacket pocket, pulled out a box that had once held packages of Seidlitz Powder, and handed it to me.

I removed the cards and put them on the table.

"Who's ready for ice cream?" Margie asked.

I'm sure it came as no surprise to her that we all were. While she and Erin went to the Creamy Whip stand, I examined the cards one by one, under Patrick's vigilant stare.

I first checked for anything written on them. Then I brushed my thumb over the corners of the cards to see if they would peel apart—maybe there was a rare stamp or something glued between the layers of pasteboard. Nothing. And the cards themselves were creased and scuffed so they weren't worth any money—not that there was such a thing as a valuable baseball card anyway. When I finished my inspection, I handed them to Patrick.

Relief showed in his face. After the cards were back in the Seidlitz box and the box was tucked securely in his pocket, he asked, "Did you find out what happened to that other Red Stocking—Dick Hurley?"

I'd almost forgotten about Hurley. "No, I'm sorry." And now I could never ask Ollie Perriman about the old utility player. "There might not be anyone who'd know about him anymore."

Margie and Erin arrived with the ice cream, and we all concentrated on eating the dessert before it melted. This course was followed by cotton candy washed down with root beer.

The kids had now consumed twice their body weight in

food and drink, so of course the next thing they wanted to do was go on the rides. Margie and I watched as they rode the Sky Rocket, the carousel, and the Dip-the-Dips. Then they talked us into joining them for a run on the roller coaster.

With daylight waning, we proceeded to an open field to catch Lieutenant Emerson and His Flying Circus in the final air show of the day. Emerson, who billed himself as "The Daredevil of the Clouds," put on a spectacular exhibition, including a stunt where he stood on the top wing of his biplane while another pilot did a double "loop the loop." For his finale, he leapt from one plane to another and then parachuted to the ground.

Finally, there were the fireworks, a marvelous display of rockets and flares that filled the night sky with dazzling colors.

By this time, Erin and Patrick were barely awake enough to walk to the pavilion and board the *Island Queen* to begin the journey back to the city.

O O O

Margie took the Kellys home while I went on to our house. I preferred to avoid the children's aunt; the woman was happy enough to let her niece and nephew spend time with us, but whenever she saw Margie or me she always made a point of mentioning that she disapproved of our living arrangement.

I unlocked the front door and poked my head in tenta-tively. There'd been no more break-ins, but neither had there been any calls from the local police or from Detective Forsch to inform us they'd arrested anyone. So the worry lingered, and the same questions ran through my mind every time I came home: has the place been ransacked? . . . is somebody inside? . . . if there is, will he have a gun?

The parlor appeared as it had when we'd left in the morning, so I hung my boater on the hat rack and went over to my desk.

As I sat down, I found myself wondering what it had been like for Ollie Perriman when his killer broke in. Had Perriman been looking through his magnifying glass, trying to identify players in an old photograph? Or maybe writing up caption cards to label the exhibits? Had he ever expected that he might not live to see the opening of his museum?

All that was going to be there of him now was the collection itself. And that behemoth bat with his name painted on the side. I remembered what Nathaniel Bonner had said when he made the presentation: that the bat from 1869 was the artifact Perriman had most wanted to find. And I imagined that the new bat, too, might end up lost someday, to be unearthed a hundred years from now by some baseball fan who would read the name and think that Oliver Perriman must have been the greatest slugger of his day. I decided that as awful as the ceremony had been, the bat was a pretty good gift.

Recalling Bonner's words, there was something I hadn't picked up on during his speech: "Fifty-two years ago yesterday," he'd said, his father had donated the original bat to the president of the Red Stockings. Ollie Perriman's memorial had been on July second. So Josiah Bonner had made his presentation on July 1, 1869. I glanced up at the old ball on top of my desk. The date painted on it was: *July 2, '69.*

"Everything okay?" Margie asked as she came in.

"All safe," I said.

"I'm exhausted. Those two are darling children, but *tiring.*"

She began undoing her hair, letting the long brown tresses fall about her shoulders. "You ready for bed?"

"Just want to look at a couple of things. I'll be up in a bit."

"I remember when you used to *want* to come to bed with me." She started to unhook her skirt.

I smiled. "You said you're exhausted."

"I am. Just checking to see that you're not avoiding me."

I got up and kissed her. "I'll be up soon."

After Margie went upstairs, I sat back down at the desk and reached for the old baseball. The coincidence in the dates seemed odd, but then I remembered that the date on the ball wasn't accurate, anyway—Spalding baseballs weren't manufactured until years after the Red Stockings folded. There was something else odd about the ball, I now realized: recorded on the others in Perriman's office were the names of the opposing teams—the Eckfords, the Mutuals, the Buckeyes. This one simply said *Cin'ti BB Club*.

I plucked the Ellard book, *Base Ball in Cincinnati,* from the shelf. Most of the volume was devoted to the 1869–1870 Red Stockings. I turned to a list of game scores for 1869 to see who they'd played on July 2. The team had returned from a triumphant Eastern tour on July 1, and played a "Picked Nine" in an exhibition game at the Union Grounds, defeating them 53–11. Before that game was the presentation of the bat, and there was a banquet in honor of the club that night. The team's next game was two days later, against the Washington Olympics. There was no game on July 2.

I turned the old ball around in my fingers. It had to be about the poorest forgery ever created. Red stitches when black was the color then in use; a brand that hadn't existed yet; a date when no game was played. And there was something else wrong that hadn't occurred to me before. Ollie Perriman had speculated that kids used the ball and restitched the cover when it came loose. But the ball wasn't in bad shape—the leather was good enough to read the Spalding trademark. So why would the stitches have gone bad? I rubbed my thumb on the seam, and felt that the threads weren't very tight.

What the hell. This ball wasn't a real piece of history anyway, I told myself as I reached in a drawer for my pocket-knife. I flicked open the blade and stuck the tip into one of the seams, tearing open a stitch. I continued ripping through the stitches as bits of red thread fluttered over the desk top.

The horsehide cover was stiff and I had to pry it off. Between the leather and the tight yarn core was a folded piece of onionskin paper. Putting the eviscerated ball down, I opened the paper. Neatly scripted in black ink was the message:

On July 2, 1869, a girl named Sarah was murdered. She was from Corryville and about sixteen years of age. She is buried in Eden Park.

Jeez. So this is what it's been about.

"Really, Mickey," Margie said from the top of the stairs. "You don't need to guard the place."

I beckoned her. "Found something."

"What?"

When she got to the desk I handed her the note. "My guess is this is what Ollie Perriman was killed for."

She read the note, then looked at me, a touch of fear in her eyes. "You *are* going to get involved, aren't you?"

"I think I already am," I said. "Whether I want to be or not." Trying to find a bright side, I added, "But at least now I have a starting point: I know what the killer was looking for."

She bit her lip and nodded. "I'll help if I can."

I gave it a day, and I gave Detective Forsch another chance. On Tuesday, I telephoned him and reported what I'd found. His response was about what I expected: he was even less interested in a murder that took place half a century ago than he was in Oliver Perriman's last week. He also pointed out that I really didn't have evidence of a crime—what I had was a note, and in his view probably the result of a prank.

To be fair to Forsch, I'm not sure any cop would have started an investigation based on what I'd found. In my mind it was clear, though, that something must have happened in 1869 that was still taking a toll in 1921. Somebody wanted that old baseball, and killed Ollie Perriman while trying to get it.

The problem was putting together the chain of events that spanned those fifty-two years.

I decided to begin by going back one link, to the man Perriman told me had given him the ball: Ambrose Whitaker, former bookkeeper of the 1869 Cincinnati Base Ball Club.

There were several listings for "A. Whitaker" in the directory. A call to the operator pinned down the "A" who was

Ambrose. She referred to him as "the railroad man," implied that he was a well-known figure in this city, and gave me both his home and business addresses. I was less interested in his phone numbers, but jotted them down as well. When going to question people, I prefer not to call ahead; I don't like to give them the time to plan their answers.

Early Wednesday morning, with the sun already bright and the heat intense, I was in the heart of downtown Cincinnati, across from the Gibson Hotel on Walnut Street. The main offices of the Mount Auburn Electric Inclined Railway Company were on the top floor of a charmless six-story brick building.

In the outer office of the railroad company, I asked an efficient-looking secretary of advanced years if I could speak with Mr. Whitaker.

"Which Mr. Whitaker?" she asked.

"Ambrose."

"Oh. You don't have an appointment, do you." She said it as a statement of fact, not a question.

"No, I'm sorry, I don't. But I'll only take a minute of his time, if I may."

"And you are?"

"Mickey Rawlings." Her lack of a reaction prodded me to add, "I play for the Reds."

"Baseball?"

No, glockenspiel. "Yes, ma'am."

"Wait here, please." She left her desk, knocked on a nearby door of elaborately carved oak, and went into another office. A minute later, she reappeared. "Miss Whitaker will see you."

I started toward the door, then drew up short. "*Miss* Whitaker?"

The secretary nodded, and I proceeded inside, the door shutting behind me. The interior wasn't as lavish as the ornate door had led me to expect. This was a place for work, not ceremony. The modern steel furniture was sparse, and there was little decoration. Two telephones were on the desk, a Dictaphone on a table behind it, and a ticker machine chattered in the corner.

A tall, trim woman with carrot-colored hair stood and offered her hand in such a way that it was clearly intended to be shaken, not kissed. "Mr. Rawlings, I'm Adela Whitaker."

She had a good grip. "Pleased to meet you, ma'am. Thank you for seeing me." I immediately worried that she might take offense at being called "ma'am"—Adela Whitaker was at that late-thirties-to-early-forties age when some women feel that "ma'am" makes them sound old.

There was no indication that she was offended; in fact, there was little sign of any emotion or expression at all. Her tight-lipped face was hard like a mask; not unattractive but somewhat forbidding. She waved me to a small armchair in front of the desk. As I lowered myself into it, I said, "I actually came to see, uh . . ." I gave a nod to the portrait on the wall behind her. It was of a homely redheaded man I assumed to be her father.

She confirmed the assumption. "My father retired two years ago, Mr. Rawlings. He's no longer actively involved with the firm."

"Oh. I see. Would it be okay if I was to call on him at home, then?"

"I'm sorry, but my father is not in the best of health. The stress of business is why he retired; so if it's a business matter, I'd prefer that you speak to me." She added as an afterthought, "Or my brother."

"I'm not sure . . . I think your father's the only one who could tell me what I want to know."

"Well, may I ask *why* you wish to speak with him?"

I sensed the question wasn't one of idle curiosity but a precaution; she was being protective of him. "You might have heard that there's going to be an exhibit of old Red Stockings memorabilia," I said. She nodded that she had. "I heard from Oliver Perriman, the fellow who was putting the exhibit together, that your father had some involvement with that club. I've been getting interested in the '69 team, so I was hoping I might ask him what it was like back then."

She appeared thoughtful. "I don't see any harm in your speaking to him, in that case. Baseball certainly isn't a topic likely to cause much excitement."

She'd apparently never seen Ty Cobb run the bases or Babe Ruth swing a bat. "I promise to leave if he gets too worked up," I said.

"Very well. You can find him at the Zoological Garden."

"The zoo?"

"Yes. That's where he likes to go on Wednesdays. He'll probably be near the band shell or in the Herbivora Building. Or if you'd rather see him tomorrow, you can try your luck at Chester Park—that's where he spends his Thursdays."

I thought to myself that I'd have time to get to the zoo and back to Redland Field in time for batting practice. I nodded at the portrait. "And that's . . ."

"Yes. His hair's a bit whiter now, but you should have no trouble spotting him."

○ ○ ○

The Number 49 trolley from Fountain Square let me out at the zoo's main entrance on the corner of Erkenbrecher and Vine. I paid the twenty-five cents admission and joined the other visitors, mostly women and children, entering the beautifully maintained grounds.

Immediately inside were formal flower beds set like jewels in the lush green grass. Beyond the gardens to the right was the Herbivora Building, less formally known as the Elephant House. It was an enormous concrete structure that looked like a Persian mosque, complete with a pointed dome. Since it was nearer than the band shell, I decided to try the Herbivora Building first.

His daughter was right; I had no trouble identifying Ambrose Whitaker. He was standing in front of a cage that held mother and baby Indian elephants, staring at the animals while they did little but stare back.

Whitaker was about my height, spare and rigid, wearing a pearl gray suit of old-fashioned cut and a homburg of the same color. He carried a silver-headed ebony cane, a watch chain was draped across his silk vest, and white spats covered the ankles of his high-buttoned shoes.

"Mr. Whitaker?"

He shifted his attention from the animals to me. "Yes?" His granite face looked no more lifelike than the portrait behind his daughter's desk, and the steel gray hedgerows he had for eyebrows were like something that belonged on one of the zoo creatures. So were his hawk nose and loving-cup ears.

"My name's Mickey Rawlings. Your daughter said I might find you here."

"Well, she was right then, wasn't she?" His tone was far

warmer than his appearance. We shook hands. "Must tell you, I'm not used to getting visitors here."

"Oh, I'm sorry. I didn't mean to disturb you. Your daughter said . . ."

"It's all right, son. What do you want to see me about?"

"A baseball."

"Pardon me?"

"You gave a baseball to Oliver Perriman. He was organizing an exhibit on the old Red Stockings. And you gave him a ball from 1869."

"Oh yes. I believe I did. A few other things, too, as I recall. No sense keeping such things for myself at this point in my life. What's your interest in it?"

"I play for the Reds, and I was going to help Mr. Perriman publicize the collection. He told me you were the bookkeeper for that team. Did you have the ball all these years?"

"Assistant treasurer, I was. And, no, I got that ball sometime later."

I knew Whitaker couldn't have had it since '69 because the ball hadn't been made yet, but I wanted to hear what he'd answer. "Do you remember who you got it from?"

"Well . . . Let me think. That was a long time ago . . . I believe I bought it at auction after the team folded. Does it matter?"

"No, just curious. The date on the ball says July 2, 1869, but I looked it up and there was no game that day. Does that date mean anything to you?"

Fissures creased his face as he smiled. "How old are you, son?"

"Twenty-nine."

"You remember anything about July 2, 1911?"

"Uh, no."

"That's only ten years ago. You expect me to recall what happened more than fifty years ago?"

Okay, it was a dumb question. But the ball was all I had, and Ambrose Whitaker was the only known connection to it. I briefly debated whether to reveal the existence of the note, but decided against it—I didn't want anyone to know the note was now in my possession, safely stuck in a volume of Mark Twain's *Life on the Mississippi.* I still wanted to see if I could get anything useful out of Whitaker, though. "I'm sorry. I've just gotten interested in that old club lately. Were you with the team long?"

"As long as the club supported a team, I was."

I'd always thought of a ball club and a team as the same thing. "What do you mean?"

"Do you mind if we walk outside?" he asked. "I'd like to be getting over to the band shell."

"Fine with me."

The baby elephant trumpeted shrilly when we left, and the sound reverberated throughout the building. As we walked at a leisurely pace toward the exit of the Elephant House, I noticed Whitaker didn't use the cane for support.

"See, the Cincinnati Base Ball Club was just that: a club," he explained. "A gentlemen's club. There were more than two hundred members and perhaps fifty of them ever played baseball. The club was primarily a social organization, not a business. Everyone who worked for it did so as a volunteer. As I did. I was only twenty when I was appointed assistant treasurer, and it was quite an honor. Mr. Champion—he was the president—served without pay also."

"But it was the first *professional* team, so they must have been paid," I said.

"The nine players were the only ones who received a

salary," Whitaker answered. "Using professionals was quite a scandal at the time. I'm sorry, there were *ten* players. I forgot about the substitute."

"Dick Hurley."

"Yes. William Hurley, actually. I don't know how he got the 'Dick' tag."

I remembered Patrick Kelly's question. "Do you know whatever happened to him?"

"Afraid I don't. He left the club in the middle of the season. Finances were always tight, perhaps he was released to save money."

"But the team went undefeated. Why didn't it make money?"

"It was expensive to pay a full team. More than $10,000 in salary, not to mention travel and lodging and equipment. We took in some money from gate receipts, and raised additional funds from the club members. Even so, the total profit in 1869 was $1.39. That's a figure I'll never forget. Won sixty-five games without a loss, and ended up with a dollar and thirty-nine cents in the till."

We emerged from the Herbivora Building into the bright sunshine. Whitaker removed his hat and ran a hand over his hair. There was an orange tinge to the gray, indicating his hair had once had the same color as his daughter's.

It sounded like we were in a jungle as we began to make our way around the lake; frenetic chattering came from the monkey house, there were eerie howls from the wolf dens, and innumerable birdcalls seemed to come from every direction. Over the noise, Whitaker went on, "The next year, 1870, things were looking better. The team was still undefeated, and crowds were getting larger, even on the road. Thought we might make a go of it. Red Stockings won the first twenty-seven games of the season—but then they went to Brooklyn to play the Atlantics. June 14, 1870." He winked. "That's a date I do remember. The first loss."

"The game was tied 5–5 after nine innings," I broke in. "The Atlantics wanted to leave the game a tie, but Harry Wright insisted on continuing. Neither team scored in the tenth. Red Stockings got two in the top of the eleventh and it looked like they had it won. But then Brooklyn scored three in the bottom half to win 8–7." I was embarrassed to realize that I'd interrupted Whitaker. "Uh, were you at that game?" I asked him.

"No, we couldn't afford travel for many of the club members." He smiled good-naturedly. "But it sounds like you were there."

"My grandfather told me about the game." He'd seen it in person. From his point of view, as a Brooklyn fan, it had been a glorious triumph made extra sweet by the fact that his favorite player, Bob "Death to Flying Things" Ferguson, had scored the winning run.

"That was the beginning of the end," Whitaker said. "The team lost a few more games, and people stopped turning out—in Cincinnati, anyway. Fans still came to see them play in other cities, but not at home." He knocked a pop bottle aside with his cane. "The streak was a double-edged sword. The novelty of it brought people out, but it also gave the impression of invincibility. Once that notion was shattered, it was all over for the Red Stockings."

"The club disbanded?"

"Again, club and team are two different things. At the end of the season, the club members voted to revert to amateur status and no longer finance a professional team. But other cities had started putting together professional nines, so there wasn't much interest in an amateur team anymore."

"You said there was an auction?"

"Yes. Terribly sad day. It was April of 1872, only three years after the streak began. The ballpark was partly dismantled—the wood had already been sold. Then everything else was auctioned off—the trophy balls, pennants . . . everything."

"And that's where you got the ball you gave Perriman."

"Yes, that's right."

"So the whole club fell apart?"

"Oh, some of the social activities continued. But it was never the same. I left the club myself after the '70 season."

"You never played?"

"Never more than a muffin." He explained that a muffin was a poor player who muffed plays. "No, my association with the club was helpful in getting me some business connections, and I pursued those."

"The Mount Auburn Automated Trolley . . ." I couldn't remember the exact name of his company.

"Mount Auburn Electric Inclined Railway. That was later. The seventies were a boom for trolleys, and folks started expanding to the hills. I worked with Bill Price on Buttermilk Mountain—"

"Where?"

"Price Hill. It was the only incline without a saloon at the top, so it was nicknamed 'Buttermilk Mountain.' We developed a cable system to draw trolley cars to the top of the hill. Worked well enough, but had to rely on mule power. Then in the eighties, I got the idea to form my own company and electrify the inclines. First one I did was Mount Auburn, and the first route we ran was here to the zoo."

We'd reached the band shell where an orchestra was warming up.

"You still own it?" I asked.

"Own a number of companies, but never wanted to change the name. Should always remember where you came from. My daughter's pushing for a more general name, though, something that sounds bigger."

"She runs the company now?"

"Yes. She and my son. You didn't see him at the office, did you?"

"No."

"Not surprised." He sat down on one of the benches, and I did the same. "I retired two years ago. Figured it's time to give my children their chance with the business." I noticed that he didn't mention anything about bad health; maybe he wanted to make it sound like he'd retired entirely of his own volition. "So now I have fun," he went on. "Look at the animals, watch the children, listen to music. You like opera?"

"No, sir." I knew that the summer season of opera at the zoo had recently started. It was cruel enough to keep animals in cages, I thought, without making them listen to opera. I also thought that Ambrose Whitaker didn't look like he was having as much fun as he claimed. Perhaps after all those years in business, he had to learn how to enjoy himself. Maybe baseball. "You ever go to ball games anymore?" I asked.

He shook his head. "I'm afraid I've lost interest."

"Well, if you'd ever like to, I'd be happy to get you tickets." Right, Mickey, this man is probably a millionaire, and you're offering him $1.50 seats.

"I appreciate the offer, son." A pleased smile etched deep

creases in his face. "Who knows, maybe I'll take you up on it someday."

On the bandstand, a singer began to screech her warm-ups. I thanked Whitaker for his time and said good-bye.

○ ○ ○

I should have left for Redland Field, but decided I had time for a quick detour to the northwest corner of the zoo.

Past a row of odd Japanese-styled structures that served as aviaries, was the Carnivora House, home to the zoo's big cats. On the lawn near the building's entrance was Margie, surrounded by about fifty children with attendant parents.

She was dressed in the outfit that she'd worn most often in her movies: pith helmet, khaki shirt, jodhpurs, and high boots. A trainer held a bushy-maned male lion on a leash while Margie gave a talk on how lions lived in the wild, describing their diet, family life, and sleeping habits. It was only her second day on the job, but her performance was polished and natural.

And she really came to life when the children started asking questions, fielding them with patience and charm. They asked everything from why didn't the lion get a haircut to how did he get the title "King of the Jungle"—her answer to the latter question was, "Because he married the Queen of the Jungle."

I thought back to when Margie told me how happy I'd looked telling baseball stories to Patrick Kelly. She looked the same with these children. And suddenly the thought struck me that if I ever had children of my own, I'd want Margie to be their mother.

Someday, maybe.

Chapter Ten

ooo

At first glance, I thought I'd entered the wrong building. The Public Library of Cincinnati and Hamilton County was constructed more like a theater auditorium than a library. It was mostly open space, with a wide central well that rose all the way from the ground floor to the roof of the four-story building. Books were shelved between the railings and sidewalls of an upper-level mezzanine that circled the well like a balcony section. There were no bookcases on the main floor, which was furnished only with reading tables, chairs, and benches.

Not sure where to find what I was seeking, I approached a high desk next to the main entrance. Before I could say anything, the matronly woman seated behind it tapped her finger on a sign that had the single word *Ladies* on it. "This is the ladies' circulation desk," she said. I was tempted to reply that I wasn't here to check out a lady. Pointing to an identical piece of furniture on the other side of the entrance, she added, "The men's desk is over there."

"I just want to know where I would find old newspapers."

The librarian hesitated. Perhaps she wasn't even supposed to speak to males. "The papers for the past week are on the tables in the back." She gestured toward the rear of the room with a slight lift of her head.

"I'm looking for 1869."

"Oh my. Those aren't generally accessible. Ask Mr. Driscoll at the men's desk. He might be able to help you."

I thanked her and crossed to the side of the room designated for my gender. Wait till I tell Margie about this, I thought. Separate circulation desks for men and women—the city fathers probably wanted to be sure that Cincinnati's gentler sex wasn't exposed to any materials that might be considered risqué. I had to stifle a laugh, imagining the poor librarian who tried to stop Margie from taking out any book she wanted.

Of the two young males behind the desk, Driscoll was the more slightly built. He agreed to bring me the old newspapers, although he seemed reluctant to do so. While I waited, I commented on the unusual style of the building to the other librarian. He told me that the structure had originally been designed as Handy's Opera House; when the opera company went bankrupt during construction, the library took over, retaining what had already been built.

Driscoll arrived with a ten-day stack of the *Cincinnati Enquirer* and the *Cincinnati Commercial* dated July 1 through July 10, 1869. Instead of handing them to me, he carried them to a reading table and laid them down gently. "These are *very* fragile," he said. "No folding! When you're finished, tell me, and I'll return them to storage."

I promised to be careful, and reached for the July 3 issue of the *Enquirer*. Driscoll remained, looking over my shoulder to see how I treated the brittle, browning papers. I handled them carefully and turned the pages slowly. Eventually satisfied that I could read a newspaper without his supervision, he returned to his desk.

By speaking with Ambrose Whitaker, I had tried going back one link in the chain of events that connected the murder of a girl named Sarah in the summer of 1869 with Ollie Perriman's death this year. Now I was trying the other end of the chain. I scrutinized every item in the *Enquirer,* looking for mention of a murdered or missing girl, or a girl named Sarah or one from Corryville. Nothing. I proceeded to the *Commercial* for the same date, with the same results.

There were no Independence Day editions. The Monday, July 5, papers had nothing about Sarah, but did report that the Red Stockings players were escorting members of the visiting Olympic Base Ball Club on a tour of the city's sights. I couldn't imagine Ty Cobb or John McGraw playing host to a visiting team like that; it certainly must have been a more gentlemanly era back then.

Through the tenth of July, there were no items in the papers that could have been related to what I'd read in the note about Sarah. To be thorough, I went back to the issues from the first two days of the month—perhaps she'd been reported missing before her supposed murder. Still nothing.

With no luck finding anything about the girl, I permitted myself to read about the team. There was extensive coverage of the Red Stockings homecoming. The July 1 *Enquirer* reported:

> *The only real sensation which our city has enjoyed of late has been that created by our victorious Red Stockings on their Eastern tour. The success which they met is unprecedented in the history of the national game, and it is but natural that after such admirable playing*

and splendid conduct the citizens of Cincinnati will feel
like giving the boys a hearty reception today.

A hearty reception it certainly was, according to the next
day's paper. Four thousand people gathered at the Little
Miami Railroad Depot and a committee of prominent citizens
met what the *Enquirer* called "*our victorious Red Stockings,*
the first nine of which met and conquered all the first-class
base ball clubs of the country." The paper went on to describe
the homecoming:

The train arrived at the depot promptly on time, when
the boys, amid the enthusiastic cheers of the spectators,
were escorted to carriages provided for the occasion,
and taken over the line of march to the Gibson House.
At the head of the procession was the Zouave Band in
an open wagon gaily decorated with flags and banners.
Before starting, this band discoursed most elegant
music, playing "Home Sweet Home," and other airs,
which, together with the cheering of the crowd, formed
a scene of excitement such as Cincinnati has seldom
witnessed. All along the line of march the streets had
put on their gala-day costumes, the buildings were dec-
orated with flags and the sidewalks filled with gaily
dressed men, women and children, all eager to give
hearty welcome to the men who had, by their unrivaled
skill and gentlemanly conduct, spread Cincinnati's
good fame throughout the length and breadth of the
land.

It must have been a glorious time to be a ballplayer, I
thought. To have a crowd of thousands meet your train and

parade you through the streets amid cheers and song. To be adored by an entire city. Someday, maybe, I'd get the chance to play in a World Series, and if I was lucky enough to be on the winning team, I might get to feel a little of the adulation the Red Stockings enjoyed in 1869.

After a brief rest at the hotel, another procession took the players to the Union Grounds for a game against *"the best selected nine of the city."*

Prior to the match was the presentation of the bat, the twenty-seven-foot trophy given by Josiah Bonner of the Queen City Lumber Company to Aaron Champion, president of the Cincinnati Base Ball Club. I noted in the article that, *"If beaten in any match, the bat is to be transferred to the victorious club,"* and wondered if the Brooklyn Atlantics ever received it.

The exhibition game, won by the Red Stockings 53–11, was reported in tedious detail. Dick Hurley appeared in the lineup of the picked nine, so he was still with the club at that point.

An even lengthier account described the banquet at the Gibson House that night, for which tickets were sold at $5 a head—probably an enormous sum back then. Besides club members, the guests included *"many of the most prominent and respected citizens of Cincinnati,"* and their names were listed in the article.

The ten players were seated at a table of honor. Each wore a medal the shape and color of a red sock, which had been ceremoniously pinned on them as a token of appreciation from the City Council. Renditions of red stockings—called *"sanguinary hose"* by the *Enquirer* reporter—decorated virtually everything: a pyramid cake, the menus, and an elaborate floral arrangement.

Following a meal that included sweetbreads, mountain oysters, and buffalo tongue, there were endless rounds of toasts. The first was to the players, each of whom was then called upon to say a few words. They all declined to do so, most of them giving the excuse that they were unaccustomed to speaking in public. I was amused to read that the substitute Dick Hurley gave the lengthiest refusal, concluding with, *"I might have made a speech if I had been called upon before supper, but, as it is, I am too full for utterance."*

The second toast was to Aaron Champion, who earned thunderous applause when he said, *"Someone asked me today whom I would rather be, President Grant of the United States or President Champion, of the Cincinnati Base Ball Club. I immediately answered him that I would by far rather be president of the base ball club."* As I read his words, it occurred to me that I would have made the same choice—except I'd have wanted to be one of the players. Even if only the substitute.

After mining the first batch of papers Driscoll had given me for all the information I could glean, I went back to the men's circulation desk and asked him if there were any Corryville newspapers from that time. He said there weren't, but brought me issues of the *Gazette* and *Daily Times,* the only other Cincinnati papers in 1869, and more copies of the *Enquirer* and *Commercial.* I checked all of them through to the twentieth of July; I would have gone further, but my eyes were starting to ache from the small print.

I left the library and walked down to Fountain Square, the "center" of Cincinnati. Many of the men and women I passed had newspapers over their heads as if they'd been caught in a rainstorm. What was raining on them was worse than water though—it came from the flocks of starlings that occupied the ledges of the buildings. The birds were so numerous and their droppings so prolific, that probably half the newspapers sold downtown were used as headgear instead of reading material. I stayed on the street edge of the sidewalk to stay out of the line of fire, then crossed to the square in the middle of Fifth Street, where the magnificent fountain was situated.

According to the clock on the Mabley and Carew Building, it was a quarter to twelve, and I still had some time before needing to leave for the ballpark. I walked around the square, immersed in thought.

I was discouraged at having found no mention in the old newspapers of Sarah or a missing girl. Was Detective Forsch right—was the note a prank? Or did Sarah's death merely fall through the journalistic cracks even more completely than Ollie Perriman's had?

For no good reason, I found myself getting angry. The civic leaders who'd attended the Red Stockings banquet all got their names in the papers, as had the businessmen who'd been at Perriman's memorial in Redland Field. It seemed like "important" people could make the news simply by showing up, but folks like Perriman and Sarah could be murdered with little or no notice.

A sudden breeze gusted, whipping water from the fountain onto those of us near it. I looked up and saw a dark cloud in the northwest; it was small and dense, but another developed nearby, and soon the sun was blocked and it felt as if the temperature had dropped a full ten degrees.

By the time I hopped a streetcar for the ballpark, it looked like there might not be a game today.

○ ○ ○

Those of us who'd gotten onto the field early were just starting
to throw the ball around when a torrential cloudburst sent
us scrambling for the shelter of the dugout.

I ended up near the middle of the bench, between Edd
Roush and Greasy Neale. Several of the pitchers were clus-
tered at one end, and Bubbles Hargrave and Heinie Groh
sat together at the other.

We watched as Matty Schwab and his grounds crew
dashed out with a tarpaulin to cover the infield. Black clouds
thickened and swirled overhead, and rumbles of thunder
grew louder. The rain came down in waves; fat drops pelted
the tarp like machine-gun fire, and a windblown mist washed
into the dugout.

"I'm gettin' the hell out of here!" Groh yelled, and he
sprinted for the clubhouse with Hargrave close behind him.

The rest of us stayed. Although we were getting wet, the
cool spray was refreshing after all the hot weather we'd been
suffering through. And it had been getting worse lately. This
morning's papers reported that Midwestern towns were
pleading for shipments of ice from other parts of the country,
and in Chicago the heat wave had claimed seven lives yesterday alone.

We sat transfixed by nature's cleansing outburst until Edd
Roush broke the silence by saying, "Looks like they ain't
never gonna get that damn trial going." Jury selection had
finally gotten under way in the Black Sox trial, but it was
progressing slowly. Only three jurors had been seated in three
days, and now the defense was rejecting all Cubs fans from
the jury pool, claiming they would have "an inherent preju-
dice" against White Sox players.

"Wish to hell they'd get it over with and give us back our title," Neale said. The burly outfielder stomped his foot on the ground for emphasis.

"Get it over with which way?" I asked. "Guilty or innocent?"

Roush turned his gloomy face to me. "Innocent, you sap. If they're found not guilty, that means we won the championship fair and square."

"No way they can find them guilty anyway now," Neale put in. "Not without the confessions." In one of those peculiarities that occasionally afflict Chicago legal proceedings, the grand jury confessions of Joe Jackson, Ed Cicotte, and Lefty Williams had somehow disappeared from the files of the State's Attorney.

"Even if they get off, it won't—" I stopped myself in midsentence. Why say what we all knew: the 1919 championship was tainted—*baseball* was tainted—by what had happened. A jury verdict wouldn't change that.

"We beat 'em 'cause we were better than 'em," insisted Roush.

"You really don't think it was fixed?" I asked.

Neale snorted. "Don't be stupid. Of course it was."

Roush said, "Hell, everybody *knows* it was fixed. But that ain't what won it for us. We'd have beaten them anyway 'cause we were the better ball club."

"Them gamblers sure found that out," said Neale. "Wouldn't have tried to get us to ease up otherwise."

"What do you mean?" As far as I'd heard, the only players approached by gamblers were the White Sox.

"After we whipped the Sox in the first two games," Neale explained, "the odds went way down. So some sports approached a few of our players, trying to get us to ease up and maybe let the Sox win a game or two."

"To get the odds back up," I said.

Neale nodded.

"If them gamblers were as smart as they think they are," said Roush, "they'd have played it straight and bet on us to win. We'd have taken care of winning the Series without any help from them. Would have saved themselves whatever they paid the Sox, and there wouldn't be all this trouble now."

"Who'd they approach on the Reds?" I asked.

Roush's eyes drilled me like flying spikes. "There's some things we keep 'tween ourselves. If certain things get out, they might get turned around, and next thing you know, somebody's accusing one of *us* of taking a dive."

"He's part of the team now, Edd," Neale said.

"Not that team he wasn't."

Neale persisted, "Neither was Rixey, and you told him about it."

"Yeah, well, Eppa don't get traded every year. Who knows where this boy is gonna be next season and who he might tell." He spat on the dugout floor, adding to the puddle produced by the rain. "I'm going inside till this lets up." With that, Roush trotted off to the clubhouse. The team's star was known for four things: he used a bigger bat than Babe Ruth, he "retired" every year to avoid spring training, he had an uncanny ability to go back on fly balls in center field, and he could be every bit as ornery as Ty Cobb.

I said to Neale, "If you don't want to tell me, that's all right. I don't want you getting in hot water with Roush or any of the others."

"Never mind Edd," he answered. "He just got a bug up his ass about that championship. We all do. Nobody gives us credit for *winning* it. They all say the Sox *gave* it to us. Hell, we busted our humps a whole season to take the pennant, then the series against Chicago, and it's like we didn't do nothing to earn it." Neale shook his lowered head. "Anyway, we all knew about the gamblers. Edd himself is the one who brought it out in the open. One of them bastards told him some fellows on our club already sold out, and that Edd might as well go along, too. Edd went to Pat Moran about it, and we had a team meeting before Game Five. Moran asked if anybody else was approached. Hod Eller was scheduled to pitch for us that game, and he said yeah, a guy on an elevator tried to hand him five thousand-dollar bills. Said he told the guy to go to hell. Moran gave Eller the go-ahead to pitch, and Hod threw himself a shutout. He won the last game of the series, too."

"The gambler who talked to Roush told him some of the Reds were already in his pocket," I said. "Do you know who they were?"

"I don't believe there were any at all. Bastard probably made it up—you know, make it sound like everybody's in on it anyway, so you might as well get your piece of the action."

"Jeez." If the gamblers' efforts had succeeded, there could have been two teams trying to lose the same World Series.

"Well, the way I figure," said Neale, "is we would have won that series anyway—we were the better ball club, I'll always believe that—and we *did* end up winning, so everything worked out."

Yeah, worked out swell. Real fine exhibition of the national pastime.

"By the way," Neale added. "I hit .357 that series."

"I know you wouldn't sell out," I said. But I also remembered that Shoeless Joe Jackson, who admitted taking the gamblers' money, hit .375.

I remained in the dugout long after Neale and the pitchers retreated to the clubhouse, just watching the rain and thinking of the news stories I'd read this morning. Two world's champions: the Cincinnati clubs of 1869 and 1919. But what a difference between the glory of '69 and the scandal fifty years later.

Chapter Eleven

We never did get the game in on Thursday, and continuing rains wiped out Friday's as well. On Saturday, we had to pay for the respite, plus interest. The heat was back, more searing than it had been all summer, and we had to face the first-place Pirates in a doubleheader to make up one of the washed-out games.

I played every inning of both contests, substituting for the injured Larry Kopf. I got his spot in the batting order, at least; his shortstop position was taken by Curt Stram, who shifted over from second base, and I took Stram's place at second. The rookie crowed about getting the glamour position, telling me that my arms and legs were too old to cover the ground at short. I pointed out to him that I had a fist exactly the same age as my limbs, and it was quite capable of knocking out his front teeth.

By the end of the opener, a pitching showpiece with Eppa Rixey outdueling Wilbur Cooper 1–0, Stram was no longer gloating. Pittsburgh's batters had kept him moving, driving ground balls to his left and right. He booted two of them, but neither of the errors caused any damage. My running was done on the basepaths, with three singles in four at bats, plus two stolen bases.

Neither team was in condition to play another game; we were all sapped by the heat, even those who remained on the bench. It was as if the steamy air was leaching energy out of our pores. So, sure enough, we all had to do more running in the second game as both pitchers kept giving up bunches of base hits. Hod Eller, who'd been denied his shine ball when baseball tried to clean up the game last year by banning such pitches, was making his second start of the season for us. No longer permitted to apply talcum powder to the ball, though, he couldn't get the Pirates batters out; he was tagged for six runs in the first four innings and was relieved by Rube Marquard, who didn't fare much better. Still, we kept the game close by teeing off on the deliveries of Pittsburgh's Jimmy Zinn. I contributed three more hits to the barrage, capped by a triple that seemed the longest run of my life. We fell short at the end, the Pirates taking a 9–7 win and a split of the twin bill.

In the locker room afterward, we were finally able to collapse. The clubhouse was almost completely silent; now and then one of the players would curse the heat, guzzle a bottle of soda pop, or peel off a wet uniform, but hardly any of us had the strength left to walk all the way to the showers. I was the first to make the trek, buoyed by my performance on the field. I'd gone 6-for-9 on the day, with no misplays, while Curt Stram went hitless and committed four errors.

After dressing, I shifted my attention from running after baseballs on Redland Field to chasing ghosts from the Union Grounds. I'd had another idea of where I might find information on Dick Hurley.

Inside Redland's main entrance was the concession area,

where construction was under way to remodel a section of it for the exhibit room. Lloyd Tinsley and another man in a business suit were there. The lanky fellow, who looked familiar, stood aside quietly while Tinsley barked orders at several workers in overalls who were tearing out one of the counters.

The Reds' business manager turned from the construction workers to me. "Ah, Rawlings. Let me introduce you." He gestured at the other man. "This is Nathaniel Bonner of the Queen City Lumber Company."

I shook hands with Bonner. "Yes, I remember seeing you at the memorial for Ollie Perriman. How did you ever make a bat that big?"

Bonner was slightly bent at the waist, as if accustomed to having to lean down to talk with people not as tall as he. "Special equipment and skilled craftsmen," he said proudly. "No job too big or too unusual for us to handle." His hair was inky black, maybe dyed, and his cheeks hollow. He looked a little like a young, beardless Abraham Lincoln. And, like Lincoln's, Bonner's appearance would have benefited greatly from some facial hair.

"Rawlings is going to be at the grand opening," Tinsley said to Bonner. I was happy to hear that; according to the papers—which were giving the exhibit more and more publicity—Edd Roush and Heinie Groh had agreed to attend, so I thought I might no longer be wanted.

To me, Tinsley said, "We were just going over how to display that bat. It would look most impressive standing up, but the ceiling's too low."

"My preference," said Bonner, "is to put it on a couple of sawhorses right in the middle of the corridor here. People can walk around it up close; even touch it if they want."

Make it easier to read *Queen City Lumber Company* on its side, too, I thought.

"Well, I suppose you're right," Tinsley said. "But if it's out in the open, they won't have to pay to come into the exhibit room to see it."

"It might get them interested in seeing the rest of the stuff," I said. "You know, like a free sample."

"Well, there's no alternative anyway," Tinsley decided. "If it won't fit inside, it will have to be out here."

With that issue settled, Bonner and Tinsley briefly discussed the arrangements for moving and mounting the bat, then Bonner left for his lumberyard.

Alone with Tinsley, I said, "I came by to ask if I could take a look at the collection again."

He hesitated. "I suppose that'd be okay. I'll have to let you in, though—we keep the office locked now." After giving the workers a few more instructions, Tinsley started toward the stairwell and I followed.

As we walked upstairs, I asked, "Still no date for the opening?"

"No. We're going to wait until after the trial; wouldn't want the opening to be overshadowed by what's going on in Chicago. And that'll give us time to finish building the exhibit room, and try to arrange for George Wright and Cal McVey to come to the opening—they both came for the 1919 World Series. Don't know if they'll be up to making the trip again, though."

The way the trial was proceeding, Tinsley would have all the time he needed to try to persuade them. In the last three days, only one more juror had been seated.

We'd reached the second floor and started down the hallway. "Mr. Bonner's going to use the time to have some more bats made up," Tinsley went on. "His company's giving free bats to the first thousand kids who come to the exhibit."

"Bet they all have 'Queen City Lumber' printed on them," I said.

"Something wrong with that?"

"I don't think Ollie Perriman would have liked it. He was putting together a *shrine*—something about memories and history." I shrugged. "Now it's business—charging admission to the exhibit, advertising a lumber company . . ." What's next, I thought, having ballplayers sell autographs? "The bats will probably be made from scrap, and break the first time a kid tries to hit a ball with them."

Tinsley stopped and gave me a hard look. "Come into my office for a minute." He led me into a room a few doors from Perriman's. It was smaller than I would have expected, and plainly furnished.

He sat down behind a desk covered with stacks of paperwork, and pointed me into one of the room's other two chairs. "You don't like baseball being 'tainted' by financial interests, I take it."

"No, I don't. It's the *game* that matters. Seems whenever it's treated like a business, things get messed up."

"Does your salary mess things up?"

"Well, no, fans buy tickets to watch me—the team— play. So that's a fair deal."

Tinsley slapped his palm on a stack of papers. "I am tired to death of ballplayers who complain about the *game* becoming a business at the same time they're drawing salaries bigger than almost anyone else can ever earn." His mouth was partly agape, and those big teeth of his exposed; for an instant, I had the bizarre fear that he might bite me.

To my relief, he took a deep breath, then patted the

papers and eased back in his chair. "Don't mean you in particular. Edd Roush holds out every spring and refuses to play in exhibition games. Then there was Heinie Groh demanding to be traded to New York. Must be nice to pick when and where you're going to play while somebody else has to make sure there's money to pay you, and feed you, and put you up in decent hotels, and arrange for Pullmans. Well, *I'm* the one who takes care of those things."

"I don't mean—"

He waved off my interruption. "Let me tell you something. I get the same salary if there's 5,000 people in the stands or 20,000. I try to make sure we draw good crowds because it's my job. If I could have been a player, I would have; but I got a head for business not baseball, so I do what I can as well as I can. Same with the vendors who sell the hot dogs and the clerks who sell the tickets. You think there's one of them who wouldn't rather be in your shoes, out on the field? But they can't. So we all do our part; there's more to a ball club than the nine men on the field."

"I never thought about—"

"Same with this exhibit," Tinsley cut me off. "If it draws people into the park, the gate receipts go up and the club benefits."

"Don't you get a share of the admission to the exhibit?" I asked.

"Yes, I do."

That didn't seem proper, somehow, but I couldn't think of anything specifically wrong with it.

"Mr. Herrmann knows about the arrangement, and he's given his approval," Tinsley said. "It's not unusual, you know. On some clubs, a coach's wife might be paid to do the team's laundry. In Chicago, William Wrigley sells his gum at the ballpark." He stood up. "Well, like I said, I guess this has been bothering me for a while. Sorry you had to be the one to bear the brunt of it."

"That's all right," I said. "Maybe I needed to hear it."

When Tinsley unlocked the door to Perriman's office, he added, "As for the exhibit, I put my own money into helping Ollie buy some of the items he wanted. And I'll be paying expenses if McVey or Wright come, as well as advertising and the construction downstairs. If the admissions are enough to cover those expenses and earn me a little extra, I won't apologize for that."

"No reason you should," I said. It was foolish of me to insist on the game being kept "pure" because it never had been. Not on the professional level, anyway. As Ambrose Whitaker had told me, there had been a lot of people working hard to make the Red Stockings financially viable, even though the players were the only ones being paid.

Once inside, Tinsley asked, "You looking for anything in particular?"

"No, just thought I'd poke around," I lied.

He left me alone, and I went directly to the desk. Perriman had mentioned having the Red Stockings score books. In the top drawer, I found them: two books, one dated 1869 and the other 1870.

I sat down and started leafing through the pages, beginning with the first entry for 1869. The names of the players were written in elegant script. They were almost the only thing I could understand, because the scoring system wasn't like anything I'd seen before. There were records of "muffed balls," "foul bounds caught," and "bases on slow handling."

But it was the players' names I was interested in anyway. After July 2, the name "Hurley" didn't appear in another lineup. I even went through the 1870 book to make sure he hadn't returned to the team that season, and found no mention of him.

The last couple of pages in the 1870 book contained detailed entries of attendance, gate receipts, and expenses. Lloyd Tinsley was right, I thought. As long as there'd been professional baseball, business considerations had been part of the "game."

Finally, I looked again at the July 1869 entries. Dick Hurley had played with the "picked nine" at the homecoming game on July 1. And he disappeared from the record book the very day that Sarah was supposedly murdered.

○ ○ ○

It was Margie's suggestion to have dinner here, and like so many of her ideas it was a good one. The Zoo Clubhouse had a fine restaurant that served full-course turkey, steak, or lake trout dinners for $1.75. The location was convenient—I'd simply taken the trolley to meet her after her final show—and the view from our balcony table overlooking the gardens was splendid.

As we started on the iced consommé, I told Margie all about the doubleheader. One of the few things I regretted about her working now was that she couldn't see me play at the ballpark. But I recounted every one of my at-bats and most of the fielding plays in enough detail so that she didn't miss much.

Soon after the main dishes arrived—Margie having ordered the trout while I opted for the turkey—the atmosphere changed, and not for the better. The nightly opera performance began at the nearby band shell. The orchestra wasn't bad, but the squalling of the vocalists was an awful thing to hear. Zoo animals joined in, adding a chorus of howls and grunts to the din, but unfortunately they weren't loud enough to drown out the singers.

The tone of our conversation changed, too. "I have a bad feeling about the Carnivora House," Margie said.

"You don't like the job?"

She jabbed her fork into the fish. "The job is fine. I love performing again, and talking with the children. It's the cats. I don't think they're as healthy as they should be."

"What's wrong with them?" I didn't like the idea of her working with lions or tigers that might be sick or injured; that's when those animals could be most dangerous.

"They're too skinny. I don't think they're eating right."

"Did you tell the keeper?"

"I sure did, and that was a *big* mistake." She rolled her eyes. "He told me that just because I was capable of standing next to an animal and looking pretty didn't mean I knew anything about them."

"How hard did you slap him?"

She let out a small giggle. "Wish I'd thought of that."

I could see that she was imagining taking a swing at the man, and she looked to be feeling better just at the notion of it.

"Or you could feed him to the lions," I said. "That should help fatten them up."

Margie's eyes showed that she liked that suggestion even better.

We finished eating quickly, then headed downtown to dance to jazz and try to get the opera out of our ears.

Chapter Twelve

000

Almost two hours before game time, I hopped off the Liberty Street trolley and walked the three blocks up Dalton. Redland Field came into view directly ahead, and it struck me how well the park fit into the working-class neighborhood. Its plain redbrick walls matched those of the Findlay Street row houses and the factories on Western Avenue.

I was coming to realize that a ball club is part of a community; their fortunes are intertwined. I used to think it was simple: fans who supported the team bought tickets and those gate receipts paid the players' salaries. But there's more to a professional baseball franchise than what transpires between the foul lines. It was apparent here: the newsboys hawking papers to early; arrivals, the vendors setting up peanut and lemonade carts, the trolley conductors—they all depended on the games for their own livelihoods. We were in business together.

Automobiles darted around the trolleys and pedestrians, heading for the tiny parking lot next to the railroad tracks west of the park. Anyone arriving by car had to come early to get parking. When Herrmann built the park in 1912, he'd neglected to take into account that more people would soon be driving automobiles. Some enterprising residents near the field rented their front yards and driveways for parking—another venture benefiting from the games.

At the corner of Dalton and Findlay, some fans turned east to buy bleacher tickets at the Western Avenue office. Most of the others turned left toward the main ticket office, which was the direction I also went.

The administrative wing of the ballpark, on the southwest corner, housed the offices, ticket windows, and clubhouse. This was of a more elegant construction, with white-stone inlays among the bricks, arches over the second- and third-floor windows, and ticket windows that looked like castle turrets.

I was half a block from the entrance when a bareheaded man in a pumpkin-colored suit stepped toward me. "Rawlings! Mickey Rawlings!" He was of medium build and average appearance in every respect but his ears: one lay flush with his head, while the other stuck out at a right angle, giving him the look of an inquisitive terrier.

I stopped. "Yes?"

He offered his hand. "Helluva game you played yesterday!"

"Thanks," I said, returning his grip. There was always close contact between fans and players in Cincinnati; we even had to go through the concession area filled with fans to get from the clubhouse to the field. But most of them didn't stop me; they went for Roush or Groh or Rixey. This was new—and flattering.

He continued pumping my arm. "You gonna be in the lineup today?"

"Sure am." I hoped.

"Well, you go get 'em." He finally broke off the grip. "Say, can I bother you for an autograph? For my kid. He'd sure be thrilled."

"Be happy to. Is he here?"

"No, home with the measles." He dug into his coat pockets. "Damn. Nothing to write on." Then he pulled a plain brown envelope from an inside pocket. "This'll have to do I guess." He handed it to me along with a pencil stub. "Could you sign this?"

I signed the blank envelope and gave it back.

"Thanks!"

"My pleasure."

He shook my hand once more, then again wished me a good game.

As I suited up for the game, I was thinking that Cincinnati would be a nice place to live and hoping that I'd get to stay here for a while. I'd always moved around so much that I never got to feel part of a community. But the notion of settling down was becoming more and more appealing to me. Maybe I'd even make things a little more formal with Margie.

O O O

On the other hand, I could see one big plus to being on a different team: I'd get the chance to play *against* Curt Stram. His youthful pride had been wounded yesterday by the difference in our game performances, and he was now trying to salvage some of it. Throughout the pregame pepper, he kept riding me, pointing out that I was dependent on the starters getting hurt in order to have a shot at making the lineup. I didn't let him get to me, though, and didn't bother responding. For one thing, the odds were that someday we'd be playing on opposing teams; at some point he'd have to face me as I came sliding into second base—and he was going to lose that showdown. The other reason I let him chatter on was because what he said was true.

And it got me thinking. Dick Hurley had been in the same situation as me, but with far greater assurance of getting into games. Hurley had been the only paid substitute on the Cincinnati roster in '69. Without gloves or other protective equipment, the starters must have suffered frequent injuries. So he couldn't have left the team because he was no longer needed. In fact, three other names appeared in the score book for that year: Fowler, Bradford, and Taylor. All three played their first games in July, the same month that Hurley vanished.

Hurley had played in the exhibition game and attended the banquet on July 1, and that's where the written record of him came to an end. The next day, according to the note I'd found, a girl named Sarah was murdered. The timing could have been mere coincidence, but I couldn't ignore the possibility, however slim, of a connection.

After infield practice, I looked around and spotted Dave Claxton hitting fungoes to the outfielders. He'd been the only one to tell me anything at all about Hurley, so I thought I'd see if I could milk his memory a little more.

I walked past Dolf Luque warming up with Bubbles Hargrave, and out to Claxton. "Want me to hit a few?" I asked.

He handed me the bat and I knocked a fly to Edd Roush. "Couple weeks ago," I said, "I asked you about Dick Hurley from the old Red Stockings. You said you thought him leaving the team had something to do with a girl. You remember what it was about a girl exactly?"

He let out a long breath. "Hell, that was ages ago. And whatever I heard was second- or third-hand."

"But what *did* you hear?" I hit a towering fly that Greasy Neale had to go back on the terrace to catch.

"Well, one version was that him and the girl eloped; other version had it that he got run off by the girl's daddy. Most of the stories favored elopement, as I recall. Him and some rich local girl ran off together." A grin cracked Claxton's face. "Decent folk didn't approve of ballplayers in those days, but, same as now, the young ladies sure liked them."

I hit the next one to Pat Duncan. So maybe there was no murder. Maybe Hurley and Sarah simply eloped. They could still be alive now, fawning over their grandchildren somewhere.

"But I wouldn't lay no stock in them stories," Claxton cautioned. "Like I say, I don't know nothing about him for a fact, just what I heard."

It was more than I'd gotten from any other source. "Thanks, Clax." I handed him back the fungo bat.

It might have been better if I'd let the old coach bat for me in the game, too. I went 0-for-4 against Babe Adams, striking out three times. To make it worse, I also made three errors at second, the last one allowing the winning run to score for the Pirates.

On the way out of the park after the game, I wondered if the man I'd met earlier was still going to give my autograph to his son. I wouldn't have been surprised if the envelope I'd signed was now in shreds, scattered on the ground with the ticket stubs and the peanut shells.

Chapter Thirteen

○○○

The smell of fresh-cut lumber reminded me of when I used to operate a lathe in a furniture factory, forming chair and table legs of oak and pine. Here at the Queen City Lumber Company, the scent of raw wood mingled with other aromas of the production process: a faint burning odor from the sawmill, where circular blades ripped through rough timber, smoke from the kilns, where finished boards were dried, and exhaust fumes from the trucks that hauled the wood from one area to the next.

The lumber company, in Camp Washington, about a mile north of Redland Field, was a sprawling complex of simple frame buildings and open-fronted shacks. Logs and cut lumber were stacked around the yard in no discernible order. Railroad sidings were west of the yard, with Mill Creek on the other side of the tracks; to the east, was the barren trench where the Miami Canal used to flow.

At ten-thirty Monday morning, I made my way to what looked like the main office, a long, two-story building off Spring Grove Avenue. It had fresher white paint than any of the other structures, and elaborate trim around the door and windows. I expected this would be my final attempt to find out what might have happened on July 2, 1869. If I got nowhere today, I would try to forget about it and concentrate on playing baseball for the current Reds.

Inside the office, I asked to speak with Nathaniel Bonner. A secretary checked, and relayed that Mr. Bonner would see me "momentarily." Half an hour later, with still no sight of Bonner, I was thinking that in the future I should call ahead and make appointments. While I waited, I prowled the lobby, looking over the pictures displayed on the walls. Many were photographs of the company grounds, showing its growth over time, with larger buildings and higher piles of lumber in the later views. Others were portraits, made by both camera and paintbrush, of Josiah Bonner and Nathaniel, recording their changes through the years. In the early ones, Josiah was pictured as a dashing dark-haired figure with a fashionable mustache gracing his upper lip; Nathaniel, even as a young man, had the same general features as his father but in a less handsome package. One photograph, obviously posed, showed the younger Bonner wielding a double-headed ax as he chopped at a tree that was already felled; he resembled a young Abe Lincoln splitting rails. In a prominent place on the wall, framed behind glass, was a *Harper's Weekly* woodcut of the great bat presentation in 1869. I was trying to identify the players in the drawing when I heard a door open and Nathaniel Bonner tell his secretary, "I'll be at the north warehouse for a while."

I checked my watch—quarter past eleven.

"Terribly sorry to keep you waiting," Bonner said as he came up to me. "Having a shipment problem."

"That's all right," I said. "I appreciate you taking the time to see me."

He started toward the door, his tall figure hunched in a charcoal gray suit that hung loose on his frame. "Wish we could meet in my office, but I have to go over to one of the warehouses. Mind if we talk on the way?"

"Not at all." He motioned for me to go first, and we both went outside. In the daylight, I noticed the scars that pitted Bonner's hollow cheeks. "Actually," I said, "I was wondering if I could speak to your father."

"You could *speak* to him," he answered, "but I'm afraid you wouldn't get much of a response."

We began to tread carefully over the bare-earth road, stepping over scraps of wood and kicking up the sawdust that coated everything like fallen snow.

"Why's that?" I asked. During the ceremony at Redland Field, Bonner had said his father wasn't feeling well, so I assumed the elder Bonner was still alive. But perhaps that was no longer the case.

"He's ill. Been confined to Parkman Sanitarium in Bond Hill for more than a year now."

"Hope he gets better."

"Thank you, but I'm afraid it's not likely. He's suffering from dementia, and at seventy-five years old there's not much chance of improvement."

"Oh. I'm sorry."

"At least he's not in any pain. It's my mother that's suffering the most. They've been married more than forty years—happy years—and now when she goes to see him, sometimes he doesn't even recognize her. She's been taking it hard; seems completely lost without him." Bonner shrugged. "Sorry. I'm sure you didn't come here to listen to me go on about family problems. What did you want to see my father about?"

"I've been interested in the 1869 Red Stockings. Ever since I met Ollie Perriman. At the ceremony for him, you mentioned it was your father who presented that original big bat to the team."

"Yes, that's right."

"He was also at the homecoming banquet for the team—"

Bonner interrupted. "How do you know that?"

"The newspapers published the guest list. Anyway, I wanted to ask him about that night."

"You're curious about a dinner half a century ago?"

"Not the dinner, a player: Dick Hurley. It's the last time he was with the team. Never played for them again and seems to have disappeared. I was wondering if something happened at the banquet."

"I wouldn't know. I didn't even know there was a 'Hurley' on that team. But then, I couldn't name half a dozen players now on the Reds." He flashed me an apologetic smile. "No offense. I just don't follow the game. My mother is the baseball fan in the family."

"That's okay." I was used to being unknown anyway. "Dick Hurley was the team's substitute."

An open truck rumbled past us hauling a load of window frames. It occurred to me that it was one of the few signs of activity I'd seen in the yard. I also noticed that the piles of lumber were smaller than they appeared in the photos from years past, and some of the sheds were empty.

"Well, I'd be happy to tell you what I do know about the banquet," Bonner said. "My father spoke of that day often— it was one of the most important in his life."

"How so?"

"It marked his entry into the most elite level of the Cincinnati business community. Some very influential men were members of that club."

"I heard it was more of a gentleman's club than a sports team," I said.

"Indeed it was. William Procter and James Gamble were members. So was Andrew Erkenbrecher, who founded the zoo. And John Shillito, who had the biggest dry goods store west of the Alleghenies. The club was a wonderful means for the city's young men to make business connections. And that's what my father did. It was his idea to present the bat. He was only a young clerk with this company back then, but he managed to convince the owners that the donation would be good for business. And he was proven right. Got wonderful publicity for the company, and great contacts for himself. Company let him make the presentation, and he told me many of the city leaders congratulated him at the banquet that night. Soon after, my father was promoted. He worked his way up quickly, and eventually became president."

"So he got involved with the club only because of business," I said. "He didn't like baseball?"

A look of distaste darkened Bonner's features. "The game itself was dreadful. Played mostly by ruffians in those days. It was the glory that could be gained for a city that counted."

"Or for a company."

"That's right."

We stopped at a rickety warehouse. Bonner excused himself and went inside. I looked around the largely empty yard, thinking that maybe the younger Bonner was hoping to do what his father had—that by getting involved with the exhibit at Redland Field, he would give his business a boost.

Bonner came out a few minutes later, and said, "By the

way, Mr. Tinsley told me about your comment regarding the bats we'll be giving out. They *will* have 'Queen City Lumber' printed on them, and I'm proud of it. This company is part of the community, always has been. And I have a fondness for the baseball team, if only because of what it did for my father in the past. But you're wrong about one thing: they will be good quality ash—wouldn't look good to have kids breaking bats that we made."

I wasn't going to argue with him. I couldn't. Business *was* part of baseball. Hell, it was industries that had given me my start, paying me to work easy jobs while playing for the company baseball teams.

I returned to my original interest. "Do you remember your father ever saying *anything* about Dick Hurley?"

"No. I doubt that he even spoke to the players. Like I said, he was there to make business contacts."

At the main office I thanked Nathaniel Bonner for his time and left to go to the park. I couldn't think of anything more to try. My quest to discover what had happened to Dick Hurley, or to a sixteen-year-old girl named Sarah from Corryville, was as likely to bear fruit as a pile of sawdust.

Chapter Fourteen

ooo

I had dinner ready and on the table when Margie came home from the zoo Tuesday night.

Her eyes showed a mixture of delight that she wouldn't have to cook and fear that I might have.

"It's safe," I reassured her. "I didn't make any of it myself." I'd only reheated some of Margie's latest batch of burgoo and picked up sandwiches from Kroger's to go along with the stew.

"That was sweet of you," she said, and gave me a kiss. "Oh, and I have a surprise for *you.*" Margie went to the parlor stand near the front door, where she'd put her handbag. She came back with the afternoon edition of the *Cincinnati Post.*

I thanked her, but was a bit puzzled. Why was a newspaper a surprise?

"Page three," she said.

I turned to that page, and there was Dick Hurley. An article about him, anyway.

Described by the *Post* reporter as "the missing sock" of the old Red Stockings, Hurley had arrived in the Queen City last night. According to the article, he was to be a guest at the opening of the exhibit honoring his old team, and Lloyd Tinsley would be hosting a dinner for him on Wednesday night.

O O O

By Wednesday evening, I was hoping that meeting the old Red Stocking would redeem what had been a miserable day.

I couldn't get to see Hurley earlier in the day because Pat Moran had called a morning practice. The Reds had lost three straight games, each defeat worse than the one before, so the manager ordered an extra workout session. Such practices generally accomplish little; no major leaguer is going to improve his fielding by catching fungoes or sharpen his hitting by teeing off on batting-practice tosses. About the most those exercises can accomplish is bolster a player's confidence. At least they couldn't hurt—except for today. A foul line drive during batting practice nailed Hod Eller in the eye, and a collision between Greasy Neale and Rube Bressler in the outfield left Bressler with a broken thumb.

The afternoon was worse, at least for me. Spittin' Bill Doak, the ace of the St. Louis Cardinals and one of only seventeen pitchers who would be allowed to use the spitball until their careers were over, struck me out the first three times I faced him. Since the Saturday doubleheader against Pittsburgh, I'd gone 0-for-14 at the plate.

At least after the game, I did wangle an invitation to the dinner from Lloyd Tinsley. He thought it would be a good publicity angle to stage a meeting between me and baseball's first professional utility player.

Evening finally came, and I walked into the plush lobby of

the Sinton Hotel, dressed in my best suit and with a hundred questions that I wanted to ask Dick Hurley.

I spotted Lloyd Tinsley and Fred Hewitt, a sportswriter for the *Post,* standing near a gaunt, elderly man seated in a leather wing chair. His dark eyes blinked and darted like a pigeon's. His hair was no longer the black that I'd seen in the team portraits. Sparse strands of white hair were combed over a scalp blotched with liver spots; a trim fringe of snowy beard covered his chin, and a mustache, twisted and waxed at the tips, lined his upper lip. The mustache was the only elegant feature about him. He was wearing a winter suit of brown tweed that was at least a decade out of style; for him to be wearing it this time of year meant it was probably the best he had—and the jacket was fraying at the cuffs. Recent years had not been kind to him, I thought.

As I approached, I heard him say to Hewitt, "Disappear? I don't know why anyone would say that. I played for the Washington Olympics in '72, I'll have you know, along with my old Cincinnati teammates Asa Brainard and Fred Waterman. If the Olympics hadn't folded by the end of May, who knows what I might have gone on to."

"Where *did* you go on to?" the reporter asked, scribbling in a notepad.

"Played a little here and there," Hurley answered. "Then I went back home to Pennsylvania. Worked as a cooper, making barrels. Later moved to Indiana."

Tinsley interrupted to introduce me to the former Red Stocking, and Hewitt went to find the *Post* photographer. Now I was nervous about meeting Hurley—and hoping that he hadn't heard about my performances on the field the past few days. It turned out I needn't have worried; he hadn't heard of me at all, although he graciously—and unconvincingly—pretended that he had.

We didn't get a chance to talk before the photographer came and put Hurley and me in a pose shaking hands. I felt like a big shot; this time I was one of those who'd be getting his name in the paper for going to an event. I'd even get my picture in it!

Nathaniel Bonner and a few others who liked to have their names published arrived, then Tinsley ushered all of us into the dining room; Garry Herrmann, unable to attend, would pick up the tab, he said.

To my surprise, I was seated next to Hurley, and the reporter was on the other side of him. I expected Tinsley or Bonner would want the choice seats, but as the dinner proceeded, I realized that they weren't interested in talking with the man; to Tinsley, Hurley's function was merely to garner some publicity.

During the first course, Hewitt asked a few more questions, mostly about famous contemporaries of Hurley's. When you're a utility player, many of the questions you get are about other, more famous, players you might have met.

Hurley kept saying, "Oh yes, I remember them well"— but in the same doubtful tone as when he'd met me in the lobby.

Hewitt then asked, "Tell me about that tie against Troy."

The old Red Stocking dutifully recounted the story of the infamous game with the Haymakers in Troy, New York. Gamblers had bet heavily on Troy to break the Red Stockings winning streak. When the score was tied 17-17 in the sixth inning, and the gamblers began to fear a loss, the Haymakers withdrew from the field in order to protect the wagers. Troy claimed a tie, but the game was officially awarded to Cincinnati. There were a couple of things I noticed about Hurley's tale. One was that there was no personal perspective to his account; it sounded like something he'd read. The other was that he claimed to have witnessed the game—although from reading the score books I knew that the match had been played in August, a month after he'd vanished.

The story appeared to satisfy Fred Hewitt, though. He scribbled a little more, then closed his notebook and concentrated on the meal.

"Did you get in the game?" I asked Hurley.

"No, no. Harry went with the regular nine. But I was ready and willing."

I was starting to have doubts about Mr. Hurley's memory. "Why did you leave the team before the end of the season?"

He stammered, then said he'd had a better offer to play elsewhere.

"I've been interested in the homecoming celebration that was given the team in '69," I said. "Can you tell me what it was like?"

"Homecoming . . ." He absorbed himself in his baked potato for a moment.

"Yes, it was the beginning of July, after the Eastern tour. There was an exhibition game and a banquet . . ."

"Oh yes, of course! Wonderful time. Great fans in Cincinnati. No place else like it."

I gave up, and followed Hurley's example in paying attention to the food. I was feeling some of the same disappointment as when Ollie Perriman told me about the "1869" baseball being a fake. Then I tried again. "A few years later, you were with Washington, I heard you say?"

Hurley then talked in detail about his brief tenure with the '72 Washington Olympics of the National Association, baseball's first major league. His recollections of this team sounded authentic.

"You've really been a part of history," I said. "The first professional team and the first professional league."

He sat up a little straighter. "That's right!" It didn't seem that the thought had occurred to him before.

I tried once more to ask him about early July of 1869, but he deflected the question and talked instead about his later days as a cooper.

As he spoke, I thought of the stories I'd read in *Photoplay* magazine about secretaries who would sometimes go to Hollywood claiming to be royalty; they'd often be lavished with attention from the stars until they were found to be frauds. I had the feeling that's what we had here. I looked across the table at Lloyd Tinsley talking with Bonner and wondered if he'd questioned the man sitting next to me to determine if he really was the missing Red Stocking. Then I realized it didn't matter to Tinsley—all he needed was a name and photograph for the newspaper.

Suddenly I felt relaxed, not minding the deception. The old man next to me was doing no more than a million men have done in saloons and barbershops, telling stories about things they'd never really done.

Hurley and I soon fell into a comfortable discussion about the making of barrels.

By the time dessert came, I was quite content. The hunt for Dick Hurley hadn't been a success, but it was now over for me. I would put 1869 behind me and concentrate on helping the 1921 Reds to finish higher than seventh place in the National League.

Chapter Fifteen

○○○

Garry Herrmann pushed a sandwich across his desk to me. "Have a little something," he said.

The "little something" was two thick slabs of black bread with about an inch of cheese between them. I didn't think I could fit it into my mouth if I'd wanted to—which I didn't. The cheese smelled like a cross between Limburger and a locker room full of sweaty ballplayers. "No, thank you," I said. It was probably bad manners to decline Herrmann's hospitality, but vomiting on his desk would be worse.

"It's Liederkranz," he said. "Very good. Go ahead."

I declined the sandwich as well as the subsequent offers of liver sausage, Thuringian blood pudding, and a stein of foaming beer. He left them all on my side of the desk anyway.

Herrmann's office on the top floor of the administrative wing of Redland Field was more like a beer garden than the headquarters of a baseball-club president. Sideboards abutted either side of his desk. One table held a variety of sausages, breads, pickles, potato salads, radishes, coleslaw, and a boiled ham. The other supported an even greater quantity of beverages—bottles of wine, buckets of beer, and amber liquids in crystal decanters. Under the table was an entire keg, and on a credenza behind Herrmann were glasses and steins of various shapes and sizes. All that was missing from the room was a singing waiter and an oompah band.

I remembered what Detective Forsch had said about the Reds' president being part of the corrupt Boss Cox machine. To me, Garry Herrmann didn't resemble a politician any more than his office looked like a place of business. His smiling florid face radiated what in Over-the-Rhine was called *"Gemütlichkeit,"* and his appearance was that of a dapper, middle-aged saloonkeeper: neat little mustache, hair slicked down and parted in the middle, and flashy clothes. Today he was wearing an emerald green suit with bright yellow crosshatching; a diamond stickpin was in his paisley tie and a pink carnation in the buttonhole of his lapel.

Herrmann took a long swallow from his stein, foam sticking to his mustache. The Eighteenth Amendment had never become law as far as Garry Herrmann was concerned; he had the wherewithal to obtain the very best of what Prohibition had outlawed and enough influence to avoid being arrested for it. "A glass of beer never hurt anybody," he said. "And two glasses are bound to be a big help." It was his motto, and he said it often.

"Can't," I insisted. "Game starts in an hour."

He put the stein down, and his smile disappeared. "You won't be playing."

It wasn't exactly unusual for me not to play, but if I was informed at all, it was typically the manager who told me, not the team president. Unless . . . was I being traded? Sold? "Is something wrong?" I asked. Please don't tell me I'm being released.

Herrmann squirmed in his seat and tugged at the sparkling

rings on his fingers. Something was definitely wrong. He reached in a drawer, and I wondered what menu item he was going to pull out next. "It's the photograph. And who's in it with you."

"Huh?" I assumed he meant the photo of Dick Hurley and me that appeared in this morning's *Post.* "What's wrong with having my picture taken with Dick Hurley?" I asked. "Mr. Tinsley arranged it."

Herrmann pulled two black-and-white prints from the drawer and slid one of them over to me. "That gentleman with you is Rufus Yates," he said.

I studied the photo. It showed me shaking hands with a man in front of the ballpark. I had no idea . . . Then I recalled the fellow with the funny ear. "Oh! That's a guy who stopped me a few days ago and asked for my autograph."

"It was Sunday," Herrmann said. "I looked at the newspaper headline." In the photo, Yates and I were standing near a newsboy, but I couldn't make out the headline of the paper the boy was holding up. Herrmann apparently noticed my puzzled look; from another drawer he pulled a large magnifying glass and handed it to me.

I checked, and saw that the newspaper was indeed the Sunday edition of the *Cincinnati Times-Star.* Its banner headline announced the peace agreement that had been signed between the Irish Republican Army and the commander of British forces in Ireland:

TRUCE FOR IRELAND IS SIGNED
Fighting Is To End Monday

"But I don't understand," I said. "What difference does it make?"

Herrmann handed me the second photo, this one of the man handing me an envelope. "What was in the envelope, Mickey?" His eyes narrowed as he studied my response.

"I don't know. The fellow didn't have anything else for me to sign, so he handed me the envelope. Said it was for his boy." I still didn't understand. "What is this about?"

"Rufus Yates is well-known in this city. He is a petty crook—and a gambler."

Jeez. Don't tell me—

"I will have to pass this on to Judge Landis," Herrmann said. There was a note of regret in his voice, which I thought was genuine. "You understand with the way things are right now, any possible"—he struggled to find a word—"*indiscretion* must be reported."

"There *wasn't* any indiscretion," I said. "I had no idea who the guy was. He came up to me, told me to have a good game, and asked me to sign something for his boy."

"Yes, well, about 'having a good game'—you have not gotten a base hit since he gave you that envelope. It might appear that your meeting with this fellow had some effect on your play."

How could I explain a slump? A four-game hitless streak wasn't all that unusual for me. I wasn't Ty Cobb or Edd Roush. Is that my defense, I thought, that I'm a lousy hitter? "He *didn't* give me the envelope," I said. "I signed it and gave it back to him."

Herrmann paused to pour himself a small glass of schnapps. "I'm no Charles Comiskey," he said finally. "If you're an honest player, I'll stick with you—as far as I can." He leaned forward. "So tell me the truth: is there anything going on here with you and Rufus Yates?"

"*No.*"

"Very well. I spoke with Pat Moran, and he hasn't seen anything funny in your play. It simply hasn't been very good of late."

"I know, but I—"

"These photos will be on a train tonight to Landis. Until he decides what to do, you won't be playing."

"What about innocent till proven guilty?"

"Not in baseball. Judge Landis is in power now." He sighed. For eighteen years, since the American League and National League made peace in 1903, Garry Herrmann had been head of the National Commission that ruled baseball. Since November, though, Judge Landis was the absolute boss of the game—a "czar," the newspapers called him. "We have to cover ourselves," Herrmann explained. "If we have any evidence of fraternizing with gamblers, we cannot allow you to play until we get approval from Landis."

"What about the road trip Friday?" We were to head East for games in Philadelphia, New York, Brooklyn, and Boston.

"Better if you stay here," Herrmann said, shaking his head. "The Judge will probably want to speak to you in person."

"And until then?"

"We—you—wait."

"Do I suit up for today's game?"

"No. Go ahead home."

What would people—my teammates—think? "What will you tell people?" I asked.

"What do you mean?"

"Can we keep quiet about why I'm not playing—say I'm injured or something? Landis is gonna clear me. He has to— a picture of me shaking a fellow's hand isn't evidence of anything. But if it gets out that I'm under investigation, some folks will think I'm not on the square."

"The handshake isn't the problem. The envelope—and your poor performance afterward—is." He downed the rest of the schnapps. "However, I see your point about being discreet. I think it's only fair to keep this a private matter for now."

We agreed that the public reason for my absence would be that I was seeing a doctor for headaches and vision problems. Then Herrmann repeated his offer of beer and his slogan about one glass and two.

I settled for one.

○ ○ ○

Chapter Sixteen

My eyes focused in and out. sometimes taking in the cornfields of central Indiana, sometimes catching my reflection in the train window as we rattled northwest toward Chicago. It jarred me every time the image of my face flashed on the glass; I couldn't believe how scared I looked.

Or how alone I felt. Contributing to my sense of isolation was the expanse of flat plains outside and the lack of company in the nearly empty railroad coach. So was the knowledge that, at this very moment, the rest of the Reds team was traveling in the opposite direction, on a Pullman to Philadelphia for the start of an Eastern road trip. They were going to be playing the Phillies in Baker Bowl while I was off to face Judge Kenesaw Mountain Landis by myself.

I had no allies in this fight to clear my name. Before I left Cincinnati, I'd asked Garry Herrmann and Pat Moran for letters attesting to my honest efforts on the ballfield. Both gave me verbal encouragement but refused to put anything in writing—because it would look bad for them if it turned out I really was tied to gamblers.

I'd also called a longtime friend of mine, a former newspaper reporter named Karl Landfors. For almost a year, Karl had been in Boston trying to help a couple of Italian anarchists named Sacco and Vanzetti who were on trial for murder; he was convinced they were being railroaded because of their political views. Karl had helped me out of some tough jams in the past, and I thought he might have some ideas on how I could get out of my current predicament. The first thing he told me, though, was the news that the Italians had been found guilty. I tried to sound sympathetic about the verdict. I also said I wasn't going to be able see him next week as we'd planned. But I couldn't bring myself to tell him *why* I wasn't going to be in Boston with the team.

I did tell Margie, the one person to whom I could confide anything. Even talking to her about it, though, I felt ashamed. Merely being under suspicion was enough to have me totally demoralized.

In the past, I'd found sufficient strength in my own knowledge of whether I was right or wrong. Not this time. It didn't matter what *I* knew, or even what the truth was. All that counted was what the new baseball commissioner would believe. And since taking office, he'd shown little inclination to be persuaded that ballplayers were innocent of any charge.

Landis placed the eight indicted White Sox—Joe Jackson, Chick Gandil, Swede Risburg, Lefty Williams, Ed Cicotte, Hap Felsh, Buck Weaver, and Fred McMullin—on the ineligible list in March. The move was widely heralded as being exactly the sort of decisive action baseball needed. I agreed with it myself; three of the players had already confessed, and there was enough evidence for a grand jury to indict the eight, so I figured it was reasonable that they shouldn't be allowed to play until their case was decided in court.

But two weeks later, Landis banned Phillies' first baseman

Gene Paulette, and the reasoning was less understandable. Paulette had "associated" with gamblers when he played for St. Louis, but there was no evidence that he'd ever done anything crooked.

Gambling-related allegations weren't the only thing that could land a player on the "permanently ineligible" list. Benny Kauff of the Giants, once hailed as "the Ty Cobb of the Federal League," was put on the blacklist for reasons that had nothing to do with baseball. Kauff was co-owner of an automobile dealership and had been indicted on charges of receiving stolen cars. In May, he was acquitted in court—but Judge Landis declared that the acquittal was "a miscarriage of justice" and kicked the former batting champion out of baseball. This action started to trigger some rumblings that the commissioner was overstepping his authority.

Landis's June victim was Ray Fisher, one of the Reds pitchers who'd helped lead them to the 1919 championship. Fisher had decided to spend this season coaching the University of Michigan baseball team instead of playing for the Reds. He'd done everything by the book, going so far as to obtain permission from Garry Herrmann and Pat Moran before talking with university officials about the job. Landis, without giving the pitcher a hearing or issuing an explanation, banned Fisher for "contract jumping." Not even the judge's staunchest supporters could defend this ruling.

By now, I didn't know what to make of the commissioner, but his actions sure seemed to be getting more eccentric. And it was now July. Was I to be this month's example of his absolute authority?

The train lurched and I saw my face in the window again. I wanted to calm the scared kid who was looking back at me, but didn't know how.

○ ○ ○

Having lived in Chicago for three years, I was aware that the Federal Building in the Loop was considered to be one of the city's architectural jewels. I'd always admired its majestic style, but it was its sheer size that struck me now. Eight floors of granite and marble covered the entire block bounded by Jackson, Adams, Clark, and Dearborn. Topping the massive structure was a dome one hundred feet across and three hundred feet high—larger even than the one that crowned the Capitol Building in Washington. Federal operations for the entire Midwest were carried out from this building, and it appeared that the U.S. government wanted to make its presence and authority known by the imposing size of the edifice that represented it. And it was in this building that Kenesaw Landis presided as a federal judge.

I went inside, passing through the octagonal rotunda decorated with mosaics and gilded bronze. Then to the sixth floor, where the U.S. District Court for Northern Illinois was in session. A secretary let me into Judge Landis's chambers to wait for him. I was twenty minutes early for my ten o'clock Monday morning appointment.

Landis's chambers were as different from Garry Herrmann's office as the building was from Redland Field. Not a sausage or beer bucket was in sight. The modest-sized room was conservatively furnished, with dark wood paneling, thick rugs, and high-backed leather chairs. Law books lined the built-in bookshelves, an unflattering portrait of President Harding hung on the wall, and a large American flag was in the corner.

I was aware as I waited that most of the baseball world was focused on another court building, the Cook County

Courthouse, four blocks to the north. On Friday, the final jurors for the Black Sox trial had been sworn in, and opening statements were scheduled to begin today. Landis wouldn't be there, in part because of defense objections that his presence would have an undue influence on the proceedings, and because he had his own court to run. Although he'd been severely criticized for it, Landis had elected to retain his federal judgeship—and the $7,500 salary that came with it—when he became commissioner of baseball. The owners were already paying him an extraordinary $50,000 a year—the vice president of the United States earned only $12,000—but rumor had it that Landis was not one to forego a single nickel if he could help it.

Kenesaw Landis, wearing the black robe of his profession, stalked into the room at a quarter to eleven with no greeting and no apology for being late. I hopped to my feet. I knew people stood when a judge entered a courtroom, and I assumed the same custom would apply in chambers.

Although this meeting with me was to be in his capacity as baseball commissioner, he didn't remove his judicial attire. Landis sat down behind his polished mahogany desk and waved me back into my chair. He looked the same in person as he did in the newspaper photos: slightly built, with a mane of white hair and a face that could chop wood. His expression was that of someone who'd been constipated since the McKinley administration.

The Judge startled me by suddenly twisting his features into a scowl that seemed to make one eye bulge larger than the other. "I see you're wearing a wristwatch," he snapped.

Was I late? I was sure the telegram had said ten o'clock. "Uh, yes sir, I am."

"Were you in the *war*, son?"

Oh, that was it. Wristwatches had become popular during the Great War, when officers found them to be more convenient than the pocket variety. Some people felt that only veterans deserved to wear the new style, and apparently Judge Landis was one of them. "Yes, sir, I was, with the 131st Infantry."

I thought that answer would be a point in my favor, but it only earned a "Hmph" in response. Was "sir" the right thing to call him? Judge? Your Honor? Commissioner? I wished Garry Herrmann or somebody had told me how to address him. I was pretty sure that the word the newspapers used for him—"czar"—was not the right one.

Landis took an accordion folder from his desk drawer and pulled out a wad of papers. The photographs Herrmann had shown me were on top of the stack. Tapping a finger on one of the pictures, the Judge said, "This is a most serious matter."

"Yes, I understand that ... sir." It seemed the safest choice.

He dug into the middle of the stack for some papers. "I have reports on this man." His eyes began to scan one of the sheets. "Rufus Yates. Used to be a ballplayer. Now he's a petty thief and general ne'er-do-well." He turned his eye to me. "Yates is also one of Arnold Rothstein's gambling contacts in Cincinnati. Tell me, how long have you known him?"

Was that supposed to be a trick question? "I don't know him at all," I said.

He pushed the photos at me. "You appear friendly."

I looked at both of them, the shot of Yates and me shaking hands, and the one which showed him handing me an envelope. "I guess that's the way it looks," I admitted. I continued to study the photos, but they didn't change. There I was with Rufus Yates, and the newsboy standing next to us holding up the *Times-Star.*

"You don't deny the authenticity of the photographs?"

"No, that looks the way I remember it." I quickly gave Landis the same explanation I'd given Herrmann: the truth.

"You sound either well rehearsed or straightforward," said the Judge.

"It's the *truth,*" I said, thinking—hoping—that a firm tone of voice might help convince him.

"Very well." He pulled a few more papers from the pile. "Let's turn to *you.*" The eye bulge again. "After you met Mr. Yates, you went hitless in your next fourteen at bats. And you made three errors the very day he handed you that envelope."

"That's true. But ..." I hated resorting to this defense. "Judge—Your Honor—I've been playing in the big leagues for ten years. And I batted over .250 in only three of them. Sometimes I just go a while without a base hit. I'm usually put in the lineup for my glove."

"The glove that made three errors?"

"One was a throwing error."

Landis looked a bit taken aback. "Well, I have checked your record," he said. "You've primarily been used in utility and you have a lifetime batting average of .247."

"It's .248," I blurted. That's it, Mickey, correct the commissioner. "As of my last game."

His mouth twitched into a humorless smile. "I'm afraid I only have your record through the end of last year. I haven't been following your slugging feats on a day-by-day basis."

I adopted a properly chastened look.

The Judge went on, "The day you met Yates, it was common knowledge that you would be starting because of an injury to Kopf. You'd gone 6-for-9 in a doubleheader the day before. The Reds were playing Pittsburgh, and Pittsburgh and New York are the leading contenders for the pennant. This could have been an important enough game for gamblers to be interested in." He hunched forward as if he was about to pounce on me from across his desk. "Unfortunately, I can't do anything about the gamblers, but I *can* take action against any ballplayer who consorts with them."

"Your Honor, it happened exactly like I said. I don't know this fellow Yates. He came up and asked for an autograph; I signed that envelope and gave it back to him. Then I went inside the park and played as good as I could. I admit I stank up the place that day, but I *tried*—I wanted to win. You can ask Pat Moran—hell, ask any manager I ever played for, including John McGraw and Hughie Jennings—I *always* give it everything I got. I play to win."

Landis eased back in his seat. "I intend to make those inquiries." He tapped a finger on the desk. "According to the information I have so far, the only problems you've had in the past have been off the field. Last year, for example, you were accused of shooting a labor leader who was trying to unionize ballplayers."

I started to protest that I hadn't done it, when Landis muttered, "Point in your favor, as far as I'm concerned." He stuffed the papers back in the folder. "I appreciate you coming in, Mr. Rawlings, but the fact remains that there are suspicious circumstances surrounding your play last week. I must consider the matter carefully, and at this point I feel further investigation is necessary." He nodded toward the door, dismissing me.

I stood, unsure what I was supposed to do. "Should I stay here—in Chicago? How long until . . . ?"

"You may go home. But be prepared to return if I call for you."

"I will," I promised. "The team's in Philadelphia now, though. Can I . . ."

He shook his white head. "Mr. Herrmann showed good judgment in benching you for the time being. It is wise to be cautious until the full story is in. Go back to Cincinnati, and after I've completed my review of the matter, I'll notify Mr. Herrmann when—and *if*—you may return to the team."

Eager to get out of Chicago as soon as possible, I went directly from the Federal Building to Grand Central Station to catch the first train for Cincinnati. I was uneasy just to be in the same city where the Sox trial was being held. I wanted no association with the scandal, and worried that I might have been seen entering or leaving Judge Landis's chambers; there were probably reporters dogging him for an opinion on the trial, and I hated to think what kind of speculation they might write about me if they knew I'd met with him.

Unfortunately, the earliest departure I could get was late afternoon, so I killed a few hours by eating lunch and then reading some movie magazines that we already had at home. I avoided the newspapers because I didn't even want to read about the trial.

But I couldn't escape it. When I finally boarded the train, a talkative salesman took the seat next to me and gave me a rundown of the day's proceedings. He said that the prosecutor had been dealt a setback when he tried to quote from carbon copies of the stolen grand-jury confessions; the defense objected on grounds that the copies were unsigned and had been repudiated by the players, and Judge Hugo Friend ruled there could be no mention of them. The state's attorney fared better when he called his first witness: Charles A. Comiskey, owner of the Chicago White Sox. One of the charges against the eight players was conspiracy to injure Comiskey's business. Although Comiskey had a well-earned reputation as a despotic tightwad, the prosecution succeeded in portraying him as a benevolent father figure. When the defense cross-examined Comiskey concerning his actual business practices, the judge sustained prosecution objections and ruled that Comiskey's finances were not relevant.

I tried to make it clear to my travel companion that I wasn't about to enter into a conversation on the scandal, but he kept up a running monologue anyway. When the fellow finally paused to ask my name, I said I was "Dr. Herrmann" and that I'd been in Chicago treating smallpox victims. I soon had the seat to myself, and was undisturbed for the remainder of the journey.

The train pulled into Cincinnati's Central Union Depot in the early hours of Tuesday morning, and I grabbed the first available cab.

I'd called Margie during a stop in Indianapolis to let her know when I'd be getting home. She was waiting in the parlor, wearing her red kimono. A worried expression was on her face.

"You didn't have to wait up for me," I said.

"Couldn't sleep anyway." She gave me a kiss and a hug, holding the embrace long enough that I had the sense she was seeking some kind of reassurance, not just welcoming me home.

"What's wrong?" I asked. "Something happen?"

Margie bit her lip and nodded. "At the zoo. One of the leopards had a litter and three of the four cubs were stillborn. The mother might not make it, either."

"Oh, damn. I'm sorry."

"Then I got in a fight with the keeper. Told him again that the cats needed to be better fed and get more exercise. He told me to stick to what I knew and stay out of his business. I tried to convince him that I did know what I was talking about—I was always involved in caring for the animals we used in the movies. But he didn't want to hear anything from 'a dumb actress.' So I called him a few things I probably shouldn't have, and it got worse from there."

I repeated that I was sorry to hear what had happened.

"I feel foolish," she said. "It's a zoo. Some animals are going to die. I should just accept that, but . . ." She took a deep breath and shook herself out of the thought. "Let me get you something to drink."

As she headed for the kitchen, she said, "Tell me how it went in Chicago."

I gave her a rundown on my meeting with Judge Landis. While I spoke, I shed my clothes, tossing them on the Morris chair. I heard the tinkle of ice chunks in glasses, the sound promising some welcome relief from the heat. Despite the windows being fully open and two fans blowing, the house was sweltering.

When I was down to my underwear, I dragged myself onto the sofa. I'd spent most of the last day and a half on trains. I was exhausted, dirty, and my body still felt like it was rumbling and lurching. My mind wasn't any calmer.

Margie came back with two large glasses of cold ginger ale. "If he's really going to do an investigation," she said, "you don't have anything to worry about." She placed the drinks on the coffee table and sat down beside me. "He'll find out that you've never done a dishonest thing in your life."

"I don't know if that will matter to Landis." I paused to guzzle down half the soda pop, feeling my insides refreshed by the coolness and the bubbles. "As it is, there's no *evidence* that I did anything wrong anyway. You'd think a judge would see that, and at least let me keep playing till there was proof that I did anything more for Rufus Yates than sign an envelope. It seems like this whole trouble is because of what other players did two years ago."

She tried a couple more times to convince me I had no cause to worry. Then we simply sat and relaxed for a little while. Margie refilled the drinks, and put Eubie Blake's latest recording, "I'm Just Wild About Harry," on the Victrola. We listened to the record five times before going upstairs.

I was so tired that I decided a bath could wait till morning, and settled for a quick wash with a wet sponge before going to bed.

Margie was almost asleep when I said to her, "There's been times before when I've been in trouble. Some of them I didn't think I'd get out of alive. But this is worse than having my life threatened. This is reputation—it goes on after you die. And it's something that you can never get back once it's gone. I know baseball isn't the most important thing in the world, but playing ball is the only thing I'm ever gonna be remembered for—and I don't want anybody to ever think that I didn't play on the square."

O O O

It was almost noon when I woke up. Margie had left for the zoo, and she'd left me a cherry pie for breakfast and a note saying that she'd promised Erin and Patrick Kelly that I'd take them to Chester Park. I was happy with the pie, but not with the promise she'd made to the kids. I thought she should have asked me first. And if she had, I'd have said no; I wasn't in any kind of mood to be around children today.

After a hot bath, a couple cups of coffee, and most of the pie, I was feeling a little better. The rumble of the train was out of my system, and the meeting with Landis felt a little more remote now that I was back in the comfort of home.

I carried a cup of coffee into the parlor and sat down at the desk, where the publications Ollie Perriman had given me drew my attention.

I started flipping through the issue of *Frank Leslie's Illustrated Newspaper* that carried the portraits of the 1869 team, then the copy of Ellard's *Base Ball in Cincinnati.* I wanted to go back for a while, step into that era and forget about the present. But it didn't happen. I read about the game against the Troy Haymakers, when the Haymakers withdrew from the field to protect the wagers of gamblers. Things weren't so much better in those days; the past was no refuge. I sighed and closed the book.

Okay, forget about going backwards, I told myself. The question for me to face now was clear: What could I do about Rufus Yates?

That photograph of Yates and me shaking hands remained vivid in my mind. When I'd seen it again in Landis's office, something about it had struck me as odd, but I couldn't tell exactly what. Now I studied the mental image until I realized what was wrong: the newsboy in the shot was hold-

ing up a paper for display, but he had never tried to sell it
to us. He must have done it for the benefit of the photographer, to establish the time of the meeting. So running into
Yates wasn't a chance encounter. It had been carefully
planned—I'd been set up.

What did I know about Rufus Yates? Only what I'd heard
from Garry Herrmann and Judge Landis. According to them,
he was a former ballplayer, a petty thief, and had connections
to Arnold Rothstein, the man who financed the fix of the
1919 World Series.

Staring absently at the baseball memorabilia on my desk,
I suddenly thought of a new angle on why Ollie Perriman
might have been killed. My previous assumption about the
motive for his murder might have been off by half a century.
Maybe it had nothing to do with whatever happened in 1869.
Maybe Perriman had something in his collection that could
implicate someone in the World Series scandal.

My thoughts were interrupted by the Kelly children at the
front door. They didn't say anything, but looked up at me as
if to ask, "Can Mickey come out to play?"

With as much enthusiasm as I could manufacture, I said,
"Ready to go to Chester Park?"

○ ○ ○

Margie was home from the zoo by the time the kids and I
returned from "The Home of Happiness," as the amusement
park billed itself.

I was grateful to her for what she'd done, and was pretty
sure that she intentionally hadn't checked with me first about
going to the park so that I wouldn't have the chance to
decline. Being with the children for a while was the best

thing for me; between answering their questions, plying them with ice cream and hot dogs, and taking them to every attraction from Hilarity Hall to the boat rides on the lake, there was no way I had time to fret. I ended up enjoying the afternoon as much as they did.

The only awkward moment was when Patrick asked why I wasn't on the road with the team. I gave him the story about having bad vision and headaches. It struck me that I was so worried about somebody thinking I could be dishonest on the field, that I was willing to lie to a child.

After Margie returned the Kellys to their aunt, it was back to trying to figure out what I could do to clear up the trouble I was in.

Over dinner, I told Margie my idea that Ollie Perriman's death might have to do with the 1919 World Series.

"How was he involved in that?" she asked skeptically.

"I don't think he was involved, but he might have gotten hold of something incriminating when he was acquiring things for his collection. A lot of what he had was recent material."

"And someone wanted it back."

"Right. Like Arnold Rothstein. They say he's the one who had the grand-jury confessions of Joe Jackson and the others stolen because he thought he might have been mentioned in them. Maybe he thought Perriman had information that could implicate him in the fix, too. According to Judge Landis, Rufus Yates works for Rothstein, so maybe he was the one who broke in and killed Perriman." Another possibility occurred to me. "You know, it could be that Yates did it on his own—not to protect Rothstein, but to protect himself *from* Rothstein."

"What do you mean?" Margie asked. "Why would he do that?"

"Edd Roush and Greasy Neale told me some of the Reds were also offered bribes to throw the series. What if Yates was the one who tried to fix things the other way? He double-crosses Rothstein and tries to get Cincinnati to lose instead. The way the odds were, he'd have cleaned up betting on the Sox."

"Except Cincinnati didn't lose, so why would Arnold Rothstein be mad at Yates?"

"I don't think Rothstein is the type to forgive a double cross just because it didn't work." I added, "But I intend to find out for sure."

Margie sighed. "Why don't you wait for Judge Landis to clear you? Maybe you don't have anything to worry about."

I told her about the Judge's decisions of the past few months and how they didn't instill any confidence in me that he'd do the right thing. "I need to look into this myself," I said. "Talk to some people who might know Yates and Rothstein."

"But if you get *more* involved," she cautioned me, "won't that make him less likely to clear you?"

She had a point. Gamblers and bookies were the ones most likely to have the information I wanted, but if Landis found out I was in contact with such men, it could be over for me. "If he finds out about it," I said. "The trick is to keep that from happening."

"Why don't you let me ask around instead? I could go to one of the vaudeville houses. The managers usually keep a few names of bookies and bootleggers and such for the visiting performers."

"Thanks, but I couldn't . . . I appreciate the offer, I just have to—"

"Do it yourself," she finished.

"Doesn't have to be all by myself, but I can't let you do it for me. I'm the one in trouble, I have to do what it takes to get out of it."

I don't think Margie quite understood, but she said that she did. "Think about it some more before you do anything, though," she urged.

"I will," I said. She did have a point. It wouldn't be wise to act in haste with so much at stake. One wrong move, and I could find myself on baseball's permanently ineligible list.

I did as Margie suggested. I thought about it overnight and talked with her again in the morning. It was clear to me—and I think to her, too—that no amount of additional time or deliberation would lead me to any different conclusion. I had to follow my instinct and act to protect myself. I could not wait idly by and leave my fate to the whim of Judge Kenesaw Mountain Landis.

Late Wednesday morning, I walked up Dalton to Redland Field and was surprised at the size of the crowd heading in the same direction. The Reds were playing more than five hundred miles away in Philadelphia. Then I noticed that the faces of those around me were mostly black, and realized they were going to see the Cuban Stars. The Negro National League team leased Redland for its home games when the white club was on the road.

We had a former member of the Stars on the Reds roster: Dolf Luque. He'd pitched for them when they were a barn-storming outfit from New Jersey, and he was one of the rare examples of a Negro League player making it into the majors.

When I reached Findlay, I looked around for the newsboy

who'd been in the photo with Yates and me, but he wasn't here. Like the crowd filing through the main gate, the paperboys were mostly colored, and *The Union,* which covered Cincinnati's Negro community, was the newspaper they sold.

Out of habit, I went to the players' entrance. When a guard told me I was at the wrong door, I explained who I was and he let me in; he looked a bit dubious about it, perhaps thinking that I was trying to see the game without paying.

On the stairs up to the offices, I passed a few of the Cuban Stars coming down on their way to the field. They were wearing red caps and stockings, and their jerseys, with *Cincinnati* spelled out across the chests, had old-fashioned collars; I recognized them as Reds uniforms from about a decade earlier.

"Here for a tryout?" one of them asked. While his teammates chuckled, I flushed; I'd seen some Negro League games before, and I knew how good those players were—if I was to be given a tryout, there was a good chance I wouldn't make the team. I smiled in reply and hurried up to Garry Herrmann's office.

Herrmann usually accompanied the team, traveling in a private Pullman car that was better stocked than most delicatessens. I knew he had to remain in town during this road trip, though, because he was on the witness list for the Black Sox trial and might have to go to Chicago on short notice.

When his secretary showed me in, Herrmann greeted me like a maître d' eager to seat one of his favorite customers. "I have some *very* nice liverwurst this morning, Rawlings. Come. Eat."

I'd skipped breakfast, figuring he might make such an offer. "Thank you." I sat down, and he handed me a napkin while preparing a liverwurst sandwich with dark mustard and a thick slice of onion.

He put a pickle on the side and offered me a beer. I opted for ginger ale, and his slight frown as he poured the soda pop told me he didn't quite approve of my beverage choice.

Like a dentist who asks questions while drilling in your mouth, Herrmann waited until I was chewing a large bite of the sandwich before asking, "So tell me: how did it go with the Judge?"

I struggled to swallow the food quickly. My guess was that Herrmann already knew how it went; I couldn't imagine that he hadn't tried to find out from Landis where things stood. But I gave him my perspective. "Not so good," I said. "He sounded like he intends to be fair, says he's going to 'consider the matter carefully.' But the bottom line is I can't play right now. He says he'll contact you when I can. I don't suppose he's . . ."

Herrmann shook his head, and a small clump of potato salad fell from his mustache. "But at least he hasn't said you can never play again."

I put the sandwich down and sipped some ginger ale. "That's why I'm here, Mr. Herrmann. See, Judge Landis already knows pretty much everything he needs to about this: that I've never been mixed up with gamblers in the past, and that there's no real evidence that I'm involved with Yates—or anyone like him—now. The way I see it, I should be clear to play today."

"The Judge is simply being deliberate." Herrmann tried to sound soothing. "It's the way things are right now."

"Well, I don't want to risk him deciding to make an example of me because of what some other guys did in the World Series."

"But you have no choice, do you?"

Yes, I did have a choice. "I want to find out for myself why this happened—why Rufus Yates approached me, and why somebody took a picture of us together and then sent the picture to you. There's a reason for it, and I want to be able to tell Landis what it is. Right now it seems like it's gonna be a coin flip as to which way he decides."

Herrmann dabbed at his mouth with a napkin. "I strongly advise that you go home and wait for Judge Landis to make his decision in his own good time."

"No. I'm sorry, but I can't do that. I want to play ball again—now. I want to look into this myself."

"Well, if you came for my permission, it is up to you." Herrmann spread his hands. "But I advise you against it. Suppose the Judge does call you to his office for more questions and now you know a lot more about this Yates fellow. It could seem suspicious. If you stay out of it, you can honestly say you know nothing—if that's the truth. Sometimes ignorance is a very good thing."

"I'm sorry, Mr. Herrmann." Ignorance never seemed to work for me. "I'd like to go ahead with this."

"Very well. You understand that if you do, it is out of my hands."

"Yes, I understand." I actually hadn't come to seek his permission. And I wasn't doing all that well *in* his hands; he wouldn't even write a letter of support for me. "I also have a favor to ask: I need your help."

"*My* help?"

"Just a phone call. I was hoping you could call Detective

Forsch at the Crime Bureau and ask him to tell me what he knows about Yates. The police probably have some records on him, but I don't think they'll let me see them unless . . ."

Herrmann smiled. "And what makes you think I have influence with the police department?"

"You have influence everywhere in this city, Mr. Herrmann."

He liked the flattery. He called for his secretary to get Forsch on the line and handed me a plate of strudel.

When Forsch was on the phone, Herrmann told the detective that I would be coming to see him and that I'd like some information about Rufus Yates. Herrmann added that he'd personally appreciate it if Forsch would extend me "every courtesy and cooperation."

When he hung up, I said. "Thank you, Mr. Herrmann."

He nodded like a ward politician bestowing a favor. I'd probably have to vote for his mayor of choice twenty or thirty times in the next election.

After thanking him for breakfast, I started to leave, then paused to ask, "In case this goes on for a while, and I can't play with the team, I'd still like to keep in shape. I saw the Cuban Stars downstairs. If they let me, can I practice with them?"

Herrmann's face reddened. "No! That would *not* help you with the Judge."

"Why?"

"The Judge does not like for white and black to mix."

"But they play in Redland Field, they're wearing old Reds uniforms . . . hell, Dolf Luque used to play with them. Isn't that mixing?"

"They pay to lease the field, and it was Lloyd Tinsley's idea to sell them the old uniforms. That is business. But we do not play together. And Luque is Cuban; he is not a Negro. No, not a good idea, you do not play with them."

I reluctantly promised Herrmann that I wouldn't try to play baseball with the Stars, then left his office to watch the colored teams practice before their game. It was going to be an all-Ohio matchup against the visiting Columbus Buckeyes.

As far as major league baseball was concerned, Negroes didn't exist—and it sounded like Judge Landis was going to make sure there were no breaches of baseball's color barrier. Although the ban wasn't based strictly on *color:* a light-skinned American Negro would be prohibited from playing in Organized Baseball, but a darker skinned Cuban was acceptable.

For some reason, the powers in baseball were trying to keep Negro players out of the view of white fans. Not even *The Sporting News*, which billed itself as "The Bible of Baseball," covered their games. If it wasn't for reports in *The Cincinnati Enquirer*, I wouldn't have known that a month before Pat Duncan hit the "first" home run out of Redland Field, John Beckwith, a shortstop with the Negro League Chicago Giants beat him to it. Maybe the big leagues didn't want Negroes in the game out of fear that some colored players might be better than the white stars.

I left the park. The issue of Negroes in baseball wasn't my battle to fight. But it was one more reason why I shouldn't place myself at the mercy of Judge Landis's sense of fairness.

○ ○ ○

I'd have rather stayed at Redland Field to watch the Cuban Stars take on the Buckeyes. Instead I was in the Plum Street side of City Hall, in the police department's Crime Bureau.

This time we met in Detective Forsch's cramped office instead of the interview room, and the two of us were alone. He was in his usual drab suit and an exceptionally cranky mood.

"Got a call from your boss," the detective said. "Wants me to give you whatever information you're looking for."

"Yes, I know. I appreciate it."

"Don't like somebody going over my head like that." He stubbed out a cigarette as if it had bit his finger. "Why didn't you ask me yourself?"

"Would you have helped me if I did?"

"Probably not. Still, you should have asked me first."

I thought a moment. "You're right," I said. "I should have. I'm sorry." And I was—Herrmann had asked Forsch to extend me every courtesy; I should have done the same for Forsch.

He hesitated while pulling another Murad from the pack, then shrugged. "No matter." After lighting up, he held the pack out to me. "Smoke?"

"No, thanks, though."

His craggy face visibly more friendly, Forsch patted a pile of folders on his desk. "Herrmann said you're interested in Rufus Yates. I pulled what we got on him. Any questions in particular?"

"I understand he has a record," I said. "What does he do exactly?"

"Nothing major. A little of anything and everything to make a buck: sell bad whiskey, burglary, loansharking."

"What about gambling?"

"Yeah, he'll set up a craps or poker game now and then, but nothing for big stakes. And it's not something we go after as long as it's just small friendly games of chance."

"I hear he's connected with Arnold Rothstein."

Forsch snorted. "Hell, ever since the Series, every two-bit hood wants to make out that he's tied up with Rothstein. Try to get a little of the spotlight to shine on himself."

"As far as you know, he isn't?"

He looked through the reports. "There's nothing we have about him being connected to Rothstein."

"Okay. You said burglary. Was he caught up in your sweep after Ollie Perriman was killed?"

Forsch smiled. "You're still on that? Thought this was about Yates."

"It is. The only reason I can think of for somebody to set me up is because I was involved with Perriman. Remember, somebody broke into my house and went through the stuff he'd given me."

"Yeah . . ."

"Well, I'm thinking: what if Yates was the guy who broke into both places?"

He smiled again. "Sorry." He pulled out a paper. "Rufus Yates was in the Work House, doing thirty days for a B & E—that's break-in and entry." As if I'd thought B & E was a railroad.

"You're sure?"

"Still don't trust me?" He slid the paper to me.

"I do," I muttered, as I nonetheless read the report. Yates had been arrested June fifteenth and sentenced five days later to thirty dollars or thirty days in the Cincinnati Work House. Apparently unable to pay the thirty dollars, Yates was one week into his sentence when Perriman was killed. And he still had more than two weeks to serve when my place was broken into. "Damn."

"Sorry to disappoint you." Forsch exhaled a stream of

smoke. "Now as far as why he'd be setting you up for something, I don't know."

"Somebody else using him maybe?" Like whoever it was that took the photograph.

"Could be. But like I say, no big-time crook is going to use Yates. He's the kind of guy who if a couple of fellows were planning to knock off a candy store they might bring Yates along to act as lookout. That's about it."

"Okay, thanks." Something else had bothered me for some time, and I thought Forsch might be the one to clear it up. "I thought burglars don't like to go in when people are home; they want them out of the house."

"Most do, that's right."

"The break-in at my house was while we were in bed. I thought that might mean the robber couldn't wait for us to be out. Maybe he was anxious to get whatever he was looking for first—before I could find it."

"Maybe. But there's also some burglars who prefer to have their victims at home. Wait for them to fall asleep, then go in. That way nobody comes back unexpectedly to catch them in the act."

"What did Yates prefer?"

Forsch shook his head. "Don't know. Never investigated him myself."

"How did he get caught last time?"

"Got the arrest report here, I think." Forsch lit another Murad. He looked over some papers, then up at me. "Yates was robbing a house in Avondale. The residents were home; one of them woke up and called us. You think that tells you something?"

I mulled it over for a few moments. "Not a damn thing," I said. "But thanks."

Chapter Nineteen

○○○

Margie seemed relieved to be getting away from me Thursday morning. The lions and tigers in Carnivora House were probably easier to get along with than I'd been lately. I was in a cranky mood, frustrated at not being with the team, and unsure what I could do to convince Judge Landis to let me play again.

This afternoon, the Reds were opening a series against John McGraw and the Giants in the Polo Grounds, which had been my home park for three years. It was agony for me to think of my teammates taking the field in New York while I was stuck here alone.

The frustration about Rufus Yates was equally intense. According to Detective Forsch, Yates wasn't the type to be more than a bit player in whatever was going on. So who was behind the scheme to set me up—and how could I track him down?

Still picking at the pancakes Margie had made for breakfast, I tried to come up with a plan of action.

Rufus Yates had to be my starting point. Landis had told me a few things about him, and Forsch had told me a little

more. That was it as far as the authorities, though; to go
farther, I'd have to talk to people on the other side of the
law. Local bookies, for example. But I couldn't contact any
of them openly. Simply shaking hands—and taking an envelope—from a low-level gambler on the street was enough to
get me in hot water already. If Landis found out that I'd gone
to a bookie, the matter of my future would surely be settled
in his mind—and it wouldn't be in my favor.

Not even close to coming up with an entire plan, I
decided I'd settle for a small first step.

There was one point on which Landis and Forsch dis-
agreed: the Judge had said Yates was connected to Arnold
Rothstein, but according to the detective he wasn't. I assumed
the local authorities would be most likely right. Rothstein
wanted the Sox to blow games; maybe Yates was on the
other side, trying to convince the Reds to take a dive.

All right, if I couldn't talk to the gamblers, I'd try those
they might have contacted: the players. I had the sense that
I wouldn't get much more out of my teammates than what
Greasy Neale and Edd Roush had already told me. Roush
had made it sound like the Reds veterans of 1919 had become
a kind of close-knit club that wanted to keep their secrets to
themselves. So how about a player who was no longer on
the team—somebody who hadn't stayed with the club long
enough to develop that resistance to talking?

I went to the bookcase and pulled out my most recent
Spalding guides. First, I made a list of the Cincinnati roster
from the 1919 World Series. Then I crossed out the players
who were still on the team this season. Next, I eliminated
those who'd played for the Reds in 1920: pitcher Dutch
Ruether, now with the Dodgers; Jimmy Ring, who was sent
to the Phillies earlier this year as part of the trade for Eppa

Rixey; and backup catcher Bill Rariden who was released. This left three players who were gone from the Reds immediately after the 1919 World Series, and whose memories should be free of influence from the rest of the Cincinnati team: outfielder and former batting champion Sherry Magee, who'd made his final big-league appearance in that series; second baseman Kid Gumbert, now with Brooklyn; and utility infielder Jimmy Smith, currently with the Phillies.

I thought these three men might be my best chances for finding out if anything had been amiss on the Reds' side of that world championship. I didn't know where I could track down Magee, but if we played the Phillies or the Dodgers, I'd be sure to talk to Smith or Gumbert. Assuming I played anywhere again.

I remembered one more thing Landis had said: Rufus Yates used to be a ballplayer. Since I'd never heard of him, I assumed his career was probably limited to semipro or the minor leagues. Yates had appeared to be about thirty-five years old, so he'd have been in his prime ten years ago. I checked a *Reach* Guide from 1912, and found him listed with Corpus Christi of the Southwest Texas League. The 1911 Guide had him with the same team. Before that, nowhere. I skipped ahead to 1913 and subsequent years. As an outfielder, Rufus Yates had a six-year career in professional baseball, never playing at a higher level than the Class A Western League. And that was with Wichita in 1915 and 1916. I'd heard something about that place recently . . . Lloyd Tinsley! Heinie Groh had told me Tinsley was Wichita's business manager before the war.

My first reaction was suspicion of Tinsley. Were the two of them still in contact? Did they have any shady dealings together in Kansas? Then I caught myself. Professional baseball is a small world, and paths keep crossing. Just because Joe Jackson once played for Connie Mack, for instance, didn't mean Mack was in on the deal to throw the World Series. Not everyone Yates met would be crooked, either—hell, Yates himself might have been completely straight back in his playing days.

Still it was something. And when you've got nothing, you can't ignore any possible lead. At the very least I might be able to get some more information about Yates from Tinsley.

O O O

When Margie came home, it was obvious that our moods had reversed from this morning. I was enthusiastic about pursuing a few more ideas I'd had about Rufus Yates, and she was in the doldrums.

"What happened?" I asked.

She collapsed onto the sofa. "You remember I told you about that litter of leopard cubs where most of them died?"

"Yes . . ."

"The mother died last night, too."

"Oh, I'm sorry."

Margie's eyes teared and she started to speak, then her voice caught and she lifted a handkerchief to her eyes. I knew how much she loved animals, and she seemed as upset about the leopard as if the cat had been a household pet.

"Let me get you something to drink," I offered. "Lemonade?"

As I stood to go into the kitchen, she waved me down. "Not thirsty." She collected herself and went on, "I went to see Mr. Stephan, the superintendent, and spoke to him about the cats being underfed."

"What did he say?"

"At least he didn't dismiss me as a dumb actress, like the keeper did. Mr. Stephan told me that animals are different in cages than they are in the wild. He said they develop unnatural habits, nervous conditions, and it affects their appetites and their health." She looked up at me. "Do you want to hear the dumbest thing?"

"What's that?"

"Mr. Stephan said he's studied the way they operate zoos in Germany, where they have natural, open settings instead of cages. He even sent his son Joe to live in Hamburg to learn the techniques they use there. During the war Mr. Stephan wanted to try setting up areas without bars in the Cincinnati Zoo, but there was such an uproar he wasn't allowed."

"Why not?"

"Because it was a *German* way of running a zoo. And anything 'the Huns' did had to be evil. He says it'll probably be years before he can try it again."

"Jeez."

"Mr. Stephan took a look at the cats himself, though, and he checked the records of their feedings to make sure everything was right."

"And?"

"He's says they do seem a little thin, but it's all being done the way it's supposed to be." She sighed. "I don't know . . . I like doing the shows, and teaching the children, but I hate to see the animals that way. Oh, and now the keeper in the Carnivora House is mad at me for going to Mr. Stephan."

"Why not quit? You don't have to work there."

She gave me a sharp look. "Because I still think something is wrong, and I'm not quitting till I find out what it is."

I couldn't help but smile. I always did like her determination.

Margie finally smiled a little, too. "How about you? Any word from Judge Landis?"

"No, but I have an idea how I might be able to find out about Rufus Yates."

"How?"

Besides talking to the Reds players and Lloyd Tinsley, there was another possible way of getting information. "Well, at first I thought I couldn't talk to any gamblers about him, but maybe I can."

"But if somebody finds out about it . . ."

"I don't think they will—as long as the fellow I meet with is colored." Maybe I could take advantage of the way black baseball was invisible to whites. There were colored gamblers and bookies, too. All I had to do was find one.

That was Margie's next question, and in answer, I showed her the amusement page of the morning *Enquirer*. There was an ad for the new vaudeville bill at the Palace Theater, including six acts of "Vodvil" and a movie "Fotofeature." Among the acts were The Ragpickin' Minstrels playing their "Darky Music."

"You said vaudeville managers know of bookies where visiting performers can go," I reminded Margie. "What about for the colored acts—would the manager know where they can lay down a bet?"

"Probably. We're not as segregated as you are—as baseball is." She thought a moment. "I played the Palace a couple years ago. Manager's name is Ralph something, I think. Would you like me to ask him?"

"Yes, please."

"Okay. So . . . why don't I smell food?"

I'd been home all day and had forgotten to get something for dinner. "Thought we'd go out to eat," I said.

Margie smiled. "And then afterward we'll go to the Palace."

○ ○ ○

The line to get into the Palace Theater stretched from its entrance on Sixth Street around the corner onto Vine. The Palace was more popular than the other major vaudeville house in the city, Keith's, with much greater variety in the acts it presented.

Since we weren't planning on seeing the shows, Margie led the way past the crowd. A young usher in a resplendent maroon uniform was near the front door trying to keep the crowd in line; the theatergoers were perfectly orderly, but the young man appeared to enjoy flaunting his authority and kept barking orders to "straighten it out" and "keep to the side."

When he tried to tell Margie to go to the back of the line, she asked sweetly if Ralph was still the manager. The boy answered that he was, and Margie gave him a quarter to relay the message that Marguerite Turner was here to see him.

The boy sputtered, "I'm sorry, Miss Turner. I didn't recognize you."

He came back a few minutes later with a large round gentleman who was badly in need of having his blond mane trimmed. "Margie Turner!" he said, beaming. "It's so good to see you again." He bowed, took her hand, and kissed it. I felt a pang of jealousy shoot through me.

After Margie made the introductions, Ralph invited us

into his office, a small room filled with posters, rolls of tickets, and photographs of the various acts that had passed through his theater.

"I read about you appearing at the zoo," the manager said to Margie. "You know, I'm still hoping you'll come back to vaudeville. There are a lot of troupes who would love to have you."

"Maybe someday," Margie laughed. "I have a strange favor to ask you now, though."

"Of course," he agreed. "You know I always keep seats available for visitors like yourself. Best in the house."

"Thank you," she said. "But we didn't come to see the show." Ralph looked disappointed to hear this. Margie went on, "We're looking for a bookie. A colored one."

"Somebody in particular?"

I spoke up, "No. Just as long as he's not white."

"My, that *is* a strange request." Ralph looked puzzled. "But I have a few names." He checked a slip of paper tacked on the back of the door, then suggested the name of a man who did business out of a West End hotel room.

I preferred a different meeting place. "You know any who might be at a Redland Field game?" If I was seen at the ballpark, at least I could try to claim that I'd only been there to watch the ballgame.

"Oh, sure! Spider Jenkins is a regular at the Stars games. You want me to write his name down?"

"I'll remember it. Thanks."

"You're welcome. Tell him I sent you, and you should have no trouble."

I thanked him again, and offered to get him tickets for any Reds games he wanted. He said he'd take me up on it. Margie then asked if the offer of theater seats was still good.

Twenty minutes later, Margie and I were in the orchestra section as the Walsh Trio, billed as "Harmony Funsters," performed on the stage. Their singing was dreadful and their jokes worse. This was a high-class vaudeville house, meaning the audience didn't throw rotten vegetables at the acts, but they made their displeasure known the same as a crowd letting an ump know when he'd made a bad call.

Still, I enjoyed it. The Walshes were so bad, they were unintentionally funny. I was feeling relaxed when it occurred to me: would giving Ralph tickets to a Reds game in exchange for fixing me up with gambler cause me more problems?

As Countess Verona, "Musical Genius of the Czimbalon," took the stage, I decided to hell with it—I'd done enough fretting lately. For the rest of the night, I'd allow myself to concentrate on the show and have a good time. I could go back to worrying tomorrow.

Chapter Twenty

ooo

I handed the usher my ticket stub and a silver dollar. "I'm looking for Spider Jenkins," I said. "Know where I can find him?"

The elderly colored man gave me back the coin. "Don't know nobody by that name."

"I hear he's the man to see about getting down a bet." I reached into my pocket and pulled out another dollar.

He studied me closely. "You a cop?"

"Do I look like one?"

"Not particularly. Except you're the color of a cop."

"I'm a ballplayer."

"You don't look like one of them, neither." After a few seconds' deliberation, he took the money and nodded in the direction of the third-base dugout. "Spider's in the front row box 'tween home plate and the dugout. White hat. Can't miss him."

I looked at the area where Spider Jenkins was seated. No matter how invisible Negro baseball was to the men who ran the white game, I was uncomfortable meeting a bookmaker in full view of everyone in the park. I asked the usher, "Could you ask him to meet me at the concession stand?"

He chuckled. "It don't work that way. You got business with Jenkins, you go to *him.*"

"All right. Thanks."

I stopped to get a bag of peanuts and a root beer before going to meet with the bookie. When I was near Jenkins's box, I made a show of examining my ticket, then sidled into the seat next to him. If anyone was looking, I hoped to appear as if I was simply sitting down to watch the game. From the corner of my eye, I saw that Spider Jenkins was dressed in the same style as white gamblers: flashy. His cream-colored suit was impeccable, the yellow tie he wore was bright enough to cause a player to lose a fly ball in its glare, and his white cap was cocked at such an angle that I didn't know how it stayed on his head.

"Seat's taken," he said.

Keeping my eyes on the field, I dug into the peanuts and cracked one open. "Hear you're the man to see about making a bet."

"You hear wrong."

I'd almost forgotten to use the name of the theater manager. "Ralph at the Palace says otherwise."

"All right . . . how much you want to get down and on who?"

I took another sidelong glance at Jenkins. He had long, skinny limbs and a face that was one of the darkest shades of brown I'd ever seen. He looked younger than I expected, possibly in his late twenties. "I don't want to place a bet. I'm looking for information."

"I ain't in the information business. What are you, a cop?"

"My name's Mickey Rawlings," I said. "I play for the Reds."

"Sure you do." I could feel his eyes studying me. "Then how come you ain't in New York with the ball club?"

"Trouble with my eyes," I lied. "I'm here to see you because I'm hoping you can tell me something about a gambler named Rufus Yates."

"Like I said, I ain't in the information business. And the business I *am* in you're hurting just by sitting there. Folks see a white fella here, they assume he's with the police, and then I don't get no customers. How about you move on?"

"Be happy to. What do you know about Yates?"

He started to stand, probably to make me move, then sat back down with a sigh. "Rufus Yates is no gambler," he said. "Gambling is an honorable profession. You place your bets fair and square and takes your chances—it's a sporting proposition. Yates is a crook. He'll steal or sell bootleg or do anything else that'll make him a buck. And if he takes a bet or places one, you know it's on something that's been fixed." Jenkins shook his head. "Ain't no sport to that."

"I hear he's connected with Arnold Rothstein."

"Hell, everybody say that. Yates probably never even met the man."

"But he might have worked for him—like in the 1919 World Series?"

"Maybe. But I don't know nothing about that Series. Buncha white boys in New York and Chicago screwed us all by fixing that one."

"Didn't you take bets on the series?"

"Sure. Everybody did. Couldn't get one down on the Reds after a while, though. Word got around fast that the fix was in."

I took a swallow of the root beer. "You know if Lloyd Tinsley placed any bets on the Sox?" Although I knew it could have been simple coincidence, the fact that Tinsley and Yates had been together in Wichita could mean they had other connections as well.

"How would I know that?" Jenkins asked.

"I expect you'd want to keep tabs on things like that to protect your own business interests. If somebody from the Reds management is betting on the Sox, that would be a sure sign something's wrong."

"I never heard nothing 'bout him doing any such thing. You ready to be getting to another seat?"

"Yeah. But first I'd like to ask you a favor: could you check around about Tinsley and Yates for me?"

"Why should I? What's in it for me?"

Good question. What could I give him in return?

"If you really with the Reds," Jenkins suggested, "maybe you can let me know next time the starting pitcher ain't feelin' so good or something like that."

So he'd have an edge in betting on the games. "Would that be 'sporting'?" I asked.

"Hey, I don't fix no games. But there ain't nothing wrong with knowing as much as you can about the teams."

"Can't do that," I said. "Look, I'll pay you straight up. If you get information, tell me how much you want for it, and I'll give you cash." I didn't want any debt hanging over me.

He chuckled. "How you gonna tell if the information's any good?"

I didn't know. But I had nothing else to go on. "I'll take your word for it," I said.

The chuckle turned into a laugh. "I don't know if you're

a cop or a ballplayer or what, but one thing I know for sure: you ain't no businessman."

All the more reason why I better hang on to my career as baseball player, I thought. "If you find out anything," I said, "give me a call. I'm in the directory."

I took another look at my ticket, then moved to a seat on the first-base side of the park. I settled back and watched the visiting Indianapolis ABCs beat the Cuban Stars 2–0 behind the pitching of Dizzy Dismukes. And I wished to hell I could have played with them.

O O O

The phone rang five minutes after I got home, and I rushed to pick up the receiver.

The first words from the caller were, "Where the hell have you been? I've been calling every fifteen minutes since two o'clock!"

It took a moment for the voice to register as that of Lloyd Tinsley. I was tempted to point out that it was none of his damn business where I'd been. My next impulse was to evade the question. Then I decided to play it safe, in case I'd been seen. "I was at Redland, watching the Cuban Stars game."

"Well, get your ass to New York. Take the first train out, and I'll reimburse you when you get here."

"But I—" As far as I knew, Tinsley wasn't aware of the reason I'd had to stay home from the trip. "My vision is, uh . . ."

"Your vision cleared up this afternoon when Heinie Groh took a fastball in the head. He's gonna be out for two weeks and we need you in the lineup. Don't worry: Moran said he wants you, and Mr. Herrmann got permission from the Judge to let you play."

"That's great!"

"Don't get too excited. Judge Landis says you're still under investigation. You're only cleared to play until he makes his final decision."

So Tinsley knew why I was really out. I wondered how many others did. "Do the fellows on the team know why I ain't been with them?"

Tinsley sounded a little less angry. "No. Mr. Herrmann, Pat Moran, and me are the only ones." Then he barked, "Now get to the train station!"

As soon as we hung up, I called Central Union Depot and found there was a 6:15 for New York. I'd make it if I hurried.

I was excited as I packed, throwing things I'd never need into my suitcase and not caring what I might have overlooked. I was back on the Reds!

And I even became optimistic about what Landis would decide. I figured the best testimony I could have in my favor was that Pat Moran *wanted* me. He knew I played to win, and Landis was sure to realize that there had to be a reason for the manager's confidence in me.

The only thing I didn't like was having to leave before Margie got home. With no time to go to a florist, I went next door and picked some flowers from the Kellys' garden. I left them for Margie in a vase, along with a note that I rewrote three times.

I made it to the station with barely enough time to buy my ticket and grab a few newspapers and magazines to read on the trip.

Maybe I was tired from the rush to catch the train, or I was just feeling more relaxed than I had in some time about being allowed to rejoin the team, but I fell asleep within fifteen minutes of boarding.

We were halfway to Pennsylvania by the time I woke up and opened the early evening edition of the *Cincinnati Post*. A two-column headline on the front page announced that Dick Hurley, the formerly "missing sock" of the old Red Stockings, had been shot.

I arrived late at the Polo Grounds Saturday afternoon. The rest of the team was already on the field for pregame practice.

Lloyd Tinsley and Pat Moran were talking together outside the locker-room door when I got there. "Glad you could make it," Tinsley said sourly.

Pat Moran expressed the same sentiments but sounded more sincere.

"Came as fast as I could," I said.

"You're playing third," said Moran. "Suit up."

I went into the clubhouse and found a pin-striped road uniform—the Reds were the only team in baseball to wear plain flannels at home and pin stripes on the road. I tried to change quickly, but exhaustion impaired my coordination. My fingers were clumsy and my vision fuzzy.

I hadn't been able to fall back asleep after reading the news about Dick Hurley. According to the *Post*, a woman had shot Hurley as he stepped off an elevator in the lobby of the Sinton Hotel. Hurley had still been alive when he was taken to the hospital, but there were few other details reported—the severity of the wound was unknown, the woman was not identified, and there was no known motive. The lack of information gave me plenty of room to speculate. Maybe the book wasn't closed on whatever it was that had happened in 1869.

Finally dressed, and with my mitt in hand, I trotted out of the clubhouse runway onto center field. The view of the Polo Grounds grandstand, with Coogan's Bluff behind it, brought my mind to focus on the game at hand. Most of the seats in the park were taken; a major part of the attraction for the fans was that Rube Marquard, once a star for New York, was going to pitch for Cincinnati.

I was too late for batting or fielding practice, so I went directly to the dugout. A few of my teammates asked about my eyes, and I told them the double vision had cleared up. I was relieved that they genuinely appeared to believe that I'd been away from the team for health reasons.

In the bottom of the first, after the Reds failed to get a runner on base in the top of the inning, Marquard went to the mound and I took my position at third base. Out to the coach's box came John McGraw. The Giants manager lit into me immediately, trying to distract me with profanity-laced insults. I pretended not to notice; I'd heard the "Little Napoleon" give the same abuse to visiting players for three years, and it sounded like he was still using the same material.

Instead of being unsettled by the needling, I was determined to play extra hard against my former team. The exhaustion of the long train ride actually helped, calming down whatever jitters McGraw's epithets and playing before New York fans might have triggered.

That calm lasted for exactly one batter. The second man up for the Giants, shortstop Dave Bancroft, pulled a blistering line drive up the third-base line. Pure reflex sent me into a dive. The ball drilled into my palm, and I held tight as I skidded on my belly. I ended up with my face inches from McGraw's feet.

"Why the hell didn't you make catches like that for me?" he screamed. One of his shoes went up, and I yanked my bare hand away. A half second later his spikes came down on the spot where my hand had been.

Picking myself up, I said, "You're slowin' down, Mac. Must be all the weight you been puttin' on."

From that point on, I don't think McGraw was aware that anyone else was on the field. His attention—and vile mouth—were targeted only at me.

The manager's rage grew in the top of the third, when I snapped out of my batting slump by hitting an opposite field double off Art Nehf. In my next two at-bats, I reached base twice more—once on a fastball that grazed the top of my head and then by taking another one on the side of my neck. The beanballs were on orders from McGraw, I was sure, so I didn't go after Nehf. In the top of the ninth, I ducked away from enough pitches to work a 3–0 count, and when Nehf finally put one over the plate I hit a single up the middle.

We were ahead 5–4 going into the bottom of the ninth. Rube Marquard, still pitching strong, struck out the first two Giants to face him. Then Highpockets Kelly came up to bat. He was New York's last hope, and the crowd was clamoring for a rally.

Kelly got all of Marquard's first pitch, lifting a high fly to deep center field. Edd Roush raced back, but the ball carried over his outstretched glove, and landed near the Eddie Grant Memorial at the base of the wall. As Roush tracked down the caroming baseball, Kelly flew around second base, and

I got ready for a throw at third. McGraw was yelling, "Spike him! Spike him!"—the "him" being me. I half expected McGraw to jump me from behind and hold me down. Roush threw to Curt Stram, who relayed the ball to me. Stram's throw was high, and I had to jump to get it. I came down off-balance, a sitting duck for Kelly's cleats. He didn't go for the cheap shot, though. He slid hard, but fair, and before I could tag him. "Safe!" called base ump Cy Rigler.

Instead of congratulating Kelly on the triple, McGraw berated him for not cutting me.

I trotted over to Marquard with the ball in my mitt. I held it over his extended glove, but didn't let go. "Stay off the rubber, Rube."

He gave me a small smile and nodded.

I trotted back to third, with the ball trapped between my mitt and my side. Marquard went to the back of the mound and pretended to scrape dirt from his cleats.

With McGraw still bawling out Kelly, I took the next step: I gave Cy Rigler a peek at the ball. If you catch the umpire by surprise, he might not see the play and call the runner safe. From the look in Rigler's eyes, he was going to enjoy this as much as me if it worked. McGraw had no friends among the umpires.

I went to the bag and gave it a kick as if it had shifted with Kelly's slide and I was merely trying to put it back on the foul line. Distracted by McGraw's wrath, Kelly accommodated me by stepping off the base. I immediately tagged him with the ball, and Rigler's thumb shot up in the air. *"Yerrrrrr out!"*

I kept a firm grip on the ball and ran to center field, my teammates joining me in the race to the clubhouse as they realized the game was over. The jeers of the Polo Grounds crowd grew to an ugly crescendo, but I could swear I heard McGraw screeching louder than the rest. As base coach, it had been his job to watch for the hidden ball trick.

O O O

I could have fallen asleep, I was so tired and content, but I wanted to savor the afterglow of the game a while longer. The boos of the New York partisans still rang in my ears; it was a sound as rewarding to a visiting player as cheers were from fans at home. Beating John McGraw would have been satisfying enough under normal circumstances. Today's game was a double victory for me, though, because no one who witnessed it—and I was sure Judge Landis would be getting a report on my performance—could doubt that I was giving my best.

On the diamond, my return to the Reds was certainly off to a good start. Off the field, however, things weren't looking so positive.

I was lying on my bed in our hotel room, still dressed, idly rolling the game ball in my fingers. At the washbasin, my new roommate, Curt Stram, was carefully navigating a razor over his cheeks, scraping off the peach fuzz. He paused often to remove excess lather with a towel and to admire his reflection in the mirror.

Since I'd left Bubbles Hargrave without a roommate when I had to stay behind in Cincinnati, Greasy Neale and Hargrave had made a trade: the two of them hooked up as roomies, leaving the unpopular Stram to room by himself. Now that I was back, I was stuck with the rookie.

"C'mon, Mick," he urged me again. "What's the point of

being in New York if you're not going to hit the town? It's Saturday night!"

"All I want is sleep tonight," I told him for the third time.

Stram continued his preparations at the mirror, carefully placing locks of his dirty blond hair over his forehead. I was amazed at how hard he worked to look carelessly handsome. If only he put as much effort into his baseball, he could become one of best.

"I hear there's a couple new girls at Daisy's," he said. "And maybe an old one for you," he added, with a laugh at his idea of a joke.

Daisy's was a house of ill-repute on Forty-first Street. I had no interest in going there with or without Stram. "What about Katie Perriman?" I asked.

His expression was blank. "What about her?"

"Aren't you and her . . . ?"

"So what if we were? She's a thousand miles away. And, as it happens, there's nothing between us anyhow."

"You told me before that there was." I didn't care whether he was faithful to her, I just wanted to aggravate him a little.

He uncorked a bottle of bay rum. "Not no more. I've had it with her. Did her a big favor and don't get no appreciation for it. To hell with her."

"What favor?"

"Just because it don't go the way she'd like, she gets all het up about it. Ought to be grateful, and all she does is gripe." He splashed bay rum over his face and neck. "Women! Gimme girls like the ones at Daisy's any day. You know where you stand with them. Not like—"

I tried again, "What's she mad at you for?"

"Can't say." He set the bottle heavily on the washstand. "It's personal."

Must have been real personal, I thought, considering Stram had never before shown a reluctance to run his mouth about private matters.

As he completed his grooming and donned an expensive suit that was a brighter shade of blue than any sapphire, I was thinking about Ollie Perriman. Because of Rufus Yates, I'd recently been focusing on the notion that Perriman might have been killed over something involving the 1919 World Series. But there remained the possibility that the motive was personal—like somebody wanting Katie Perriman's husband out of the way.

Stram asked one more time if I'd join him. I again declined and added a warning that if he woke me when he came in, I'd put soap in his toothpaste. He assured me he wouldn't be back till morning.

When he left, I opened the windows wider to let out the smell of the bay rum and went down to the lobby to phone Margie. It was the first chance I'd had to talk to her since leaving Cincinnati.

I began with a detailed recounting of the day's game. Then I caught myself, and told her that I missed her and apologized for having to leave for New York so abruptly.

"I understand," she said. "It was sweet of you to leave me the lilies."

"I thought they were daffodils."

"At this time of year? Daffodils don't bloom in *July.*" She sounded like she was telling me something as obvious as that the earth was round.

I knew if a bat was ash or willow or hickory, but with flowers I pretty much went by color. "Well, they were yellow," I said. "So I thought they were daffodils."

She laughed. "By the way, it's best to cut the roots off

before putting them in a vase. Oh!"—her tone grew serious—
"I thought you might be interested: that old Red Stocking
Dick Hurley was shot yesterday."

"I know. I read about it on the train. Not much detail,
though. Did he live?"

"So far. He's in Old City Hospital. And they caught the
woman."

"Any news on *why* she shot him?"

"No, just—hold on—" I heard the receiver clatter on the
table. When Margie got back on the line, she said, "I have
the article here. Her name is Mrs. Charlotte Ashby. She lives
in Walnut Hills, and she's described as 'elderly.' There's no
theory about motive."

She promised to save the newspapers for me, and we
talked for a while longer before grogginess overtook me and
I headed up to bed.

O O O

Sundays were no longer a day of rest for major-league ballplayers in New York. A year ago, the state legalized Sunday
baseball games, leaving Boston, Pittsburgh, and Philadelphia
as the only big-league cities that still prohibited them.

This Sunday, we played the opener of our series against
the Dodgers in Ebbets Field. With Eppa Rixey outpitching
Brooklyn's Burleigh Grimes, we took a 2–0 win over the
defending league champions. I had another good game, picking up two hits in four at-bats against the spitballer Grimes.
I also got my first chance to see one of the former Reds who'd
left the club after the 1919 World Series: second baseman Kid
Gumbert.

After showering and changing, I waited for Gumbert outside the players' gate. When he came out, he was with several of the other Dodgers; all of them appeared glum over the loss. Gumbert's nickname of "Kid" was about twenty years outdated; he was now a grizzled veteran whose face looked as worn and scarred as an old baseball. He walked with a stiff waddle, his knees probably destroyed by base runners breaking up double plays.

"Hey, Kid!" I called as he began to pass by.

Without looking at me, he growled, "No autographs."

"Fine, then I won't give you one."

His head jerked and he looked at me quizzically.

"I'm Mickey Rawlings," I said. "I just played third base against you."

"Oh, sorry. Didn't recognize you out of uniform." I was getting used to that; it seemed nobody believed I was a ballplayer unless I was wearing spikes and flannels.

"I was hoping I could talk to you."

He shook his head. "I'm on my way for a beer."

"Sounds good. I'll buy." I knew that Judge Landis was an ardent Prohibitionist, but I wasn't worried about being spotted in a speakeasy; if Landis was going to blacklist every player who had an illegal beer, there wouldn't be enough left to field a team in either league.

Gumbert readily accepted my offer, and we soon found a gin mill on Empire Boulevard. There was a bare patch on the front of the building where a sign had once hung that identified the saloon.

We went in and sat down at the bar. Other than the removal of the sign outside, there were no other indications that the proprietors had heard of the Eighteenth Amendment.

Gumbert raced through the first beer and made a good start on the second, barely acknowledging my presence.

"This is my first year with the Reds," I said.

He belched loudly.

"You were with the club in 1919," I went on.

"Yup."

"I been hearing some things, and I was wondering if you could tell me your take on them." I nodded for the bartender to back him up with a full glass.

"What kind of things?"

"That the White Sox weren't the only team offered money to take a dive in the World Series."

Gumbert said firmly, "Nobody on the Cincinnati club did nothing crooked."

"That's what I hear. But there *were* offers made, right?"

He drank from the third beer, more slowly. "Wouldn't know."

"How couldn't you know? There was a team meeting about it before one of the games."

"If you know that, what are you talking to me for?" The beer wasn't mellowing him; he was starting to sound irritated.

"Were *you* approached by gamblers?" I asked.

Gumbert appeared to be debating with himself, before deciding to talk. "Hell, I'm too old to run scared." He shook his head. "I didn't do nothin' wrong."

"Run scared from what?"

"From what that Judge Landis is talking about: 'guilty knowledge'—if you know something and don't tell about it, he'll kick you out of the game."

"Oh, yeah. Well, whatever you say won't go no further than me."

"All right," Gumbert said. "There *was* a team meeting. And some of the fellows admitted they were offered money to blow the series. But every one of them denied going along. I

ell you, that was the most pressure of them games—worrying
about making an error or swinging at a bad pitch and having
the boys think you sold out."

"Must have been especially tough on Hod Eller," I said.
"He was offered five grand to blow a game." I thought if
Gumbert knew I had some information, he might be forth-
coming with more.

"Yeah, but he came through fine," he said with admira-
tion. "You know, if anybody *had* folded, they'd have been
beaten to death in the clubhouse—I guarantee you that.
Anyway, there were more fellows approached than admitted
it; that ain't the kind of thing you want people to know—it
can leave a stink on you even if you're on the square."

"I know what you mean," I said. "Been going through
something like that myself."

He didn't push me for details, and I wasn't about to offer
any.

"So nothing ever happened," I said.

"Wouldn't say that. When the gamblers found they
couldn't pay us off, they took a different approach: they tried
to get our pitching staff drunk."

Jeez. "But it didn't work?"

Gumbert laughed. "Hell, Dutch Reuther and the others
could outdrink any of them hoods. So they did. And by game
time they were just fine." With that, he polished off the third
brew.

I thought for a few moments, then asked again, "Were
you approached?"

He nodded. "Yeah. And I turned him down cold."

"You know who he was?"

"You think them fellows give their names?"

"No, guess not. How about what he looked like? Anything stick out about him?"

"Nah, he didn't look like nothing. Just average—" Gumbert frowned in thought. "Stuck out . . . yeah, matter of fact there was something that stuck out: his ear. One of his ears stuck straight out."

○ ○ ○

Tuesday was to be our final game in Brooklyn. I'd continued to keep my mind and eyes open for anything that could provide a lead on the death of Ollie Perriman, hoping that somehow it would lead to an explanation of how I came to be set up with Rufus Yates.

I'd talked to Curt Stram some more—or tried to, at least. I'd asked him if Katie Perriman had ever mentioned that her husband had enemies, or if she knew who'd been interested in his baseball collection. According to Stram, the only times she mentioned her husband were to complain about how he neglected her.

I spent the last morning in New York trying to learn a little more about Dick Hurley. The New York Public Library carried old issues of the *New York Clipper,* the theatrical and sporting paper that covered baseball in its earliest years. The year I was interested in was 1872.

I pored over the box scores and accounts of the Washington Olympics games. There weren't many of them; the club folded in less than two months with a record of two wins and seven losses. In two of those games, Hurley played the outfield. He never got a base hit or scored a run, but there he was, just as the old man I'd dined with at the Sinton Hotel had said. And his teammates included former Red Stockings Asa Brainard and Fred Waterman.

The question that troubled me was: why would Hurley be so accurate about 1872 and so vague on 1869? Why would a handful of games with an insignificant ball club be more memorable to him than a season with one of the greatest teams in history?

Unable to find an answer to that question, I checked some newspapers from 1919 that covered the World Series. Not to see if there was anything about a scandal—those reports didn't develop for some time afterward—but to read about the two surviving Red Stockings who'd returned to the Queen City for the Series opener.

There were several lengthy pieces devoted to the recollections of Cal McVey and George Wright, but neither one of them mentioned Dick Hurley. I did note that Wright had traveled to Cincinnati from Boston, where he owned a sporting goods business.

And Boston was the next stop on our road trip.

Finished at the library, I returned to the hotel to pack before heading to Flatbush for the series finale. I also placed a phone call to my friend Karl Landfors; I told him I'd be coming to Boston after all, and that there'd be a ticket for him at Braves Field tomorrow.

Chapter Twenty-Two

OOO

I was already moving in toward the plate when Dolf Luque released the pitch. Hank Gowdy squared to bunt, and dropped a beauty that died in the thick grass. It was only supposed to be a sacrifice to move Billy Southworth to second, but I had to race in and barehand the ball. Off-balance, I threw to Jake Daubert just in time to nail Gowdy at first.

A couple blades of grass stuck to my hand and I brushed them off on my jersey as I trotted back to my position. It struck me that I had played on this very turf when I'd first broken into the big leagues, with the Boston Braves in the fall of 1911. The park was different—the team then played at the South End Grounds on Walpole Street—but the infield grass was the same, having been transplanted here when Braves Field opened a few years later.

"Hey, Rawlings!" came a shrill cry from the stands. "Why didn't you *roll* the ball to first—it would gotten there faster!"

It wasn't a pleasant-sounding voice, but I was happy to hear that Karl Landfors had made it to the game.

Luque then got Frank Gibson on a pop-up and fanned

Walt Holke on three straight pitches to end the game and chalk up a 5–2 win.

Half an hour later, I met Karl outside the park on Gaffney Street. "You sure got a good set of lungs," I said. "Didn't know a string bean like you could be so full of hot air." I'd been trying to teach him about baseball for ten years. He still couldn't keep score, or fathom the infield fly rule, but at least he was making an effort to heckle, and I thought he could use the encouragement.

He grinned at the compliment and pushed his horn-rim spectacles higher on his long, thin nose. Karl was making some progress as far as baseball went, but his wardrobe was as limited as ever: a somber black suit draped his skeletal frame, and a derby of the same color perched on his head, hiding a scalp nearly as free of hair as a skull. "Sorry I was late," he said. "Got held up at a meeting."

"Free ticket for a ball game and you go to a meeting? That's downright un-American." As a muckraking reporter, Socialist pamphleteer, and sympathizer to just about any hopeless progressive cause, he'd often been accused of being unpatriotic. At least with me, he knew I was only kidding.

But he was serious when he replied, "It was actually a rather important strategy meeting."

"About the trial?" The Sacco and Vanzetti case had occupied most of his attention since he joined their cause last summer.

He nodded. "Yes, we're planning the appeal. It looks like—"

I interrupted, "How about we head downtown while you tell me?"

He agreed, and we got on the Beacon Street Subway. During the fifteen-minute ride, he told me about the trial of the Italian anarchists that had ended with their conviction for the murder of two men during a payroll robbery in South Braintree.

We came out of the subway at Park Street. I suggested dinner, but Karl said he'd filled up on fried clams during the two innings he'd been at the game. So we opted for a walk through the Boston Common.

"This appeal," I said. "You think you have any chance?"

"If it were strictly a matter of law, yes. The trial was an utter travesty, and Judge Webster Thayer was blatantly biased. He even bragged to one of his cronies that he'd get them hanged. That's the prosecutor's role, not the judge's."

"Jeez, Karl. That's awful."

"Thayer also liked to refer to them as 'those anarchist bastards.' Unfortunately, that's what most people think of anarchists, so politically I don't think we have a chance with the appeal. The rest of the Defense Committee is more hopeful." He sighed. "Perhaps I'm just tired. I haven't had a break for a long time."

"Why not take one? Get away for a while."

"No. There's too much work to do."

A stray baseball came into our path, and a couple of boys who'd been playing catch yelled, "Little help!"

Karl stooped down to pick up the baseball, then tried to hand it to me.

"You throw it to them," I said with a smile. "According to some bum at the ballpark, I'd do better rolling it."

"Very well. I shall." He methodically removed his coat and hat, and gave them to me to hold. Then he went into a peculiar windmill windup that made it look as if he was trying to screw himself into the ground. With a high-pitched grunt, he let loose. The ball traveled a good forty feet before plopping to the earth.

The two kids ran in to pick up the ball; one of them said loudly to the other, "My sister throws better than that."

Karl actually looked proud. His glasses had slipped down his nose, and he puffed from the exertion.

"Not bad," I said. "Next time I'm in town we'll work on your hitting."

He put his derby back on, at a bit of an angle, and draped his coat over his arm as we resumed walking. He complained that he thought he'd pulled a muscle in his arm. I refrained from pointing out that he had none to pull.

We crossed Charles Street to the Public Garden. "I got a problem with a judge, too," I said. "Judge Kenesaw Mountain Landis."

"That—that—" Karl's face reddened, and a vein bulged from his temple. I hoped he'd come up with an appropriate cussword before it burst. "That *addlepated despot!*"

I wasn't sure what that was, but I thought I got the gist of Karl's meaning. "I figured you'd know about him from the Wobbly trial," I said. During the war, Landis had presided over the sedition trial of Big Bill Haywood and almost a hundred other members of the Industrial Workers of the World.

"Landis is every bit as bad as Thayer," Karl said. "He's bigoted, and a showboat. After the war, he tried to have Kaiser Wilhelm extradited to Chicago. Landis wanted to indict him for murder because a Chicagoan had died when the *Lusitania* sank. Then there was Victor Berger, the congressman from Milwaukee—Landis sent him to prison simply for being opposed to the war."

I told Karl about Rufus Yates and the photograph that had been taken of us. "You think I can trust the Judge to do the right thing?" I asked.

He shook his head. "Landis's prejudices are many—he hates immigrants, Negroes, unionists, suffragists, Socialists—and his rulings are capricious. As my friend John Dos Passos says, 'that judge hands out twenty-five year sentences as lightheartedly as he'd fine some Joe five bucks for speeding.' No, Mickey, you cannot rely on him to make a fair decision."

"You sure it's not because you and him have different politics that makes you say he can't be trusted?"

Karl thought for a long moment. "I disagree with his politics. And I admit I detest the man personally. But my dislike for him is because of how he abuses his power, not simply because of a difference in philosophy." He pushed up his glasses. "You don't have to take my word for the fact that Landis goes by his whims instead of the law. Check into all the times his rulings have been overturned by higher courts. He probably has had more decisions reversed than any other judge on the bench."

I found that bit of information discouraging. "We don't have that in baseball," I said. "There's no such thing as an appeal. Landis is the final authority."

Karl looked at me. "Then I strongly suggest you do whatever is necessary to ensure that he arrives at the correct decision."

O O O

The problem was I didn't know what was necessary, because I didn't know why I'd been set up with Rufus Yates in the first place. So I had to keep skipping around in time, from 1869 to 1919 to 1921, trying to cover all the bases.

Thursday morning, I began an effort to learn more about the old Red Stockings from that team's most illustrious player.

I found Wright & Ditson Sporting Goods on Washington Street, near Filene's Department Store in the heart of Boston's shopping district. The large, orderly shop contained merchandise to appeal to every interest: baseball, football, and basketball gear for those who played sports; tennis and golf equipment for those who merely liked to stroll about on lawns. There were rows of shiny bicycles and shelves stocked with elegant uniforms. The only thing missing was George Wright.

I explained my interest in meeting Wright to a salesclerk who got on the telephone to see if he could arrange an interview for me.

While I waited, I explored the store, accompanied by a second clerk. I asked him about Wright's baseball career after leaving Cincinnati, but the young man said he knew almost nothing about it. He did tell me that the former Red Stocking had introduced golf to Boston, brought ice hockey to the United States from Canada, and was the country's leading manufacturer of lawn tennis equipment. Golf appeared to be the clerk's favorite pastime, and he insisted on showing me a set of clubs. He was describing the virtues of a particular mashie niblick, when the first clerk arrived with the news that Mr. Wright would be pleased to meet me tomorrow at Franklin Park.

I left the store wondering how anyone could play a game that used something called a "mashie niblick."

O O O

The golf course at Dorchester's Franklin Park, a couple miles southeast of Braves Field, was crowded with men wielding such clubs. Most of the golfers were of middle age or beyond, dressed in funny suits with oversize caps.

George Wright had finished playing for the day and the two of us were sipping lemonades on a patio behind the clubhouse. Our table overlooked the course, which was certainly picturesque: manicured green grass blanketed the fairways, and clusters of elms and maples dotted the rolling landscape.

I was barely aware of the surroundings, though, because my attention was fixed on the noble face before me. Wright had deep-set, intelligent eyes; a strong nose projecting over a handsome mustache; and thinning silver hair neatly groomed. The seventy-four-year-old former shortstop, who still appeared fit enough to field the position, had removed his cap, but he still wore his golfing outfit: brown tweed Norfolk jacket, knickerbockers, argyle stockings that came up to his knees, a stiff white shirt, and a neatly knotted cravat.

I was awed to be in the presence of this baseball legend, and had difficulty finding anything to say. I finally asked him about playing in 1869, and he willingly began regaling me with tales of the old Red Stockings.

As he talked, I relaxed a bit and noticed a couple of things. One was that he spoke with practiced ease; he'd probably been telling the same stories at banquets and business lunches for years. The other was that, unlike Dick Hurley's supposed recollections, George Wright's words conveyed the *feel* of what it was like to have been a member of the team.

He went on to describe his later baseball career, including the competition between him and brother Harry in 1879, when both were National League managers. George came out on top, leading his Providence Grays over Harry and the Boston Red Stockings for the championship.

I was reluctant to interrupt his stories; I could easily have listened to them for hours. But when he paused to hail a waiter for fresh drinks, I asked, "Do you still go to the ball games?"

"Not many," he answered. "Business, golf, and grand-children keep me quite busy."

"You play a lot of golf?"

"Nine holes every day." He smiled. "But never more, or I might not be able to play nine the next day." Waving his hand at the grounds before us, he added, "I do more than play—this course is my own design. Next year, it will open to the public."

I was disappointed that another sport had stolen the affections of this baseball pioneer.

Wright reached into an inside pocket of his Jacket. "I do get to a few of the Braves and Red Sox games," he said. He showed me a couple of passes. One was for Fenway Park; the other was a solid silver "Lifetime Pass #1" for all National League ballparks. "The game has grown so much," he said. "When I was a boy, I played at Elysian Fields in Hoboken. Beautiful spot for baseball, but it was just a pasture sur-rounded by trees—no fences, no seats for spectators. Now to see these big new parks like Fenway and Braves Field . . . it's remarkable to me." He leaned back. "You know, there's still not one of them that can compare with the old Union Grounds in Cincinnati, though."

"What was it like?"

"Union Grounds was a pretty little park, but it's not the structure that made it so special. It was everything that surrounded a ball game in those days: the parades, being taken to the game by carriage, bands playing, banners waving, the crowd cheering . . ." His eyes looked upward, and I was happy to see that they did still have a spark of passion for the game, at least for the one he used to play. "To take the field and see the flags flying from the cupola over the Grand Duchess—"

"Grand Duchess?"

Wright explained that it was the nickname for the grand-stand which was reserved for the ladies. "And, oh, how the ladies adored us," he added with a twinkle in his eyes. "They'd wave red handkerchiefs, and some of them would wear red stockings. Of course they had to lift their skirts above their ankles for us to see them, and that was considered quite provocative in those days."

"Speaking about the ladies," I broke in, "I heard that's why Dick Hurley left the team—something about a girl named Sarah. They eloped, some say. Do you know if that's true?"

"I don't recall the name of the girl," he answered. "But I do believe I heard something about an elopement."

I then asked him about the homecoming on July 1, 1869, and the banquet that night. He gave me a recounting of the parade, the exhibition game, and the dinner. Although I enjoyed hearing it from his perspective, he didn't say anything that I hadn't already read or heard about. And, again, it all sounded smooth and polished.

"Mr. Wright," I said, "this might be important. Could you please try to think back if anything happened that night with Dick Hurley? Did you see him with a girl at the banquet? Or did anything unusual happen?"

He frowned and studied me for a moment. "You sound serious."

"Yes, sir. Mr. Hurley was shot last week. And it may have to do with something that happened in the summer of '69."

"Shot!" Wright repeated. "Did he survive?"

"So far, but the last I heard, he's still in the hospital. He came to Cincinnati for the opening of an exhibit on the Red Stockings, and a woman shot him at his hotel."

"Oh, my." Wright appeared to be searching his memory. His tone no longer sounded like he was giving a banquet speech when he said, "I believe the story about Hurley running off with a girl was just a rumor. The team never discouraged it, though." He smiled wryly. "Been telling the same story myself for so many years, I suppose I got to believing that's what really happened. But it's not why he left the club."

"Do you know the real reason?"

He answered sadly, "My brother fired him for drunkenness. We were trying to make baseball respectable, and Harry had no tolerance for drunkards. In fact, Harry Junior, my nephew, was a fine ballplayer and could have made the big leagues in the eighties, but his father wouldn't let him play because of all the rummies in the game. We weren't exactly saints, mind you. Charlie Sweasy and Asa Brainard in particular could be problems. But Hurley embarrassed the team in public."

"What did he do?"

"He was so inebriated at that homecoming banquet that he couldn't walk under his own power and had to be carried out. In front of the city's leading citizens. Harry fired him the next morning. We didn't want to humiliate him by giving the reason publicly, and of course it would have reflected badly on the team to say why he'd been dismissed. So Hurley just quietly went away. Must say, I prefer the story that he ran off with a girl."

"Thanks, Mr. Wright. I may be seeing you soon in Cincinnati. I hear you might be coming to the opening of the exhibit for your old team."

"I'm not sure if I can. I'm awfully busy here. But I do hope we get a chance to chat again. Not many people ask me about my baseball days anymore."

O O O

During my nightly phone call home, I asked Margie if there was any news yet on why Charlotte Ashby had shot Dick Hurley.

"No," she answered. "According to the papers, she hasn't said a word to anyone about why she did it. I do have some news for you though."

"What's that?"

"Spider Jenkins, the gambler you met at the Stars game, called. He was pretty skittish—wanted to talk only to you, and really didn't want to give me a message. But I coaxed him into it. Hope you don't mind."

"Of course not. What did he say?"

"Lloyd Tinsley did bet on the 1919 World Series."

"Huh! So maybe—"

"But he bet on the Reds."

"Oh." So he and Rufus Yates weren't in on a fix together. According to Kid Gumbert, Yates had wanted the Reds to lose the series. Tinsley had bet on them to win. "Did he find out anything about Yates?"

"Not yet. He said he'll keep looking into both Tinsley and Yates. Oh—he also says you owe him twenty-five dollars for the information. You can leave it with Ralph at the Palace, he said."

"Pretty steep, but okay." I had told Jenkins to name his price, after all, and a deal was a deal.

"How's Karl?" Margie asked. The two of them had met several times when we lived in Detroit.

"Uh, you'll be seeing him for yourself soon. He's coming to stay with us for a while." I held my breath.

She didn't yell at me for not asking her about it first. "That's wonderful! It will be nice to see him again. And I wish *you* were here tonight already." I assumed her desire to see me had a romantic basis, but she added, "I could use your help. I'm going to the zoo later to dig up a wildebeest that died last week."

"You're *what?*" And I thought I did some crazy things.

I still wasn't sure if she was kidding me about her plans for the night when we hung up, and I went back to the room.

After packing, I checked the schedule to see when our first games in Redland Field would be. Then I looked at the date of the game when I'd met Rufus Yates outside the park: July 10. Something seemed wrong with that. I flipped the calendar back to June. According to the report Detective Forsch showed me, Yates had begun a thirty-day sentence on the twentieth of that month. Thirty days. So how did he get out after only twenty?

Chapter Twenty-Three

○○○

"Thanks for letting him stay," I said to Margie.

She handed me a stack of plates and bowls to set on the dining table. "It will be fun to have a houseguest."

Margie had to be the most optimistic person on earth to think that it could possibly be "fun" to have Karl Landfors around.

Karl and I had arrived in Cincinnati only a couple hours earlier, and I was already irritated with him. After the long train ride from Boston, we both badly needed a bath. Out of hospitality, I let him go first, and he remained in the tub for so long that I was going to have to wait until after dinner to wash off the soot and dirt from the train.

The table was set, Margie's latest batch of burgoo was ready, and the drinks were poured by the time Karl came back downstairs wearing a clean change of clothes. The degree of cleanliness was the only variable in his wardrobe, which consisted entirely of black suits, white shirts, and black ties.

"Smells wonderful," Karl said as he sat down. He tilted

up his long nose and sniffed in about half the room's air supply. "What is it?"

"Burgoo," Margie answered. "Something like mulligan stew."

"Except you probably never had mulligan stew with squirrel in it," I said.

Karl dropped the napkin he'd been primly folding. "Squirrel?"

"Or worse. You never know what critters might end up in the pot." I asked Margie, "You didn't put in any of that wildebeest you dug up, did you?"

She smiled. "Just the eyeballs for flavor."

Karl approached his first few bites skeptically, but then appeared to enjoy the food. Throughout the meal, I said little, letting Margie and Karl catch up. She told him about her job at the zoo; he talked about the Sacco and Vanzetti trial and the Defense Committee's planned appeal.

After dinner, we went into the parlor for coffee and peach pie. Margie and I took the sofa while Karl sat stiffly on the edge of an armchair. We'd barely sat down when Margie popped back up. "Oh!" she said. "I have something to show you." She went over to the sideboard and came back with a small stack of newspapers. "You made the headlines."

Uh, oh. I'd made headlines before, and they rarely involved good news.

"No, you'll like it," she said, apparently noticing my expression. "It's about that hidden ball trick you pulled."

I certainly did like it when I saw the two-column headline:

Rawlings Outwits Giants
McGraw Howls Over Game-Winning Play

Not only was it great to see my name in print like that, it was especially nice to see it given top billing over John McGraw's. The article accompanying the headline referred to me as "the crafty veteran." I liked "crafty," but seeing myself called a "veteran" was probably like the first time a woman hears herself addressed as "ma'am." On the whole, I was thrilled with the coverage, though, and I glanced around the parlor to see where best to display that game ball.

"The other stories are in there, too," Margie said. "About the Dick Hurley shooting."

"Shooting?" Karl asked. In Boston, I'd only mentioned my problem with Judge Landis and Rufus Yates. I hadn't yet told him about the death of Oliver Perriman or the attempt to kill Hurley.

While he nibbled his dessert, I filled him in on Dick Hurley's disappearance in the midst of the 1869 season, the arrival in Cincinnati of a man who claimed to be Hurley a couple of weeks ago, and on the contents of the note I'd found in the old baseball. As I talked, I skimmed over the newspaper articles about the shooting. They reported that while Hurley was recovering in Old City Hospital, Mrs. Charlotte Ashby had been charged with attempted murder and was being held in Central Station. She was refusing to make a statement to police, and the motive for her action remained a mystery.

"So your theory," Karl said in a dubious tone, "is that the shooting was to get revenge for something Hurley did fifty-two years ago?"

"Not necessarily 'revenge,' " I said, "but at first I did think it might be related to what happened to Sarah—especially if she and Hurley had eloped. Now I have no idea why he was shot. I talked with George Wright in Boston, and he told me Hurley was kicked off the team for drunkenness. So there probably never was any elopement." I took a sip of coffee. "And as for this fellow who was shot, I suspect he's a fraud anyway. Maybe Charlotte Ashby knows his true identity, and wanted to kill him for some reason that has nothing to do with the real Dick Hurley."

Margie said, "Maybe you should tell that to the police— about him being an impostor."

"I don't know for a *fact* that he is, it's just the sense I have from the way he talked. A lot of what he said didn't ring true." I dug a fork into the pie. "Sure would've helped if Lloyd Tinsley had checked him out first, but all Tinsley wants him for is publicity."

"Tinsley is the business manager," Karl said. I'd pointed out most of the team, including Tinsley, Pat Moran, and the coaches, to him in the club car during the trip from Boston.

I nodded. "He also has a stake in the exhibit Ollie Perriman was setting up—a hundred percent stake now that Perriman's dead." I gave him a brief rundown on Perriman's death, and on the break-ins at Redland Field and our home. "I thought maybe that could be a motive for Tinsley to want Perriman dead—to get the exhibit. But now I'm pretty sure he had nothing to do with it."

"What makes you sure?" Karl asked.

"*Pretty* sure. I'm not *certain* about anything in all this." I paused to organize my thoughts before continuing. "I figure Perriman was killed for one of two reasons: either somebody wanted him dead, and the break-in was to cover up the motive for the murder, or somebody wanted to steal something from the collection and killed Perriman while trying to get it. If Lloyd Tinsley wanted something from the collection, he could have taken it anytime; no need to kill Perriman.

And the only reason I could think of for Tinsley wanting him murdered is to inherit the collection—but that doesn't make sense because he'd do better to wait until Perriman finished organizing it."

"Is there anyone else who would have motive to murder Perriman?" Karl asked. "Or do you believe he was simply killed in the course of a robbery."

Margie looked over at me, then said, "Well, his wife might have been having an affair with one of the players."

"Curt Stram," I said. "There *was* something between him and Katie Perriman, and whatever it was turned sour." I told them of my talk with Stram, and about him saying that he'd done her a favor, and now she was mad at him. "Could be one of them wanted Perriman out of the way."

Karl was rubbing his nose and blinking rapidly as he tried to absorb everything.

I pushed away my empty plate. "I think Rufus Yates is the key in all this."

"The gambler you were photographed with," Karl said. He appeared relieved at the mention of somebody he'd already heard about.

"Yes. He was definitely involved in trying to get the Reds to throw games during the 1919 World Series—I talked to one of the players he tried to bribe. And Yates is only part of it. There's also whoever it was who took the photo and sent it to Garry Herrmann. For a while I thought it could be Tinsley, because Yates once played for a team he ran in the minors. I figured maybe it went something like this: Tinsley and Yates were partners in trying to get the Reds to throw the Series, Ollie Perriman came across evidence of it among the stuff he gathered for his collection, and so Tinsley had Yates kill him." I shook my head. "But that doesn't work.

Yates was in jail when Perriman was killed, and, according to a local bookie, Tinsley bet *on* the Reds, not against them."

Karl looked puzzled. "Isn't any kind of betting in baseball enough to get you kicked out?"

"Not back then it wasn't. Lots of managers and players bet on the games. As long as you bet on your own team to win, it was always okay."

"So where do you go from here?" Karl asked.

That was the question. "I'm not sure. There is something new that's come up about Yates: he was supposed to be serving a month in jail—thirty days or thirty dollars—but he got out more than a week early. And I've been wondering: how did he come up with the money after twenty days in jail? If he had enough to pay the fine when he was sentenced, why not pay it right away and avoid serving time? And if he didn't have it, where did it come from? Maybe somebody paid the fine for him. And maybe knowing who put up the money will tell me who his partner is." I leaned back in the sofa, my head tilted against the cushion. I felt tired and grimy and didn't want to talk or think about it anymore. "Thing is, I don't know where to start."

Apparently the grime hadn't escaped Margie's notice. "Maybe with a bath," she suggested.

O O O

We all retired early. Karl Landfors was settled in the guest room, and Margie and I were in bed.

"Do I smell better now?" I asked her.

"You weren't bad before. I just thought a hot bath would do you good." Margie began to massage the back of my neck. "Besides, it gave Karl and me a chance to talk."

"About what?"

"Among other things, we decided to help you." Her fingers dug deeper.

"Mmmm. That feels good. Help me how?"

"Karl's going to look into how Rufus Yates got released early. And I'm going to talk to Katie Perriman; maybe I can find out what the 'favor' was that Curt Stram did for her."

"Thanks, but I—"

Her fingers left my neck, and she curled up close to me. "Something else probably do you good, too."

"Uh, Karl's right across the hall." His proximity put a damper on my enthusiasm for the way Margie and I traditionally celebrated my return from a road trip.

"So? The door's closed—it's not like he's going to see us."

"I know, but . . . he'll hear." With Margie and me, there was little chance of it being a quiet celebration.

Her hands flew up under my arms and she tickled me until I was choking back the laughs and bouncing to free myself from her. "Stop," I said. "He's gonna think we're . . ."

She halted the tickling. "Well, if he thinks that's what we're doing anyway, then we might as well."

Margie always did make such good sense.

I approached Redland Field with fresh enthusiasm Monday afternoon. This was the first time I'd be playing in the park since my encounter with Rufus Yates had landed me on the "injured" list. I was eager to see how the fans would greet me. They were usually generous with applause when a player returned from an injury. And maybe they'd pour on a little extra because of my hidden-ball play in New York.

Even the weather was encouraging. The heat wave had broken while we were on the road, and the temperature was now in the mid-seventies. The sky was clear and the breeze mild. A perfect day for playing baseball.

My high spirits took a dip when I hit Findlay Street and spotted the face from the photograph. It was fixed in my memory, and I had no doubt this was the same newsboy who'd appeared in the picture with Yates and me. He had a batch of papers under one arm and a single issue held up in a hand smudged with black ink. The boy's ragged corduroy knickers appeared to be a size too large for him, and the only other garment he was wearing—a yellowed undershirt—was at least a size too small.

Along with a dozen or so other newsies, he was yelling, "Paper! Getcha paper!" Each boy tried to shout louder than the others. He spotted me as I neared, and tried to hand me a copy of the *Times-Star*. "Paper, mister?" There was no indication that he recognized me.

"Do you remember me?" I asked.

"Nope. Should I?"

I took the newspaper from him and dug into my pocket. The prospect of a sale brought a little brightness to his eyes. "About three weeks ago," I said, "I met a man just about where we're standing now. Somebody took a picture of us— and you're in the picture holding up a paper."

"Yeah . . . So?" He eyed my pocket, waiting for his money.

"You didn't try to sell us the paper. Looked like somebody only wanted you to hold it up next to us."

"Yeah, I remember," the kid said. "The guy"—he pushed one of his ears forward to give the impression of Rufus Yates—"said it was a joke on you. Gave me a buck to do it."

I thanked the boy and handed him twice that amount.

O O O

There wasn't much applause when I stepped into the batter's box for the first time, but I didn't take it personally. By the bottom of the third, it was already clear that this wasn't going to be the kind of game where there would be a lot to cheer about. Nor was there anything to jeer. The game had simply settled into a leisurely, lackluster battle between two equally mediocre ball clubs: the sixth-place Cubs and the seventh-place Reds.

The pitching matchup was nothing to get excited about,

either. Chicago's Lefty Tyler and our Hod Eller were among the league's least effective hurlers. This was August 1, and the men were tied in victories with two each—an average of half a win a month.

As the game progressed, there were few strikeouts, plenty of routine grounders and fly balls, and no spectacular catches or extra-base hits. By the seventh inning, with the score tied at 3–3, it had the feel of one of those sandlot marathons that kids play—where they go on for twenty or thirty innings, with the fun of playing more important than the final outcome. It was the kind of game that didn't provide much entertainment for spectators, but was an easy one to play in, and I was starting to wish it would continue into extra innings.

I also wished that Margie and Karl Landfors could have been there. But she was at the zoo, and he was trying to find out how Rufus Yates had gotten out of jail early. I'd been starting to suspect that Karl hadn't come to Cincinnati merely to take a rest from the Sacco and Vanzetti case, as he'd told me before we left Boston. In fact, it wouldn't surprise me if Margie had contacted him earlier and asked him to come and help me. But I wasn't going to ask either of them about it. I was just glad he was here.

○ ○ ○

My hope for extra innings was denied when the Cubs put together three bloop singles in the top of the ninth and the resulting run held up to give Johnny Evers's ball club a 4–3 win.

I left the park feeling as fresh as when I'd arrived. I'd played the full nine innings at third, but hadn't been pressed either physically or mentally. I'd made no errors and, in keeping with the routine nature of the game, had gone my traditional 1-for-4 at the plate.

There was still a trickle of late-departing fans heading down Dalton as I started for home. I'd crossed Sherman Avenue when a Liberty Street trolley pulled up a block ahead and began to take on passengers. I picked up my pace, hoping to catch it, when a big fellow came up behind my left shoulder and jostled me. "Excuse me," I said, trying to step a little faster. He came up again, nudging me harder and throwing me off stride. I turned. "What are you—?"

He said nothing, and his broad face was expressionless as he gave me another push. The man kept bumping me like a cowboy using his horse to nudge a stray calf back into the herd.

One more shove propelled me into a narrow alley between a run-down apartment building and a secondhand furniture store. Standing about twenty feet inside the alley entrance was Rufus Yates. I'd just recognized him when I was slammed from behind and sent stumbling forward, my boater falling off in the process. By the time I regained my balance, I was face-to-face with Yates.

He gave me a smile that was full of teeth and devoid of sincerity. "Glad you could stop by." His clothes—a sky-blue double-breasted suit and a cream-colored fedora—were out of place in the filthy alley, but Yates himself appeared quite at ease, as if it was his natural habitat.

I shot a glance behind me to see if there was a way I could get past the thug who'd steered me here. His muscular bulk, outlined beneath a thin green turtleneck sweater, blocked any exit in his direction. Behind Yates, at the other end of the alley, trash bins and ash cans spilling over with garbage presented a greater obstacle.

"What do you want?" I asked.

Yates tilted up his hat with a forefinger. "I want you to stay out of my business. You been asking questions about me, and that's gonna have to stop. There's nothing about me you need to know."

"There's a picture of us that's causing me some trouble," I said calmly. "You got to expect me to be curious about why it was taken."

Yates shook his head; the ear that stuck out looked like it was waving at me. "What I *expect* is that you're going to stay the hell out of my business from now on. And Knucksie here is going to make sure of it."

Knucksie—that's the nickname for a knuckleball pitcher. I shot another look at the big man. His round, placid face was unfamiliar to me. Did he play in the minors—a teammate of Yates? Maybe with Lloyd Tinsley's Wichita club? I turned back to Yates. "Is it your business I'm supposed to stay out of, or Tinsley's?"

I watched closely for his reaction, but I couldn't tell if the name of the Reds business manager meant anything to him. My question brought another smile to his mouth. "I tell you to quit poking around, and the first thing you do is ask me a question. Not a promising start, is it?" He called past me, "Knucksie, explain to him that I mean business."

The big fellow lumbered toward me. For the first time, his face showed expression: a gleam came to his eyes as he pulled a set of brass knuckles from his pocket. His name had nothing to do with baseball.

I frantically looked around for a way out. If I tried to climb over the trash pile, he'd be on me in seconds. A fire escape? No, too high for me to reach. A door? The only one

was on the side of the furniture store. I could make it . . .
maybe . . . but if it was locked, I'd be trapped.

I judged that my best chance of escape was to try to slide
past Knucksie, who now had the shiny implement secured
over his fingers.

Yates moved aside to make room for his accomplice. I
started to edge backward. When Knucksie was within a few
feet of me, I made a feint for the doorway of the furniture
store. He moved to block me, and I tried to roll around him
toward the alley entrance. I was almost past him when his
right fist flashed out and landed a glancing blow to the side
of my head; the impact of metal on skull sent me reeling. I
staggered to the opposite wall, my hand clasped over my
ear.

He came over to where I was leaning against the building.
I pulled my head away from the wall; getting it caught
between the bricks and another brass knuckle punch would
have been like putting it in a nutcracker. He grabbed my
shoulder with one hand and swung with the other. I jerked
my arm up to protect my head, but this time the blow came
to my stomach. I doubled over, and thought I tasted spleen
rising in my throat. Hard as I tried, I couldn't remain standing.
Determined to stay as upright as my body would allow, I
dropped to one knee and rested in that position.

Knucksie stepped away and looked at Yates, who
appeared satisfied with the "explanation" I'd been given.

Yates walked to where my straw hat was lying on the
ground. He picked it up and made a show of dusting it off
with his pocket handkerchief. I fought to breathe again as
he brought it to me. "Any more questions?" he asked.

Finally able to get some air into my lungs, I wasn't about

to waste any of it by talking. I forced myself up from my knee, but remained bent over.

My silence met with Yates's approval. "Good," he said. "Now we understand each other." He reached out to hand me my hat, affecting a courteous manner.

Angry as the beating had made me, it was this gesture that sent my anger boiling over into rage. I grabbed his extended wrist with both hands and swung him face first into the wall. The crunching sound of the impact was more satisfying than the crack of a solid base hit. I followed with a flurry of hard jabs to his kidneys, getting in five or six punches before I was pulled off and sent flying through the air. My fall was broken by a packing crate that shattered, injecting a number of splinters into my back.

Rufus Yates abandoned all pretense of courtesy. "Kill him," he ordered Knucksie.

The big man hesitated.

Yates screamed, "Kill him!"

A window creaked open from one of the apartments several stories up.

"I don't kill for nobody," Knucksie said. "You want that, you get somebody else."

Yates turned on him, shrieking, "I said *kill him*, you stupid oaf. *Do it!*"

I got to my feet, unsteady, but feeling stronger, encouraged by the argument between the two hoodlums.

From the window above, a man shouted, "What's going on down there!"

Yates yelled back, "None o' your business, you old fool! Get your head back inside before I shoot it off!" It was an idle threat; if he'd had a gun, I was pretty sure he'd have used it on me already.

"I'm gonna call the cops!" The window slammed shut.

With Yates and Knucksie both still looking up, I sprinted past them, ignoring the pain that jolted me with every step.

"Stop him!" Yates cried.

I was almost to the street when I heard Knucksie answer, "Go to hell."

His response was reassuring, but I still didn't slow down until I was safely seated on a trolley headed home.

I'd reached several conclusions by Tuesday morning. One was that I didn't ever want to be on the receiving end of a brass-reinforced punch again. The second was that, despite conclusion number one, I was not going to drop my questions about Rufus Yates—no petty hoodlum was going to scare me off when my career was at stake. And, third: there was no sense trying to figure out how Yates had heard that I'd been asking about him. I'd talked to a number of people— the newsboy, Spider Jenkins, Detective Forsch, Kid Gumbert—and by the time you tell three people anything, you might as well consider it public knowledge.

Two people I hadn't told everything about yesterday's encounter with Yates were Margie and Karl Landfors. I'd described it only as "a bit of a run-in," and they were gracious enough not to ask about the purple lump that had blossomed above my ear. They'd both left early this morning; Karl was pursuing a courthouse contact regarding Yates's early release, and Margie was off to meet Katie Perriman before going to the zoo.

Nor had I reported the assault to Detective Forsch, since I

assumed it wouldn't do much good. I was now reconsidering, though, and decided to give him a try.

When I got the detective on the phone, I told him about the episode in the alley.

"You want to press charges?" Forsch asked.

That hadn't been my intent, but it might not be a bad idea—pressing criminal charges against Yates should at least demonstrate to Judge Landis that I wasn't in league with the gambler. "What would that involve?"

He let out a whoosh of air that must have produced a spectacular smoke cloud. "The procedure or the reality?"

"Reality."

"You file a complaint, Yates produces a dozen witnesses who swear he was elsewhere at the time, and the case is dismissed."

"Doesn't sound worth the trouble."

"Probably isn't."

"In that case, let's skip it." Then I got to the main reason I'd called. "In the alley, Yates was screaming he wanted me killed. You think he'd follow through on that?"

"Nah, he doesn't have it in him," the detective answered. "He'll use a blackjack in a robbery, or have somebody beaten up if they owe him money, but he's no murderer. The fellow he was with might be, though. You catch his name?"

Strangely, I felt I owed Knucksie something for refusing to kill me. "No, I didn't. But I don't think I have anything to worry about from him."

After we hung up, I felt I was getting through this okay. I'd survived yesterday, and I was unlikely to be murdered today. And, if anybody had seen me with Yates, it would have been obvious that we were not on friendly terms, so I didn't have to worry about another report to Landis that I'd met with him.

Other than the bruise to my head, there appeared to be no damage, and I was eager and able to play in the afternoon game. Until then, I relaxed over coffee and a plate of butter cookies, reading the morning papers. And there was plenty of news in them to interest me.

The leading baseball story was about the Black Sox trial in Chicago. The defense was scheduled to complete its closing statement today, and then the case would go to the jury. Soon it would finally be over.

What didn't look like it would be resolved anytime soon was the attempted murder of Dick Hurley by Charlotte Ashby. She was still refusing to make any statement about her action in the Sinton Hotel. According to the papers, the police were now speculating that her silence was because she was covering up for somebody and had possibly carried out the shooting on behalf of another party.

I still hadn't figured out what had really happened in 1869. Except that the real Dick Hurley had been fired instead of eloping. Was there really a girl named Sarah who'd been murdered? If so, did it involve the Red Stockings in some way? And, fifty-two years later, did it result in Oliver Perriman's getting killed?

Maybe the false Mr. Hurley could give me a clue.

O O O

Five of the hospital room's eight beds were occupied, and four of the patients had visitors. Dick Hurley was the only one who was alone.

He lay in a bed near the window, staring out at Music

Hall across Plum Street. His pale skin and white hair blended in with the color scheme of the room. The walls, the chairs, even the iron rails of the bed were all painted white; I knew it was to make the place look sanitary, but it also gave the room a funereal air. The white-linen sheet that covered Hurley from foot to chin looked like a burial shroud.

"Mr. Hurley?"

I said his name once more before I caught his attention. It took another moment until he recognized me. His dark eyes, which had been so bright and lively when I'd seen him before, now appeared dull and sluggish. "Michael, isn't it?" he said in a hoarse whisper.

"Mickey. Mickey Rawlings. We met at the Sinton Hotel."

"Of course. At the dinner. How are you?"

"I'm fine. I came to see how *you're* doing."

"Improving, the doctors say." He waved a shaky hand at a chair next to his bed. "Sit. Stay a while." As I sat down, he asked, "How was the game today?"

"Good. Beat the Cubs 5–1." I'd come to Old City Hospital directly from the ballpark.

"Who pitched?"

"Alexander for Chicago, Rube Marquard for us." I couldn't help but add, "And I tripled in two runs." It was immodest, but a triple off Grover Cleveland Alexander was something to brag about.

"Good for you!" Hurley sounded delighted.

Several more visitors came into the room to see one of the other patients. Hurley looked over at them, and a touch of sadness came into his eyes. Turning his gaze back to me, he said, "Except for the police and a couple of reporters, you're the first visitor I've had."

"Mr. Tinsley hasn't come by?"

"No. But he's doing plenty for me—the doctors tell me he's going to pick up my medical bills." He tucked the top of the sheet under his whiskered chin. "I was getting pretty lonely here, though. You don't know how alone you are until you're in a hospital, just about on your deathbed, and there's no kin or friends standing by you." He adjusted the sheet again. "But listen to me feeling sorry for myself. You're here now, and I do appreciate that." A coughing fit racked his body.

I felt a little guilty that I wasn't really here on a social call. "How are you coming along?" I asked.

"Considering I had a bullet in my lung, not bad. Chest hurts, and breathing's a bit of a chore, but I'm doing better every day. Docs are still worried about pneumonia, so I might be here a few more days."

I leaned forward and asked, "Do you have any idea why that lady shot you?"

"No." He attempted a wan smile. "And where I come from, a 'lady' doesn't shoot people."

"Did you know her?"

"Never saw her before in my life."

"She just walked up to you and fired? Didn't say anything?"

Hurley hesitated, then shook his head.

I glanced around the room; no one was paying attention to us. "Do you think she tried to kill you because she had a grudge against the real Dick Hurley?"

His body twitched. "The real—?"

I nodded.

"You know? How?"

"From when we talked at the dinner. Some of the things you said weren't quite right. I don't suppose Lloyd Tinsley questioned you too closely when you showed up and told him you were Hurley."

"No . . . He didn't take much convincing. But what would he have asked? It's not like I was pretending to be Harry Wright."

True, he'd only claimed to have been a utility player. Who would question such a modest claim as that? "Why'd you do it?"

"I got the idea two years ago, when I read about how nice Cal McVey and George Wright were treated when they came to Cincinnati for the World Series. The newspaper stories said that the other Red Stockings were all dead, except maybe for Hurley, and nobody knew what happened to him." He coughed again. "Then a few weeks ago, when I heard about the museum that was going to honor the team, I thought why not. I knew the real Hurley, so I figured I could answer questions about him—"

"You knew him from the Washington Olympics?"

He nodded. "I *was* a ballplayer—I'm not faking that. I was backup pitcher to Asa Brainard. Never got in a game, though. Club folded nine games into the season. Never got the chance . . ." His eyes locked on mine. "I'd have give anything to play just one game—hell, to throw one pitch for a major-league team. Spent a lot of years tramping around the country with semipro clubs, but never got another shot at the top." He nestled deeper in his pillow.

There were many times when I complained about not getting enough playing time. This man's words reminded me that I was lucky to be a big-league ballplayer at all. "What's your real name?" I asked.

"Cogan. John Cogan. And you won't find it in any record book."

"Nice to meet you, John. And as far as I'm concerned, you can still go by 'Dick Hurley'—I won't be telling anyone otherwise."

His mustache slowly pulled up in a relieved smile. "Thank you, son."

I then turned back to the shooting. "Was there anything more to what happened in the hotel?"

"There was, yes. But it didn't make sense to me. Before she pulled the trigger, that woman said 'This is for Sarah.' "

Jeez. The Sarah from the note? "Did you tell the police?"

Cogan looked ashamed. "No. I would have had to admit I didn't know who Sarah was. Thought the cops might figure out I was a . . . fraud."

"Anything else you can tell me about it?"

He shook his head no, then turned to stare out the window.

I stood up, planning to leave, then I caught sight of the other patients with family and friends around to cheer them. "Warm in here," I said. "Mind if I take off my jacket?"

Cogan, appearing a bit surprised, said, "Not at all."

I draped the coat over the back of the chair, then sat back down and asked, "What were some of those semipro teams you played with?"

He told me stories about his playing days for more than an hour until the nurse came and announced that visiting hours were over.

OOO

Margie had prepared another local delicacy for supper, one that I like better than burgoo because it had no vegetables at all in it. The sausage and oatmeal pancakes, called "goetta," were a fried, mushy mixture that reminded me of Philadelphia scrapple.

She and Karl already had the table laid when I got home, so we immediately sat down to eat. As we dug into the goetta, we gave our reports on the day's progress.

I went first, recounting my meeting with John "Dick Hurley" Cogan and getting in mention of my two-run triple off Grover Alexander.

Karl followed. His report was brief: Rufus Yates had paid off his fine on June 30, in cash. There was no record of where he'd got the money.

"Well, I had lunch with Katie Perriman," Margie said. "Nice woman, I thought. So nice, I hated to bring up the question of whether she'd had an affair with Curt Stram. But I did, and I got some answers. I mentioned to her that you and Stram were now roommates, so she assumed he already gave you an earful and I think that helped open her up— she seemed almost eager to talk, to counter whatever he might have told you."

"He *suggested* a lot," I said. "He didn't say much directly."

Margie smiled. "She did. They did have a brief affair— but not a *romance*. It was so brief, it lasted less than an hour, Katie said."

"What happened?"

"In February, there was a party at the Emery Hotel. Some of the Reds players who live in the area—including Stram who'd just signed with the team—were there, and so were the Perrimans. Ollie Perriman spent the entire time with the ballplayers, ignoring Katie. She was already upset with her husband for spending so much time and attention on his collection, and she felt he was embarrassing her in public at the party. So . . . she got a bit drunk and she made one of those monumental errors of judgment that can haunt you for a long time. She and Stram went off to a room together . . ."

"And that's it?" I asked.

"Isn't that enough?"

"What about the big favor Stram said he did for her?"

"From what I gather, Mr. Stram thinks awfully highly of himself: the 'favor' was that he had sex with her."

Landfors coughed on a mouthful of food. Even among radicals, "sex" wasn't a word you often heard from a woman's mouth.

"But it sounded like something went wrong," I said. "That she was mad at him about something."

"She is. He continued to contact her, and he didn't take it well when she made it clear that their tryst at the Emery was a one-time mistake. Katie didn't like the way he kept pressuring her to get together again, but I think there was something more that made her mad, too. She didn't say what it was, though."

"Well, what do you think?" I asked her. "Could she and Stram have killed Ollie Perriman?"

"Katie is devastated by her husband's death. And she's feeling terribly guilty about what she did with Curt Stram." She shook her head. "I don't think Katie Perriman had anything to do with it."

"What about Stram?"

Margie shrugged as if to say, "Who knows?"

Chapter Twenty-Six

Baseball got top billing over opera in the Wednesday morning *Enquirer*. The death of tenor Enrico Caruso had made the front page, but the newspaper's main headline read:

White Sox Players Go Free;
Cheers Greet Jury Verdict

Late last night on its first ballot, the jury had returned a verdict of "not guilty." According to the paper, five hundred spectators had packed the courtroom awaiting the decision; when it was announced, they erupted in a "joyful din," crying "Hooray for the clean sox!" and tossing hats and confetti into the air. Among those cheering the loudest were the bailiffs, who'd been given the go-ahead by Judge Hugo Friend to join the celebration. And the judge himself congratulated the defendants and told the jury that he agreed with their verdict. The acquitted players rushed to the jury box, thanking their "liberators" and shaking their hands; the jurors in turn hoisted Shoeless Joe Jackson and Lefty Williams on their shoulders.

The other judge with an interest in the case, baseball commissioner Kenesaw Mountain Landis, "could not be reached to give his views on the acquittal." Nor could American League President Ban Johnson or White Sox owner Charles Comiskey.

I read every word of the coverage, even studying the definitions of "statutory conspiracy" and "common-law conspiracy," and I wasn't sure how I felt about the result. But I certainly didn't feel like cheering.

When I started to go through one of the stories again, I noticed next to it a brief update about Charlotte Ashby. While the investigation into the "Hurley" shooting continued, she was being transferred from Central Station in the basement of City Hall to the more secure environs of the Cincinnati Work House.

O O O

A small marker near the main gate noted the date that the Cincinnati Work House first opened. And I noted the coincidence: it was in 1869, the same year that the Red Stockings made baseball history and a girl name Sarah was allegedly murdered. The mammoth stone prison, in Camp Washington not far from Nathaniel Bonner's Queen City Lumber Company, looked far older than a mere half century. It had the appearance of a relic from the Spanish Inquisition, a medieval castle that had gone to seed.

At the entrance, I told a potbellied jailer that I'd come to see Mrs. Charlotte Ashby. He let me in and led me to a small office.

"You can talk to the prisoner for fifteen minutes," he droned, "in the presence of a guard. There's no touching allowed, and you can't give her anything or accept anything." He opened a book like a hotel register. "I need to see some identification."

I took a folded paper from my jacket pocket and handed it to him. At the top of the document, in Gothic lettering, was *Honorable Discharge from the Army of the United States*. A small, black-and-white photograph glued to the paper showed me from the waist up, wearing a greatcoat. He looked at the photo, then up at me. "You look different out of uniform."

"Yeah, a lot of people tell me that."

But there was enough of a resemblance to satisfy him. He returned my discharge paper and filled out a line in the register, recording the date, time, my name, and the name of the prisoner I was visiting. Then he turned the book around and handed me a pen. "Sign here, Michael Rawlings."

"It's Mickey," I said quietly. The U. S. Army didn't get my name quite right on any of my paperwork. Uncle Sam didn't seem to like the idea of a soldier named "Mickey."

I was next searched for contraband and led by another turnkey through a dank stone corridor. The antiquated jail had the look and feel of a place where people were still put on the rack, and I found myself half-expecting to hear the screams of tortured prisoners.

We arrived at a room like a small dining hall. There were a dozen benches and tables bolted to the floor. A solitary guard, with a shotgun cradled in the crook of his arm, sat atop a stool at the far end. Although there were only two other people in the room, a middle-aged male prisoner and a man who appeared to be his lawyer, the guard looked like he was expecting a full-scale riot—he also looked eager and willing to use his weapon to quell any such trouble.

My escort pointed me to a table in the middle of the room, and said, "Wait there." I sat, uneasy under the gaze of the armed guard, waiting for Charlotte Ashby.

The jailer soon returned with a slim, handsome woman of proud bearing and advanced years. Her silver hair was neatly combed but fell long and limp about her head; she probably wasn't permitted hairpins. She wore a plain, shapeless gray dress, and her shoes, without laces, clomped loosely on the floor. The closest thing to jewelry were the shackles on her hands. I removed my hat and stood when she came into the room. The jailer led her to the other side of the table from me, warned against any physical contact, then left us under the watch of the guard.

Charlotte Ashby spoke first. "I am only here because it allows me to leave my cell for a little while. I don't know who you are, I don't care, and I have nothing to say to you." There was no offense in her tone, just a simple statement of fact.

"My name's Mickey Rawlings, ma'am. I'm not a reporter, and I'm not with the police. I'm a baseball player—with the Reds."

Her shrug indicated that she still didn't care.

"The reason I came to see you," I persevered, "is because I'd like to ask you about Sarah."

We stared at each other for more than a minute. She cracked first. "What about her?"

"I understand she was murdered. On July 2, 1869."

Mrs. Ashby struggled to keep her composure, but failed. Her body trembled, her eyes became watery, and she began breathing in ragged gasps. "Do you know that for a fact?"

"Not for certain, no. But I came across some information that that's what happened." When she calmed down a bit, I asked, "What do *you* know about Sarah?"

In a faint voice, Mrs. Ashby answered, "I know she disappeared that night. And I suspected the worst."

"You and her were friends?"

"Yes, almost like sisters. Sarah—Sarah Mary Devlin—was fifteen at the time, and I was a year younger. We grew up together—"

"In Corryville?" The more Charlotte Ashby thought I already knew, the more she might be willing to tell me.

She nodded.

"What was her relationship with Dick Hurley?" I asked. "When you shot him, you said you were doing it for Sarah."

The old woman began folding and unfolding her thin hands, then rested them flat on the table one on top of the other. "Like a lot of girls, Sarah and I got caught up in the craze for the Red Stockings that summer. Even wore red stockings ourselves. Some of the older girls went further in showing how much they liked the players, but with Sarah and me it was innocent. She was a good girl, Sarah was." Mrs. Ashby took a handkerchief from her dress pocket and wiped away a tear. "The day the Red Stockings came back from their trip East, the whole city went on holiday to celebrate. Sarah and I followed the parade, we saw the game, and later that night we went to the Gibson House where there was a banquet for the club. Couldn't get in ourselves—tickets were five dollars apiece—but we stayed outside with a small crowd of fans. It was fun just being near the team. Well, like I said, I was a year younger, and as the night grew late I started worrying that I was going to catch it from my parents for being out. Sarah kept telling me a little longer, a little longer—she wanted to see the players come out again. All she wanted was one more look at them. But come midnight, I went home by myself. She stayed.

"Next morning, Sarah was banging on my bedroom window. I let her in my room, and she told me she met one of the players—"

"Hurley?"

"Sarah wouldn't say. What she did say was that she and the player were going to meet again that night—just the two of them."

"July 2."

She bit her lip and nodded. "I tried to talk her out of it. I was always the less daring, I suppose, but actually meeting a ballplayer, alone, it just wasn't to be considered."

"But she went."

"Sarah was *so* excited. There was no changing her mind."

"And she wouldn't give his name?"

"No, and I pressed her for it. All she'd say about him was that he might not be the best player on the team, but he was sure one of the handsomest. Anyway, I talked to her again that night before she went to meet him. She was dressed up in her finest frock and wearing red stockings of course. I tried again to talk her out of going, but she thought it was going to be a wonderful adventure." Her voice faltered. "I never saw her again."

"I've looked in the newspapers from back then," I said. "There wasn't anything in them about her being missing."

"Her family wouldn't report it. They thought she'd run off with a boy, and they were too ashamed to have that printed in the newspapers. I told them about the ballplayer, but they thought I was telling a tall tale. I kept trying to tell people—the police, the newspapers—but they wouldn't believe me either. That's why I won't talk to the police now; they had their chance."

"You thought the player was Dick Hurley because he left the team at the same time?"

"No," she answered. "He was only the substitute—I didn't think of him at all. What I did was try to narrow down the possibilities by figuring out which players it *couldn't* have been. Sarah said he wasn't one of their best, so I eliminated George Wright and Asa Brainard and a couple of the others. She said he was handsome, so Fred Waterman and Charlie Sweasy were out—I knew the type she liked. It wasn't until sometime later that I saw a picture of all *ten* players. And there was Dick Hurley, with his dark wavy hair and mustache, handsome as all get-out. That's when I realized why she hadn't given me his name: because he wasn't one of the first nine. She wanted it to seem like she got a bigger prize than the substitute."

The guard barked, "Two minutes!"

Mrs. Ashby continued, "The years went by, and I never heard anything more about Hurley. But I never forgot Sarah. I knew she was either dead, or he'd done things to her that made her ashamed to come home. Then last month I read about him coming back to Cincinnati for this museum. And I knew what I had to do."

"You decided to shoot him."

"Nobody else did anything for Sarah, so it was up to me. I didn't mind going to jail for it. I've outlived two husbands, lost one son to the Spanish and another to the Germans. There's nobody who'll miss me, and I don't believe being in prison can be any worse than living alone in a house where you've once had a family." She pulled herself straighter. "I only wish I'd killed him."

"Mrs. Ashby," I said, "that wasn't Dick Hurley you shot. Just an old man trying to get a little attention for himself by pretending to be one of the famous Red Stockings." I didn't like breaking my word to Cogan, but I didn't want her taking another shot at him if she ever got the chance again.

The jailer came by and started to lead Charlotte Ashby out of the room. She turned back to call, "What was the information you found about Sarah?"

She was pulled away before I could answer. I thought maybe I should come back to tell her about the note. Maybe she'd want to know where her friend was buried.

Chapter Twenty-Seven

○○○

Judge Kenesaw Mountain Landis was no longer without comment on the outcome of the Black Sox trial. His statement appeared in the next morning's paper:

> "*Regardless of the verdict of juries, no player that throws a ball game, no player that entertains proposals or promises to throw a game, no player that sits in a conference with a bunch of crooked players and gamblers where the ways and means of throwing games are discussed, and does not tell his club about it, will ever play professional baseball.*"

I thought the phrase "regardless of the verdict of juries" was an odd one for a judge to use, but it fit Landis's autocratic reputation. As baseball commissioner, he wasn't bound by the legal system, and could make any ruling he wanted to in the interests of the game. And, the more I thought about the case, the more I agreed with Landis—to a point.

The crux of the matter for baseball was whether the White Sox players had attempted to lose the World Series. But since there was no *law* against throwing a sporting event, they couldn't be prosecuted on that charge. In Judge Friend's instruction to the jury, he told them that the state had to prove the players had intended "to defraud the public and others and not merely to throw ball games." As one of the newspaper editorials noted, that was like saying they had to decide whether an accused killer had intended to murder his victim or merely cut his head off.

So maybe baseball did have to operate under a different standard, and Landis's decision to override the conclusion of the jurors was proper. The leaders of the game, both major league and minor, sure seemed to think so. The papers carried statements from the presidents of the Pacific Coast League and the American Association hailing Landis's decision and vowing that the acquitted players would be barred from their leagues as well.

What troubled me, however, was that Landis had simply declared all eight players guilty, even though there was overwhelming evidence that some were innocent. Judge Friend had stated that he would not have allowed a guilty verdict against Buck Weaver or Happy Felsh because the cases against them were so weak. Weaver had been approached about throwing a game, refused, and played to the best of his ability. But he was being blacklisted for "guilty knowledge." And the jury never even had to decide on utility player Fred McMullin; the case against him had been so lacking that the prosecution dropped it. Yet he was also barred.

Judge Landis was going to sweep the game clean, but I worried that he was using a broom too broad. And that I might be swept out, too.

My worries deepened when Detective Forsch phoned and told me Rufus Yates had been found shot to death.

O O O

This time I was tempted to accept the cigarette Forsch offered me. I waved it off, though, and he lit one up for himself. He then told the two uniformed officers who'd escorted me into the interview room that they could wait outside.

"So where were you last night?" the detective began.

"Home."

"All night?"

"Yes."

"Anyone with you?"

"Yes. Margie Turner. She's my, uh ..." Jeez, I wished they'd invent a word for it. "... we live together. And Karl Landfors, he's a friend visiting us."

"Both of them might lie for you. Any other witnesses who can swear you were home?"

"Yes. I always invite one complete stranger to spend the night in case I should ever need a witness like that."

Forsch blew out a stream of smoke. "Don't be a wise-ass, Rawlings. I'm not looking to screw you. As far as I'm concerned this is a formality. But we're gonna run through some questions."

"All right. Sorry." I did feel on safe ground. Not only could I prove where I'd been last night, I didn't expect Forsch would be under much pressure to solve the murder. The death of a hood like Yates surely couldn't be considered a great loss to the community.

"It's curious," the detective went on. "First you were asking about him, then you had a run-in with him where he wanted to kill you ... And now *he's* dead."

"Asking questions doesn't mean I killed him."

"There's more. Your address was found in his room."

"It was?"

"Written on the back of a betting slip."

Back to the gambling. Was this going to get to Landis? "I don't understand. Why would—" Maybe Yates *was* planning to come see me and do what Knucksie had refused to do.

Forsch pulled a piece of yellow paper from his pocket. "You have any explanation for this?"

I looked at it. The slip recorded a two-dollar wager on a horse named Celtic Treasure. Written in a childish scrawl above the betting particulars was my address. Then I noticed the date of the bet: July 1. "This is the day after Yates got out of jail," I said. "And it's two days before my house got broke into. He's the one that did it."

Forsch shook his head. "He still had a couple weeks to go on his sentence."

"He paid the fine and got out early. I checked." It was my turn to ask a question. "You *sure* he was in jail when Oliver Perriman got killed?"

"Yes, that I do know. He'd been in there a week before, and he was still there the day after."

I was trying to make sense of this, but was getting nowhere. I wanted to go home. "Anything else?" I asked.

Forsch toyed with the cigarette pack. "One thing more. It's not a matter for this department, but you might be interested . . ."

"Yes?"

"Couple of private investigators came by about a week ago. They were looking for information on Rufus Yates. Of course, we don't share our files with just anybody, so I wanted to know who they were working for." He pulled another Murad from the pack, letting me stew in suspense. "They were sent here by the baseball commissioner. Seems they were checking if some ballplayer was in cahoots with Yates. Wouldn't give the name of the player." He lit up. "But it occurs to me that if Landis thinks a ballplayer is hooked up with a gambler, and when he starts an investigation the gambler ends up dead ... well, that might seem awfully convenient for the player, wouldn't it?"

"Yeah, it might at that," I said.

The interview over, I left City Hall, but didn't go home. I stopped at a Central Avenue lunch counter for coffee and time to think. I wanted to go over everything Forsch had said about Yates while it was still fresh in my mind.

I had no worry about the police seriously thinking I'd killed him. And although I briefly considered that Yates's pal Knucksie might come after me to avenge his death, I quickly dismissed that too; from what I'd seen, it was clear that the two of them didn't exactly have a close friendship. What did worry me was what Judge Landis might imagine. But I didn't know what I could do about that.

Then I tried to think how I could make use of the new information. It seemed obvious that somebody had paid off Yates's fine and hired him to break into my place.

Rufus Yates goes to jail on June 20 to serve thirty days; he's still there on June 28 when Ollie Perriman is found dead, gets released on June 30, has my address on a betting slip dated July 1, and breaks into my home on the night of July 2. And what's he looking for? That old baseball. Not the ball, but the message inside. A note about a murder in 1869, inside a baseball that Ambrose Whitaker bought in 1872, but wasn't—

Damn, you're an idiot, Mickey.

O O O

Under the nervous gaze of Mr. Driscoll, the librarian at the men's circulation desk, I searched through old copies of the *Cincinnati Enquirer* for any item related to the auction. According to Ambrose Whitaker, it was held in April of 1872. I hoped his memory was right—if it was a different month or a different year, I could be here a long time.

His memory was accurate. The Sunday morning paper for April 14, 1872, carried the sad news:

> *DEPARTED GLORY*
> *Sale of the Red Stocking Traps and Trophies*
> *In the glorious April sunlight of yesterday afternoon a little knot of men gathered at the old Union Grounds to witness the disposal at auction of the "traps and trophies" of the Cincinnati Base Ball Club, whose sobriquet "Red Stocking"—the synonym of victory—was once on every tongue. A red flag fluttered drearily from "The Grand Duchess," where the never-lowered streamer "Cincinnati" was wont to proudly flaunt the breeze . . .*

The article went on to report that the lumber of the half-dismantled ballpark had already been sold. It also listed the items that were auctioned: trophy balls, medals, streamers, and a set of goblets. The baseballs went for bids of one to ten dollars, most selling for three.

I stared at the ancient paper, and I reread the article several times, a number of thoughts running through my head. Part of what I felt was a sense of loss that much of the charm of that era was gone—from the polite rituals that surrounded the matches, to a grandstand called "The Grand Duchess," to the flowery style of writing. And it was sad that only two years after the Red Stockings had been the peerless club in the baseball world, their fortunes had plummeted to such depths. It also occurred to me that in the same month the auction was being held, the real Dick Hurley was playing for the Washington Olympics, and a young John Cogan was on the bench hoping for a chance to take the mound.

Mostly what I thought about, though, was that there was no way Ambrose Whitaker could have bought a baseball at an auction held in 1872 when Spalding didn't manufacture the ball until 1876.

I played all nine innings Thursday afternoon and didn't remember one of them. The fact that I was allowed on the field at all was the only positive aspect to the entire day; it meant that I wasn't on Judge Landis's blacklist—yet.

My thoughts were occupied by the death of Rufus Yates and on what could follow from that development. I tried to convince myself that his murder might have nothing to do with me—he was, after all, in a line of work with a high mortality rate and might have simply been killed in a dispute with another hood. But I had the sense that his death was more likely related to the scheme to set me up. Yates was supposed to convince me to stop poking around, and I'd left evidence on his face that he'd failed. Maybe his partner in the scheme wasn't confident that Yates could keep me from digging further and decided to kill him to keep his own identity a secret. Whatever the reason Rufus Yates had been killed, Detective Forsch was right: from Judge Landis's perspective it might look awfully convenient for me that he died before investigators could question him.

When I got home after the game, Margie and Karl were

both out. I put in a call to Forsch to see if there was any progress on the Yates shooting. He told me there were no suspects, but the assumption was that the gambler knew his killer and had let him in his apartment. Yates had been shot twice in the chest while sitting in an easy chair. There was no sign of a forced entry, and enough cash was in the room to eliminate theft as a motive.

After getting off the phone with the detective, I thought some more. Lately, much of Yates's activity had been related to me: the break-in at my house, arranging the photograph outside Redland Field, the encounter in the alley. According to both Forsch and the colored bookie Spider Jenkins, Yates was never more than a hired hand. He must have had his fine paid by somebody who wanted him out of jail to do a job. Since his first task after getting out of jail was breaking into my home, I figured that stealing the note about Sarah was what he'd been hired to do.

I went over to the bookcase, pulled out *Life on the Mississippi*, and removed the piece of onionskin I'd tucked between its pages. I reread the words:

On July 2, 1869, a girl named Sarah was murdered.
She was from Corryville and about sixteen years of age.
She is buried in Eden Park.

I began to wonder if perhaps I'd been looking at the message the wrong way.

Karl Landfors came in, lugging a bundle of groceries. I helped carry them into the kitchen, and noticed with dismay that they consisted mostly of Moxie. Karl was the only person I knew who liked the soft drink. He brought a bottle of it into the parlor and I grabbed a ginger ale.

"Take a look at this," I said, handing him the note.

Karl gave it a quick glance. "You've shown it to me before."

"Read it again. There's no mention of *who* killed Sarah."

He pushed up his glasses and reread the message. "So?"

"Maybe it's not an accusation. Maybe it's a confession."

"By whom?"

"Ambrose Whitaker. He lied about where and when he got the ball, so he is covering something up. And let's go back to 1869: he'd been at the Red Stockings' homecoming banquet, and he was about the age of a player. Maybe he decided to impress a girl by claiming to be on the team."

"If he was going to impersonate someone, why not one of the stars?"

"Too likely to be recognized. A substitute wouldn't be." As John Cogan had said about his recent impersonation of Dick Hurley: *It's not like I was pretending to be Harry Wright.*

"But if Whitaker wrote the note, why steal it back? Even if he changed his mind about having written it, he'd know that his name isn't mentioned—there's nothing to implicate him."

"Maybe he thought it could be traced back to him because he was the one who donated the ball."

"I don't know," Karl said. "Pretty halfhearted confession, if you ask me." He frowned. "And why put it in a baseball? Good chance nobody would ever find it."

"Maybe in his mind it didn't ever have to be found. It could have just been something he had to say."

"What do you mean?"

I hesitated. I'd known Karl for years, but never found it easy to speak with him about personal matters. "I've told you about my aunt and uncle that I grew up with." He nodded. "Well, my uncle didn't talk a whole lot except with customers at his general store, and only if the conversation was about baseball or politics. Never said much around the house. So after my aunt died, I was real surprised to find him writing a letter to her. I asked him about it, and he said he was telling her things he wished he'd said to her while she was alive. And it wasn't the first one he wrote. He'd been writing a letter a week, and even put them in the mail, with just her first name on the envelope. He must have known they'd all end up in the dead letter bag at the post office, but he got out something he felt he had to say."

"Like putting a note in a bottle," said Karl.

"Right. Maybe Ambrose Whitaker did something similar, except he changed his mind and—" Another idea struck me that made more sense. "Or maybe he wasn't the one who wanted it back. What if it was somebody who didn't know there was nothing incriminating in the message?"

"Such as?"

"One of his kids, Aaron or Adela." Maybe one of them wanted it back either to protect their father or to protect the family's name—and business.

Adela had seemed a sharp businesswoman, the type who'd want to protect her interests. Aaron I knew almost nothing about, except that he apparently had no involvement with the family business. What *was* he involved with? And was it something that might bring him into contact with someone like Rufus Yates?

I told Karl what I knew about the Whitaker family and asked him to check into them further.

He looked like a hound dog about to hit the trail. Nothing a muckraking Socialist likes better than the prospect of digging up dirt on a "robber baron."

○ ○ ○

Friday night, well after dinner time, Karl Landfors came home with his tail between his legs.

"No luck?" I asked.

"I spent all day looking into the Whitaker family, and *nothing.*" He tossed his derby on one end of the sofa and plopped down on the other.

"What do you mean 'nothing'—there's got to be some information on them."

He looked around. "Where's Margie?"

"Called a little while ago. She's staying late at the zoo." I moved to get up from my chair. "Got sandwiches if you're hungry."

Karl waved me back down. "The Whitakers are the kind of business people who give capitalism a good name," he said with disgust. "Kills my appetite."

"I'm sorry," I said in mock sympathy.

"They pay decent wages," Karl went on, "their facilities have the most modern safety features, they don't employ children . . . I just can't find anything on them."

"That's now," I said. "What about in the past? Nothing shady?"

"Nothing!" Karl spat the word. "Ambrose Whitaker worked hard as a young man, built the streetcar company that made him wealthy, and kept working hard to make it grow. Nothing illegal—well, maybe a little. To do anything in this town you had to grease the Boss Cox political machine, but he only made the minimum payoffs necessary to get things done. Never established real political ties. He had a good reputation—treated his workers fair, and supported several charities. A couple of years ago, he turned the business over to his daughter Adela and son Aaron. His health was deteriorating, and he wanted to pass it on."

"What was wrong with him?"

Karl shook his head. "Don't know. 'Poor health' is all that I've read about it; never saw any mention of a specific ailment. Anyway, brother and sister were supposed to share the business, but Adela is the one in control. She's modernizing and branching out into new areas. She recently made a substantial investment in a company called Formica out near Chester Park."

"And her brother?"

"Let's just say that for the family to remain prosperous, it's probably best that he leave his sister to run things."

I thought for a few moments. "What about their personal lives?"

"Mrs. Whitaker—Ambrose's wife—died about fifteen years ago. Adela has never married, although she's had the same suitor for the past five years; I think she prefers to be independent. Same as her father had, she has a reputation for honesty and fairness. She even pays their female workers the same as the men. Stubborn, though, from what I hear, and a hard negotiator."

"And Aaron?"

"Well, because he stays out of the business, I couldn't find out as much about him. He's married, two children. No mistresses that I heard of. He likes to spend time with other men. Hunting, fishing ... he has a horse ranch outside Covington. I think he fancies himself a country gentleman." He spread his hands. "That's all I have."

"All right. Thanks, Karl."

"If only there was *something* scandalous in their past," he said wistfully.

I tried to console him that we might find something yet.

○ ○ ○

Aaron Whitaker wasn't what I'd expected. I thought he'd be rich, spoiled, and perhaps a bit dandified. That's not what I found when I ventured across the river into Kentucky to visit him at his horse farm Saturday morning.

He was outside the stable, working on the cinch of a finely crafted saddle that was resting on a fence rail. I hadn't pictured him as the sort of man who worked with his hands, but his fingers were callused and his skin rough. Whitaker's dungarees and red-and-black flannel shirt were well-worn. In both dress and build, he could have passed for a lumberjack. He was tall, muscular, with a weathered face and full orange beard.

The farm, south of Covington and bordering the Licking River, wasn't a showplace, either. It was of modest size, with a small ranch house, a decrepit red barn, and a stable that was in better repair than the other two structures. Across the dirt driveway from the stable was a pasture where several magnificent horses grazed on the high grass.

"Are those racehorses?" I asked.

"My horses are for riding, not racing," Aaron answered. "Give me the awl, would you?"

I handed him the tool. His answer was a disappointment. I'd wondered how any of the Whitakers would have contact with someone like Rufus Yates. Aaron seemed the best bet; if he bred racehorses, he might have known Yates from the tracks—and hired him to steal back his father's confession. "I hear there's a big demand for them," I said. The racetracks had been shut down during the war so the animals could be used by the army for hauling supply wagons. Now the racing business was booming again.

"I get offers," he said. "But there's not enough money in the world to get me to sell my horses to the tracks. I'm not in the breeding business."

"How much are you involved in the family business?"

"I'm not." He looked up at me. "You said you met my father and sister. Didn't they tell you I stay out of it?"

I admitted they had.

He jabbed the point of the awl into the leather. "I'm forty-four years old. I've never had a head for business, and I don't suppose I'll ever develop one. My sister does, and I'm grateful to her for it. She runs the company, I stay out of her way, and she keeps me on a salary that's far more than I deserve." He chuckled. "Hell, maybe I *am* worth it—if I got involved in the business, I'd be sure to lose more money than what she's paying me."

Aaron Whitaker sounded comfortable with the arrangement.

"Now," he said. "You told me our family might be in some trouble. What is it?"

"I'm not sure exactly. But I've been hearing that there was a scandal some time ago that might come out."

"*Scandal?* About what?"

I'd been hoping he could tell me. "It involves your father."

He paused from his work and wiped his forehead with a bandanna. "I don't believe that's possible. My father and I have had our differences over the years, but I've never heard anyone question his integrity. I can't imagine he ever did anything wrong."

"If he did," I said, "and if it becomes public, that would probably hurt the family business, wouldn't it?" And if that happened, Aaron could lose his income.

He answered calmly, "I don't see how. Even if there was some kind of scandal in the past, that's not going to stop people from riding the trolleys."

"You're not worried about it?"

"So far, it doesn't sound to me like there's anything *to* worry about. Don't get me wrong—just because I'm not active in the company doesn't mean I don't care about it. Or about my father and sister. If you get any *specific* information that something might be wrong, let me know." He gave me a hard look. "Because if there is real trouble facing our family, I'll do whatever it takes to protect them."

○ ○ ○

By Sunday, there were signs in the newspapers that life was starting to return to normal. Reports on the aftermath of the Black Sox trial were dwindling; the major baseball stories were the home run hitting of Babe Ruth, who was on a pace to eclipse the record of fifty-four he had set last year, and the retirement of Cubs manager Johnny Evers. There was nothing in the papers about the Hurley shooting or the death of Rufus Yates; the crime news of note were the massacre of a family in Kentucky by a deranged blacksmith, the capture at the Sinton Hotel of New York bootleggers who were recorded on a Dictaphone trying to bribe Prohibition agents, and a melee that followed another cross burning by the Ku Klux Klan in Dayton. Political news was also routine; on the national level, there were arguments to make beer legal again in order to collect taxes on it, and in local affairs the city council was leaning toward building a canal parkway instead of a subway.

On the diamond of Redland Field, there was a return to normal as well. Heinie Groh was healthy enough to play third base again, so I was back on the bench as the Reds continued the drive for sixth place.

After the game, I decided to see Charlotte Ashby again. At least I could answer her question about how I knew about Sarah and tell her that her childhood friend was buried in Eden Park.

There was only half an hour left for visiting when I arrived at the Cincinnati Work House. When I went in, I already had my discharge paper in hand to show the jailer. He made the entries in his register and turned the book for me to sign.

After scrawling my name and sliding it back to him, it occurred to me: maybe Rufus Yates had a visitor when he was here. How else would he have gotten money to pay the fine while he was confined to jail?

"Can I take a look through that book?" I asked.

The jailer shook his head. "You ain't authorized."

"How can I get permission to see it?"

"From somebody who *is* authorized."

I considered for a moment. "Would the president be authorized?"

"Of the *United States?*" He appeared to be seriously wondering if there was a chance that I knew the president. "Yeah, I guess he would."

I pulled a five dollar note from my wallet. "Hope that includes a dead president."

He glanced at the portrait of Benjamin Harrison. "Better

than most live ones." He pushed the register to me and tucked the money in his pocket.

It was June 30 that Yates had gotten out of jail, so I looked at the entries for that date. And there was the answer: Rufus Yates had been visited by Nathaniel Bonner of the Queen City Lumber Company.

Chapter Twenty-Nine

○○○

"**M**r. Rawlings?"

"Uh, yeah, this is me." My answer was tentative; the phone call had awoken me and I wasn't entirely sure who I was.

"This is Adela Whitaker. We met in my office about a month ago."

"Yes, of course. How are you?"

She skipped the social niceties. "You spoke with my brother on Saturday, told him there might be some scandal about to come out regarding our family."

"Yeah, I talked to him."

"I would appreciate it if you could stop by my office today to discuss the matter." The words were polite; the tone was steely.

"Sure." I was planning to speak with her again anyway. Doing so at her invitation might make her more willing to talk. Although probably not by much.

"You remember how to get here?"

"Yes."

"Very good. I'll see you at 9:45."

"Well, I—" Since she'd already hung up, I decided 9:45 would be fine.

OOO

Adela Whitaker greeted me with a firm handshake. "Thank you for coming, Mr. Rawlings."

"Glad to." I hoped an offer of coffee would follow, but it didn't come.

Having met her brother, it struck me what a contrast there was in their surroundings. Aaron was an outdoorsman who dabbled at horse ranching; she cloistered herself in a modern office that looked like it ran with the efficiency of a military organization.

"I won't take up any more of your time than necessary," she began. I took that to mean that she wanted me in and out of her office as quickly as possible. "Can you tell me the nature of the trouble you think my family might be facing?"

I could tell her something about it, but wasn't sure I wanted to. "It involves your father, Miss Whitaker."

She toyed with a fountain pen on her desk while keeping her stern gaze on me. "Details, Mr. Rawlings."

"It dates back to the 1869 Red Stockings," I said, "when your father was their bookkeeper. My understanding is that a serious crime was committed, and your father had something to do with it. It's been covered up all these years, but now a lot of material has been gathered on the old team, and whatever happened may become known to the public."

"You're holding back, Mr. Rawlings."

"Yes. Aren't you?"

A flicker of a smile tugged at the corners of her mouth. "Let's put our cards on the table."

"Okay." I leaned back and adopted an expectant expression.

"Very well," she said. "I'll go first." The rigid set to her jaw softened and a smile took over her face; she looked like a completely different woman. "Before I do, however, I would like to apologize. I have a tendency to treat everyone who comes in here as a business competitor, and I'm afraid I can be a bit brusque at times."

"In my line of work," I said, "people throw baseballs at my head and try to plant their spikes in my shins. And 'brusque' is the way they talk when they're being friendly. You've been acting just fine to me. No need to apologize."

"Well, thank you. I've occasionally been accused of playing 'hardball,' but I suppose that's a relative term." She smiled again. "So far, I've never tried to spike anyone." Then her tone became serious. "Back to the matter at hand: you are not the first person to tell me my father was involved in something criminal back in his younger days."

"Who else told you?"

While Miss Whitaker considered whether to reveal the name, she began doodling on the desk blotter, making geometric figures with hard strokes. "Nathaniel Bonner," she said. "He's president of Queen City Lumber Company."

"Yes, I know. I've met him."

The pen stopped moving. "You and he aren't . . ."

"No. I was helping Ollie Perriman with his exhibit. Nathaniel Bonner is donating some bats for the grand opening, and that's how I met him. I don't have any other connection to the man."

"I'm relieved to hear that," she said.

"Why?"

"The reason Mr. Bonner came here was to blackmail me.

He told me that long ago my father had engaged in criminal activities and that unless I paid him a substantial sum of money each month, he would expose my father in the press."

Blackmail. So that was Bonner's angle. "Did you go along?"

"I did *not!*" There was a ripping sound as the nib of the pen scratched deeply into the blotter. She laid the pen down. "For one thing, he refused to tell me the particulars of the crime—he merely claimed that it was terrible enough to ruin the family. For another, I do not believe that my father could have ever been involved in anything as awful as Mr. Bonner implied. I told him to bring me proof and then I'd reconsider. I also told him that if he didn't, I would file charges of attempted extortion against him."

"When was this?"

"In the spring. I never heard from him again, so I assumed there'd been nothing to it—simply a feeble attempt to extort money."

"Did you tell the police?"

"No. If it had gone any further, I would have."

"You wouldn't have paid?"

"No. Even if he had brought me proof, I wouldn't have paid blackmail. And it's not a matter of the money; it's a matter of principle. I'll pay generous wages for honest work, but I will not pay a penny to an extortionist."

"What if Bonner did go public with the information?"

"Then my father would face up to it. That's the way he is, and it's the way he raised Aaron and me. My father wouldn't *want* me to protect him by paying blackmail." She folded her hands together and eased back in her chair. "Now you tell me, Mr. Rawlings: *is* there something that Mr. Bonner might have on my father?"

"Yes." I couldn't bring myself to tell her about Sarah and the possibility that her father was a murderer, though. "But Nathaniel Bonner might have done at least as bad as what your father did. And if I can think of a way to do it, I'd like to nail him for it."

"I assure you, Mr. Rawlings," she said, "so would I." There was a sparkle in her eyes and a firm set to her jaw. Maybe she'd never actually spiked anyone, but something told me she had what it took to do it.

O O O

Good news greeted me when I entered the clubhouse at Redland Field. "Yer playin' second today," Pat Moran told me. "Stram's out sick for a while."

"Great!" My reaction was in response to getting in the game, not to the rookie's misfortune, but I realized it might not have sounded that way. So trying to sound concerned, I added, "What's wrong with him?"

"He got himself another groin injury," the manager answered with disgust.

"Oh."

"Starts takin' his shots tomorrow."

Oh! *That* kind of "groin injury." The phrase was often used to keep the public from finding out why a player was really out. The kind of groin injury Curt Stram was suffering from, the only kind that required shots, was syphilis. And the way Moran put it, this wasn't the first time Stram had come down with it.

By the time I took the field, I was enjoying the dual satisfaction of replacing my obnoxious roommate in the lineup and having finally found out what had gone wrong

with the "big favor" Stram had done for Katie Perriman—
he'd probably given her the disease.

After the game, while I was drying off from the shower,
the manager came up to me again. "Herrmann wants to see
you."

"Okay. Do you know—"

Moran averted his face and walked away. Whatever Garry
Herrmann wanted to tell me, it wasn't going to be something
I wanted to hear.

When I entered his office, and the Reds president didn't
offer me any beer or sausage, I knew it was going to be bad.
"This was your last game for a while, Mickey," Herrmann
said.

"Did Landis—?"

"He has not reached a final decision. But there has been
a new development. A man has come forward who says you
tried to hire him to murder Rufus Yates."

"*What?* Who?"

Herrmann glanced at a paper on the desk in front of him.
"Earl Uhlaender."

The name meant nothing to me. "Who the hell is he?"

"A hoodlum. Detective Forsch tells me he goes by the
name 'Knucksie.' He's made a statement to the police and
to Judge Landis's investigators. Says you and Yates had a
violent encounter last week. Swears you later offered him five
hundred dollars to kill Yates. Also swears he didn't accept."
Herrmann eyed me steadily; there was no sign of the Teutonic
good humor he was so famous for. "The suggestion has been
made that perhaps you found someone else to do it—in
order to keep Yates from talking about your relationship with
him."

"There wasn't any—" I realized it was pointless to go on. I'd told it all to Herrmann before. "What happens now?"

"Mr. Uhlaender has agreed to travel to Chicago. The commissioner would like to talk with him personally. Until then ..." He spread his hands. "You don't come to the ballpark."

I left his office angry. And one of the things I was angry about was that I'd actually been grateful to Knucksie for not killing me when Yates wanted him to. I wished I had told Forsch about him. It would do me no good to tell the detective now; he'd only think I was trying to get back at the thug for the charges he was making.

○ ○ ○

I wanted to rant and rave and cuss, but no one was at home to listen and commiserate. Margie had left me a note saying that she and Karl were at the zoo and didn't expect to be home until late. No further explanation.

So I heated up some of Margie's latest batch of burgoo and tried to make sense of things.

I couldn't understand why Earl "Knucksie" Uhlaender would claim that I'd wanted to hire him to kill Rufus Yates. One possibility was that he truly believed that I was behind Yates's death, and with no arrests in the case, decided to provide the police with fabricated testimony in order to get me. I didn't find loyalty to Yates a likely motive, though; the two of them hadn't seemed close pals by any means. There was something else odd about Knucksie coming forward. The crooks behind the fix of the 1919 World Series kept their mouths closed about what had gone on; none of them provided information to Judge Landis. So why would Knucksie? The only answer I could think of was that somebody was paying him to do so.

As for who that somebody might be, my gut feeling was that it was most likely the man who'd visited Yates in prison: Nathaniel Bonner. I started to put together a possible sequence of events.

In the spring, Bonner visits Adela Whitaker. He demands hush money or he'll reveal a crime from her father's past. Adela turns him down and says come back with proof. But he doesn't come back. So maybe the proof he thought he had was missing.

According to Katie Perriman, somebody who wanted to buy the collection had been calling Ollie in the months before he died. It could have been Bonner: his evidence of what happened in 1869 was missing, so he thought it might have gotten into the mass of materials Perriman had accumulated.

Perriman refused to sell the collection, so Bonner—or somebody in his employ—searches the office and kills Perriman in the process. Whatever he was looking for wasn't found. Two days later, Bonner visits Rufus Yates in prison and gives him money to pay off his fine. Then both men continue the search: Yates by breaking into my house, and Bonner by getting involved in the exhibit at Redland Field.

So far, it all seemed plausible. As for killing Yates, and setting me up for it, all I could think was that maybe Bonner felt I was getting too close. Since I'd talked with him at his lumberyard, he knew I had in interest in the events of 1869. And I was probably being watched—hell, Yates and Knucksie even knew which side of Dalton Avenue I habitually walked on, because they chose the right one to lay their ambush for me. So Bonner probably also knew I'd gone to the Cincinnati Work House and that I'd recently met with Adela and Aaron Whitaker.

I couldn't piece it all together, though. There were gaps and inconsistencies in the scenario that I couldn't yet resolve. The problem was I didn't think I had time to wait for more information—not with Knucksie on a train to Chicago to tell Judge Landis that I tried to have a man murdered.

So I thought of how I could fill in the pieces, and as the night drew on, I came up with a plan.

As I picked up the telephone, I thought it was probably a good thing that Margie and Karl were still out. They'd certainly have tried to talk me out of proceeding.

Then I went ahead and placed the first call. Let's see how far Adela Whitaker will go to do something about Nathaniel Bonner.

Chapter Thirty

OOO

I'd been asleep when Margie and Karl got home Monday night, and although she'd tried to explain what had happened at the zoo, I was too drowsy to comprehend. It wasn't until morning that I got the full story of their adventure.

Over a breakfast of coffee and chocolate cake, Margie said, "I never would have believed anyone could steal their food like that."

"From the animals?"

"Yes. And we caught them red-handed."

"What exactly happened?"

"Well, an anteater died yesterday, so I knew something would be going on last night. That's why Karl and I went— to stake out the place."

Margie seemed to enjoy using the phrase "stake out the place." I didn't get the connection. "The anteater died of starvation?" I asked.

"No, old age, the vet said." She backed up, and started again at an earlier point in the chronology, "You remember when I went to dig up the wildebeest?"

I said that I did. It was when I'd been in Boston—and I'd thought at the time that she was kidding.

"Its carcass wasn't there. In fact, I found there were hardly any animals buried in the plot where they were supposed to be."

"So where'd they go? Cremated?"

"Sausage."

"*What?*"

"The attendant who was supposed to bury the animals sold them for meat. They went into Maynard Kimber sausages."

Kimber, I recalled, was one of Garry Herrmann's guests at the memorial for Ollie Perriman. I wondered what Herrmann would think if he knew that his friend was putting anteater in his beloved wurst. "Yech," I said.

Karl spoke up, "Read *The Jungle* sometime if you'd like to know what other things end up in sausage casings."

Margie went on, "He had a nice business for himself. The zoo has almost two thousand animals in the collection. Every week, several of them die from age or disease. The attendant saved himself the work of digging graves and made extra income by selling the meat."

"But how does stealing food from the animals come into it?"

"The keeper of the Carnivora House found out what was going on and he wanted in on the deal. A big cat is fed about six pounds of fresh meat a day—and it's prime meat. The keeper skimmed off more than a pound a day from each animal. With twenty or thirty big cats in the collection, it added up. And he got a better price than the attendant got for dead animals."

"So what happened last night?"

"We caught them! A panel truck from Maynard Kimber was picking up the anteater, and we saw the driver give the attendant his money. The attendant tried to run off, but Karl tackled him." She gave him an admiring look, and he blushed.

"Why didn't you tell me about this?" I asked. "I'd have gone with you."

"You already had enough to worry about with your own situation," Margie said. "Anyway, we called the police and the zoo superintendent, Mr. Stephan. The driver got away, but the attendant confessed to everything. There should be a few more arrests soon." She was beaming and Karl was looking awfully pleased with himself.

I congratulated them on their success, and silently hoped that my upcoming engagement this afternoon would have an equally successful outcome.

O O O

Adela Whitaker sat behind her desk and I was in one of the two chairs in front of it. Neither of us spoke, and I had the feeling that behind her iron facade she was as nervous as I was. I kept glancing up at the portrait of her father; his stolid, homely face had a calming influence on me.

We were waiting for the phone to ring, but were both startled when it finally did. Adela picked up on the first jangle of the bell. She listened a moment, then said, "Send him in."

Nathaniel Bonner came into the office, ducking his tall frame as he passed through the doorway. Today his resemblance to the sixteenth president was closer to the Lincoln of the war years, with worry creasing his features.

Bonner and I exchanged curt nods. Adela said to him,

"Please have a seat." Once he'd done so, she went on, "As I mentioned on the telephone, I've decided to take you up on your offer. Mr. Rawlings here confirms that there is merit to your claim regarding my father's past indiscretion."

"I have no idea what you're talking about, Miss Whitaker," Bonner said.

She frowned. "I'm referring to—"

"Nice place," he interrupted, looking around. "I've thought of getting some of the modern amenities for my own office." He then looked from me to Adela. "Don't think I'll get a Dictaphone, though. Too noisy. You mind turning that thing off?"

Adela looked disappointed. Then she turned a switch on the machine behind her desk, and the whirring of the recording apparatus came to a stop.

Visibly more relaxed, Bonner asked me, "*Do* you have information, or was this just a ruse hoping I'd say something incriminating for the machine?"

"I know *you* don't have what you were looking for," I said. "Otherwise, you wouldn't have paid Rufus Yates's fine, or hired him to break into my house." I wasn't willing to say much more; there wasn't much that I knew for certain, and so I had to make it last, giving him one crumb at a time to make him think I knew more than I did.

"What Mr. Rawlings is proposing," Adela said, "is that, since he has the evidence that can verify your claim, you pay him a finder's fee, as it were. I think his proposition sounds reasonable."

He turned to me. "What size 'finder's fee' did you have in mind?"

"Whatever you were going to pay Ollie Perriman for the

entire collection. What I have is the only part of it you really wanted anyway."

Bonner slumped back and thought it over. He finally said quietly, "It would have been so much easier if he would have sold. Everything that followed is on his head—Perriman brought it all on himself by being too stubborn to sell."

Adela put in, "If he'd sold you his collection, you would have recouped the cost with the money you expected to get from me."

"Exactly," Bonner said. "What happened is partly your fault, too, you know. You threatened to charge me with attempted extortion. So I *had to* find the ledger"—he smiled—"so it could be genuine extortion."

Ledger? What ledger? I didn't know what he was referring to, but I tried not to look surprised. "You couldn't let Perriman know exactly what you wanted," I said, "so you had to try buying the whole lot. The day Perriman was killed, there was an announcement in the newspaper saying the exhibit would be opening soon. I take it that's when you decided you couldn't wait any longer."

He nodded. "Once it was on display, there wasn't much chance of ever getting it back. So I paid him a visit that night. Tried to get him to tell me where the ledger was."

"And he wouldn't." My mind was racing, trying to determine what ledger Bonner could be talking about. The one in which Perriman recorded his collection had still been in the office, so that couldn't be it.

Bonner shook his head. "Claimed he didn't know what I was talking about. And I did try to get it from him. Tied him up, punched him around a little . . ."

"Tried burning the old uniform, too?" I asked.

"Figured if he didn't care about himself, I'd see if he

cared about his precious relics. Set a match to the shirt, but he still wouldn't talk. So I put the fire out—that ledger was somewhere in the room, and it wasn't going to do me any good as a pile of ashes."

"And then you killed him."

"Wasn't planning it that way," Bonner said. "I brought the gun with me as a precaution—I don't make a habit of breaking into places at night. Then when Perriman wouldn't talk, I realized he'd tell what I'd done. And by that time I was furious that he didn't give me what I wanted. So ... I shot him."

"And later you found out that he'd given part of the collection to me. Why bring Rufus Yates into it? Why not do it yourself again?"

A distasteful expression curled his lips. "I didn't care for the experience. I decided it would be better in the hands of a professional."

Adela said, "You are not only a blackmailer and a murderer, Mr. Bonner. You are a coward."

His eyes narrowed. "My price just went up, Miss Whitaker." Then he leaned back farther in his chair and clasped his hands behind his head. "Now let's decide exactly how much it's going to cost you to keep the world from finding out your father built this business on money he embezzled from the old Red Stockings."

Embezzlement? This was supposed to be about the murder of Sarah Devlin.

He stretched out his long legs under her desk, then jumped at the clattering sound when his foot struck something. He was quickly on his knees, pulling out the base of a candlestick telephone. "What the hell is this?"

"It's a line to my secretary's office, Mr. Bonner. She has a Dictaphone also."

Bonner dashed to the door and pulled it open. Aaron Whitaker was standing outside, blocking his path. He had a shotgun in his hands and the muzzle was aimed at Bonner's chest. Aaron stepped forward, forcing Bonner back into Adela's office.

Adela calmly said, "We didn't know if you would be armed, Mr. Bonner. Now, my brother will keep you here until the police arrive." She looked at me. "Detective Forsch was the name, correct?"

I nodded, and she told her secretary to put in a call to the detective.

With a few exceptions, the meeting with Bonner had gone the way we'd planned. Adela and I expected him to notice the first Dictaphone; the idea was that once he discovered it and the recorder was turned off, he might feel secure that he'd thwarted our scheme and open up about what he'd done to Ollie Perriman. I didn't count on his long legs knocking over the phone under the desk, though. I'd hoped to get a lot more information.

I tried a few more questions while we waited for the police to arrive, but Bonner had clammed up completely.

Forsch arrived with several patrolmen. We gave him our statements and the disk from the secretary's recording machine, and he took Nathaniel Bonner into custody. Bonner refused to make any comment to the police, telling them to contact his attorney.

I was still trying to figure out the strange turn this had taken. Especially Bonner's charge about embezzlement from the Red Stockings. And what ledger had he been looking for?

Then I looked up at the portrait of Ambrose Whitaker and realized he wasn't the one who had killed Sarah Devlin.

O O O

At home that night, I finally told Margie and Karl all that had happened. I was uncertain whether confronting Nathaniel Bonner had been an overall plus or a minus. On the plus side, I had learned some more, and I had another idea on the role Sarah Devlin's murder played in things. But Bonner had thrown that curve about embezzlement, and failed to tell me anything that would get me out of trouble with respect to Rufus Yates. And, perhaps the biggest negative, I'd sure antagonized the man who might have given me more answers. If he continued to keep silent, some questions might never be resolved.

That's what the three of us discussed: the pressing need to find out more about Yates. And a question that was bothering me: how did he and Bonner happen to know each other—what was the connection between them?

Margie volunteered to contact the manager at the Palace Theater again and ask if he knew any other bookies she could contact about Yates. Karl was going to get in touch with Spider Jenkins to see if he had been able to dig up any additional information.

As for me, I was going to look for the ledger that had been the true target of Bonner's search.

There was nothing in the Wednesday morning newspapers about the Bonners or the Whitakers. Either the police department was being cautious in releasing information to the press, or the families had enough influence to keep the stories squelched for a while.

Lloyd Tinsley did make the front page. According to the paper, a date for the opening of the exhibit had finally been set: August 30. That date, three weeks away, had been chosen because it was Cal McVey's birthday, and the former Red Stocking had confirmed that he would attend the opening. Also scheduled to appear were Edd Roush, Eppa Rixey, Heinie Groh, and "Dick Hurley," who'd been released from the hospital two days ago. George Wright was still a maybe. There was no mention of me.

For now, the disappointment over being scratched from the grand opening was minor. Because the article did give me an idea on how I might be able to check out the ledger Nathaniel Bonner had been looking for.

OOO

John Cogan, "Dick Hurley" to everyone else, readily agreed to serve as my accomplice. I picked him up at the Sinton Hotel, and the two of us traveled by taxi to Redland Field. It pained me to know that I wasn't welcome at the park, but I put that aside.

The two of us found Lloyd Tinsley in his office, going over some paperwork. He looked up, obviously surprised to see either of us at the ballpark.

"Sorry to bother you," I said. "But Mr. Hurley here was hoping for an advance look at the collection."

"Yes," Cogan chimed in. "If I might, I'd like to spend a little quiet time looking over the mementos from my old team before it's opened to the public."

"I suppose that would be all right." Tinsley rose from his seat. "Why are *you* here, Rawlings?"

"At my request," Cogan said. "He told me at the dinner you so generously gave me that he was familiar with some of the items. So I asked him to show me around, and he kindly consented. With your permission, of course."

Tinsley's big jaw chewed from side to side. "Fine by me," he decided.

The business manager led us to Perriman's office, unlocked the door, and accompanied us inside. Tinsley remained with us, watching, as I pointed out to Cogan some of the 1869 relics Ollie Perriman had shown me. Each object inspired a long-winded "recollection" by the Dick Hurley impostor; some of the things he said I knew to be wrong, but Tinsley didn't. And for my purpose, it was the length of the yarns that counted, not their accuracy.

As I expected, Tinsley grew tired of listening; the same as at Cogan's dinner, when he'd barely spoken to the old-timer, he just wasn't interested. "I'll be in my office," he said. "Come let me know when you're finished."

When he was gone, Cogan winked at me, and whispered, "I'm afraid I've bored him."

"Yes, nice job." I immediately went to Perriman's desk, opened the top drawer, and pulled out the 1870 score book. "Could you check to see that he doesn't come back?"

Cogan walked to the door. As he did, I flipped to the back of the book, to the tallies of attendance and gate receipts that I'd seen before. I looked closer now, and saw that the pages were not originally part of the book but had been inserted and secured with tape. I carefully pulled out the two pages, folded them, and tucked them in an inside pocket of my jacket.

I replaced the score book in the drawer, then Cogan and I chatted for another fifteen minutes or so. We returned to Tinsley's office, where Cogan thanked him and said he'd better be getting back to his hotel room for some rest.

As Cogan and I left the park, I had mixed feelings. The mission had been a success, but it still nagged at me that the Reds were playing a baseball game this afternoon, and I couldn't be part of it.

O O O

I met Karl Landfors for lunch at Heuss House, a small German restaurant in Over-the-Rhine.

After ordering, I asked him, "Anything on Rufus Yates?" Ralph at the Palace Theater had given Margie the names of all the bookies he knew, and Karl was going to try to contact as many of them as he could about Yates.

"Not yet. But his former colleagues aren't early risers. I

have some leads, and I'll keep checking them out this afternoon and tonight. You have any luck?"

The waitress brought a beer for me and a glass of white wine for Karl. There were some communities where the Eighteenth Amendment was probably never going to be acknowledged.

I pulled the ledger sheets from my pocket and passed them over to Karl. "What do you make of these?"

He pushed his spectacles up on his nose and gave the pages a once-over. "What do I look like, an accountant?"

On a good day, he did; most days he resembled an undertaker. "I tried to read them on the trolley," I said. "Looks to me like they're for the same days, only the numbers are different."

Karl put the pages side by side and began to study them closely. The waitress returned with our meals, neither of which included sausage. After Margie's revelation about the zoo, I had the feeling it would be a long time before I'd even try a hot dog again.

While picking at a plate of noodles and cabbage, Karl completed his examination of the accounting entries. "I'm no expert," he said. "But I think what you have here is from a double set of books." He shoveled a pile of red cabbage into his mouth, and juice dripped down his chin as he went on, "The pages each have the same dates and game locations, but different attendance figures and gate receipts. Somebody was skimming off the difference between the higher and lower amounts."

"There's something else I noticed," I said. "All the dates are after July 2, 1869."

He glanced again at the entries. "You're right. But it could simply be that the earlier pages are missing."

"Could be. But these were the only ones in the score books."

I polished off the last of my potato pancakes. "Well, I'm off to the zoo."

"Going to see Margie?"

"Her too. But first I'm going to talk to Ambrose Whitaker."

○○○

The onetime Red Stockings bookkeeper was in a back-row seat outside the band shell, listening to an orchestra rehearse something that involved far too many trumpets. He was wearing a quaint three-piece suit, a homburg crowned his head, and his hands were clasped over the silver head of his cane.

Whitaker recognized me when I approached, and invited me to sit next to him.

"I guess Adela and Aaron must have told you what's been happening," I said.

"No . . . They don't tell me much anymore. Certainly nothing they think might upset me—they don't think my health can stand it." He smiled. "It's rather nice, really, the way they're protective of me."

I hesitated. I didn't want to trigger a heart attack or anything.

"But they underestimate my endurance," Whitaker said. "So why don't you go ahead and tell me?"

Okay, if he says he can handle it. "You wrote that note in the old baseball," I began. "Didn't you?"

His eyes remaining focused on the orchestra, Whitaker nodded.

"I thought maybe it was a confession," I continued, "but the man who met Sarah Devlin that night passed himself off as Dick Hurley. You didn't look anything like Hurley." It wasn't only that fact that Ambrose Whitaker had red hair, while Hurley's was black. Charlotte Ashby told me that Sarah claimed the player she going to meet was "one of the handsomest" on the team. It was when I'd looked again at his portrait in Adela's office that I realized there was no way, with his ungainly features, that Whitaker could have ever fit that description.

He murmured, "Her last name was Devlin, was it? I'd have contacted her family if I'd known."

"Other than the players, there weren't many young men at the banquet, were there?"

"No, mostly judges and business leaders. I was one of the youngest there."

"You and Josiah Bonner, who presented the giant bat." The pictures I'd seen of Bonner at the Queen City Lumber office showed him with dark hair and a mustache—he bore a fair resemblance to the *Frank Leslie's* illustration of the real Dick Hurley. "Josiah Bonner was the one who killed her, wasn't he? And you knew about it."

Whitaker's granite face betrayed nothing; his expression was as fixed and steady as a statue's. Then he gave a barely perceptible nod. "More than knew about it. I helped bury the poor girl."

"Tell me what happened." Since he'd at least taken the small step of leaving the note in the baseball, I thought Whitaker might be wanting to get it all off his chest.

His gaze dropped from the band shell to the ground at his feet. "In the summer of 1869, Josiah Bonner and I were a couple of up-and-comers in the Cincinnati business world. Both of us in our early twenties, and both getting a nice boost from our association with the Base Ball Club.

"Well, July 1 was the homecoming, and Josiah had his moment in the sun when he presented the team with that bat on behalf of the Queen City Lumber Company. That night, there was the banquet at the Gibson House. First time either Josiah or myself were among so many of the city's leading politicians and businessmen, and we were both convinced that we'd soon be part of that elite circle. With the company, and the champagne, and the excitement of the day, it was a heady experience.

"After the banquet, Josiah and I went outside, and there was still a crowd around the hotel door, mostly young ladies."

"George Wright tells me the ladies were ardent fans," I said.

"They were indeed," said Whitaker. "And that's how the trouble started. Josiah and me were among the few men at the dinner who were about the same age as the players; some of the ladies assumed we were part of the team when we came out, and they tossed flowers and garters at us. One girl asked if we were Red Stockings. I answered that I wasn't. Josiah was a faster thinker than I was, and he wasn't about to pass up an opportunity with a young lady. Claimed he was Dick Hurley, and I backed up his fib—it's what you do for a friend, and I didn't see any harm could come of it. Josiah and the girl went for a stroll, and I went on home.

"Next day, Josiah comes by and tells me things went well enough that he and the girl were going to see each other again that night. My family had a new phaeton, and he wanted to borrow the carriage to take her out for a midnight drive. Also wanted to borrow my best cuff links and a gold watch I'd been given for my birthday. I didn't mind lending him my things, but I knew my parents wouldn't agree to giving him the carriage, so I arranged for him to pick it up after they were asleep. I also told him that if he was planning to court the girl, he ought to fess up as to who he really was. He made it clear his intentions were of the short-term variety, however. Sorry to say, I didn't think there was anything wrong with that at the time—I was envious of him more than anything." He sighed. "Of course the older I got, the more I knew it wasn't right—he was dishonest, she was too young. I've wished a million times that I'd tried to stop him."

"You think you could have?"

"If I'd known what was going to happen, I'd have damn well made sure I stopped him." He folded his hands a little tighter over the head of his walking stick. "Couple hours before dawn, Josiah came knocking at my window. Said there'd been an accident: the girl had a seizure and died. He wanted me to help bury her.

"At first I argued, saying he should take her to a doctor or contact her family. He said she'd told him she had no family, and he didn't even know her last name. Only her first: Sarah. Josiah was all agitated, worrying that a scandal would dash his own future. Don't know why I agreed to help him—maybe it didn't seem real or it was the hour of the night or it was because of our long friendship—but I did. Got a couple of shovels and the two of us drove to Mount Adams with Sarah's body wrapped in a blanket behind the seat.

"We dug a grave, and then I froze. I couldn't touch her, couldn't help Josiah lay her in the ground. He did it himself, and in the course of moving her, part of the blanket fell away. She didn't die of a seizure. There was a red stocking knotted around her neck."

"Did he see you notice it?"

"Didn't say so at the time, but he noticed."

"You never went to the police?"

"I wanted to. The next day, I told Josiah he ought to confess and make the best of it. Said if he didn't, I'd go to the police myself and report what happened. That's when I found out that he was totally amoral."

"What'd he say?"

"It's what he'd done. When he put her in the grave, he put that watch of mine under her. It had my name and birthday engraved on it. If I ever told anyone and they dug her up, they'd find the watch. Josiah said he would swear that *I* killed her."

"Jeez. Couldn't you dig her up yourself and take the watch?"

"No. I considered it, but I knew I couldn't. Josiah knew it, too. He saw that I couldn't even touch her to carry her to the grave. No way could I dig her up and go feeling around for a watch."

This wasn't the way I'd imagined his story would go. After the meeting with Nathaniel Bonner in Adela Whitaker's office, I'd been trying to figure out who had killed Sarah if not Ambrose. What led me to think it was Josiah Bonner wasn't merely his resemblance to Dick Hurley or the fact that he was one of the few men at the banquet young enough to pass for a player. I believed the attempted extortion by his son—and the fact that it occurred only after Josiah was hospitalized—had to be more than coincidence. The scenario I envisioned was that Josiah Bonner and Ambrose Whitaker had been at a standoff over the decades; Bonner with evidence of Whitaker's embezzlement from the team, and Whitaker with the knowledge that Bonner had killed Sarah.

But it sounded like Josiah Bonner already had an effective way of keeping the former bookkeeper silent without the threat of going public about the embezzlement. So how did that fit in?

"Josiah Bonner wasn't the only one with a secret crime, though, was he?" I took the ledger pages from my pocket and held them out to him. "You were stealing money from the ball club." Since Ambrose Whitaker appeared relieved to be finally telling the story, I hoped he'd give the rest of it.

His bushy eyebrows merged in a frown. "Haven't seen these in fifty years," he said. "Yes, I took money from the club. Only way I had to pay Josiah."

"*Pay* him?"

"It was a small step for him from threatening to use the watch to implicate me if I went to the police to blackmailing me for cash. More cash than I could raise legally."

"So you took it from the team."

"Yes. And like I said before, the club was not a great financial success. The funds I took might have kept the club going for a while longer. Josiah came to think that, too. When the club started selling off its mementos, he managed to get the accounting ledgers. And when the new Reds team joined the National League in 1876, he said he would expose me as being the cause of the earlier club going bankrupt. By then, I'd started working on the inclined railways, and was earning a good living. Bonner wanted regular payments. And when I started my own business, he took 'consulting' fees. With the money he got from me, he bought controlling interest in the lumber company."

Josiah Bonner sure had Whitaker in a tight grip. "How long did it go on?"

"Until a few years ago. Josiah got sick, and had to go into a home. Hardly knows his own name anymore. So I stopped making the payments."

We sat in silence for a little while. He appeared to have gotten anything he wanted to say out of his system. And I was out of questions.

I finally thought of one more. "You went through all the trouble of putting that note in the baseball," I said. "Why didn't you give the details—and the names?"

He looked at me sadly. "Because I don't have any more guts now than I had in '69."

"Yes you do. You've told what happened now." I folded the pages from the account books. "If anything else comes up, can I talk to you again?"

"Certainly, son." He looked disappointed when I put the ledger sheets in my pocket; I was pretty sure he would have liked to have them.

O O O

Margie was a trouper, all right. I could see that her heart wasn't in it, but she went through with her performance, first telling a group of enthralled kids an entertaining fable about how tigers got their stripes and then explaining how the pattern really helped the animals stay hidden in tall grass.

I joined her after the show, and the two of us went into the Carnivora House, where she changed from her jungle outfit into a loose yellow summer dress.

"That was my last performance," she said when she came out of the ladies' rest room.

"What happened?"

"I quit." She packed her clothes and a few other items into a canvas satchel. "The zoo isn't pressing charges against the keeper for the meat theft."

"Why not?"

"They decided it wouldn't be good publicity for either the zoo or the sausage makers. Mr. Stephan said that as much as he would have liked to see the men in jail, they wouldn't have served much time—if any—and that it was probably better to make another arrangement."

I took the satchel from her. "What arrangement?"

"Both the keeper who was stealing the meat and the attendant who was selling the dead animals have been fired, and they have to pay back all the money they got. And Maynard Kimber is going to make an additional donation to the zoo to hire another full-time veterinarian."

"Maybe that will do more good in the long run."

"I understand the reasoning," Margie admitted. "I just wish Mr. Stephan would have taken my suggestion, too."

"And what was that?"

"To put the keeper who was stealing the animals' food in a cage for a few days—with nothing to eat."

I could tell that if it was up to her, she would have done exactly that. "C'mon," I said. "Let's go home."

Chapter Thirty-Two

OOO

I had no intention of going public with the fact that Josiah Bonner had murdered Sarah Devlin fifty-two years ago. To what end? It was unlikely that a prosecutor would file charges against him at this late date, especially since he was ailing and probably didn't have much time to live. And if Bonner had dementia, like his son said, he would probably be found unfit to stand trial anyway.

No, it wasn't Josiah Bonner I wanted to get. My target was Nathaniel.

OOO

Margie and I stayed up late waiting for Karl to get home. He finally got in at three o'clock, looking tired and a bit inebriated. He also had a cocky smirk on his lips that I knew meant he'd turned up something worthwhile.

"That was an adventure," he said, plopping onto the sofa. "Quite a bunch of characters you have in this city."

"Any trouble?"

Karl affected a miffed expression. "I've exposed crooked

politicians, union busters, and slumlords. You think I can't handle a few sports and bookies?"

Oh yeah, I could picture him fitting right in with the city's gambling element—like a glass of Moxie in a gin mill. "What did you find out?"

"Rufus Yates did have a connection to Arnold Rothstein. A distant one, but important." Karl gave us his report like a professor lecturing a class of dullards. "At the start of the 1919 World Series, rumors were rife that the fix was in. Bookmakers all around the country were watching closely to see who placed bets and on which team. If a major gambler like Rothstein put a large sum on the underdog, the odds would have changed drastically. So Rothstein, who operates out of New York, tried to get all the local Cincinnati boys he could to front for him. It was expected that folks here would bet on the hometown team, so that didn't raise any eyebrows."

"Must have taken a lot of people to put all that money down," I said. "I heard there were hundreds of thousands of dollars bet on the series."

"One man put down over twenty thousand of that," Karl said. "Not all with one bookie, but I've been totaling up his bets."

"It wasn't Yates," I said. "They'd know *he* couldn't come up with that much money on his own."

Then I realized who it had to be. Karl and I said in one voice, "Lloyd Tinsley."

No one would have questioned a Reds official placing bets on his own team.

"Yates must have gotten Tinsley to front for Rothstein," I said. Maybe they'd been involved in similar activities together back in Wichita. Or maybe Tinsley thought he'd never take over Frank Bancroft's job as business manager and decided to make his fortune by accepting Yates's proposal. "Wonder how much Tinsley got out of it?"

"I understand ten percent of the winnings is the standard fee for such a service," Karl said. One night with the sporting types, and he thinks he's an expert.

Margie spoke up. "What about Rufus Yates approaching the Reds players to try to get them to throw the series the other way? That doesn't make sense."

Karl answered, "It was a token effort, and it didn't come until a couple of games into the series. The word was out about Rothstein fixing the series, and the odds had dropped. Yates just wanted to get the rumor mill going the other way— to swing the odds back in Rothstein's favor, not to change the outcome."

We finally all decided to call it a night. On the way upstairs, I asked, "How much you lose, Karl?"

His shoulders sagged. "Hundred and twenty."

I didn't think his newfound expertise had come cheaply. "I'll give it to you in the morning. And thanks for all you did tonight."

"Hope it helps."

"Me too." I only wished I knew how it could.

O O O

I was wishing even harder when I read the telegram that arrived for me in the morning. It was from Judge Kenesaw Mountain Landis. He wanted to see me in his office ten o'clock Monday morning. This was Thursday, and I'd have to be on a train by Sunday. That meant I had three days to find a way of convincing him that I had nothing to do with

Rufus Yates when he was alive and had no involvement in his death.

My first step was to put in a call to Detective Forsch. I asked if Nathaniel Bonner had admitted setting me up with Yates.

"No," the detective answered. "Matter of fact, he isn't talking at all. His lawyers are doing that for him. And one of the things they're saying is that they want kidnapping charges filed against you and Aaron and Adela Whitaker."

"*What?*"

"His lawyers claim that the three of you coerced his 'confession' from him at gunpoint."

"That's not true! Aaron didn't put the shotgun on him until he tried to leave. Everything he said was voluntary—you heard it."

"No, I didn't. The recording you technical geniuses made sounds like one long hissing noise. You must have had the phone too far away."

Jeez. "What if the three of us testify about what he said?"

"Well, that's something. But not a whole lot. We can't just go by what somebody says they heard. We got to have proof."

"Well, that's not—"

He cut me off. "I wouldn't complain about that if I were you. Remember, there's this Knucksie goon who says you tried to hire him to kill Rufus Yates—but I haven't arrested you, have I?"

"No."

"That's because there's got to be credible evidence. You and the Whitakers holding a man at gunpoint and then testifying that he confessed something isn't all that credible is it?"

"But we didn't—Well, not when you put it that way, it doesn't."

"That's the way his lawyers will put it."

"So what's gonna happen?"

"We'll hold him a little longer. *Maybe* we'll charge him with attempted extortion, but no way is the district attorney going to go ahead with a murder charge based on what we have now."

' "Did you search his place? Maybe he still has the gun that killed Ollie Perriman—or Rufus Yates."

"Thanks for the tip on how to do police work. Of course we searched. They were both shot with a thirty-eight. There was no thirty-eight in Bonner's house." Anticipating my next question, he added, "Didn't find one at the lumber company either."

"All right. Any idea when you might go ahead with the extortion charge?"

"By end of tomorrow. The D.A. says we can't hold him over the weekend without a charge."

"At least that will keep him in jail for a while."

"Not after tomorrow, it won't. He'll post bond as soon as we charge him."

"Damn." The man who'd admitted murdering Oliver Perriman would be out in twenty-four hours.

○ ○ ○

Margie and Karl offered a number of suggestions on what to do, but when it came down to a final decision they left it up to me. I was the one who'd had the most contact with Bonner, Tinsley, and the Whitakers, and it was my career that depended on proving to Judge Landis that I was clean.

I thought over all sorts of possibilities before settling on the one that seemed most likely to succeed.

I asked Karl, "You know anybody here where you can get something printed up real quick?"

"I used to know a fellow who put out Socialist handbills. But he got sent to jail for it during the war, and I don't know if he's back in business."

"Could you try to track him down?"

"Sure. What do you need?"

I explained what I had in mind. Then Karl left to track down his friend, and Margie went to the library. Neither of them said so, but I could tell they weren't optimistic that the scheme would work.

I wasn't either, but there was one man who could help me sell it. I called Ambrose Whitaker.

○ ○ ○

Friday morning, Ambrose Whitaker and I paid a call on Nathaniel Bonner in Central Station, the holding area in the basement of City Hall for prisoners awaiting trial. Overall, security wasn't as tight as at the Work House, but our meeting was under the watchful eye of an armed police officer.

Bonner said with a smirk, "You don't have another Dicta-phone with you by any chance."

"Tried to hide one in my pocket," I said, "but the guard took it in the search."

Ambrose Whitaker began, "Thank you for seeing us, Mr. Bonner. I know you are going to find what we have to say to be quite interesting."

"Nothing else to do in here," Bonner said. Still smirking,

he added, "But make it quick. My lawyer says I'll be out of here in a couple hours."

We were out of earshot of the guard, but Whitaker kept his voice low when he continued, "You were quite right about me embezzling from the Red Stockings fifty years ago. But do you know why I did it?"

Bonner snorted. "For the money."

"That's right. To make blackmail payments to your father."

The smirk vanished. "What are you talking about?"

Whitaker then related the same story he'd told me about Josiah Bonner and Sarah Devlin. It was clear from the younger Bonner's expression that this was news to him. I didn't think he was aware of what his father had done; otherwise, he wouldn't have run the risk of exposure by trying to blackmail the Whitakers. It was also clear that he was debating with himself, trying to decide if it was possible that what he was now hearing was the truth.

"What's your point in spinning a yarn like that?" Bonner asked. "You're slandering a man who can't defend himself anymore. I don't believe a word you say."

"The point," Whitaker went on calmly, "is that I am prepared to give a formal statement regarding the events of 1869, and of subsequent years when I paid blackmail money to keep your father in business. Unless . . ."

"Unless what? You want money? You're going to try a little blackmail of your own?"

"I don't want money," Whitaker answered. "And you may call it what you like. The fact of the matter is that unless you give a complete and honest account about the deaths of Oliver Perriman and Rufus Yates, I will proceed to tell my own story."

Bonner shook his head. "The ramblings of an old man. Nobody'll believe you."

"There's more," I said. "Charlotte Ashby—the woman who shot Dick Hurley—was a friend of Sarah Devlin's. She'll confirm a lot of what Mr. Whitaker is saying."

"Like what? That some girl met a fellow who claimed to be Dick Hurley in 1869? Hell, that could have been anyone. Including you, Whitaker." Despite his defiant words, Bonner's expression was downcast and his tone lacked conviction. I had the sense that he was starting to realize that what Ambrose Whitaker was saying was the truth.

I took a small notebook from my pocket, and pulled a scrap of ancient paper from the protection of its pages. "Got this at the library," I said. "It's the newspaper account of the banquet. Says the players were given pins in the shape of red stockings. Also says toward the end of the party, Dick Hurley was so grateful to your father for including his name on the big bat that he gave him his pin." I held out the paper. "Read it yourself. The library has more copies, by the way, so there's no sense destroying it." As he studied the clipping, I added, "Charlotte Ashby will testify that the 'player' Sarah met was wearing such a pin."

He looked at the paper long and hard, then handed it back to me. I quickly slipped it back in the notebook before Bonner could notice that his thumb had smudged the ink.

"So what?" Bonner said stubbornly. "My father isn't competent to stand trial. Doesn't matter what you say, or what kind of evidence you have, no judge in this county is going to let a murder charge against him proceed."

"You're quite right," Whitaker said. "My intention is to testify at *your* trial, to describe the origin of your extortion scheme. And I am prepared to show where your father and

I buried Sarah Devlin. I'm sure an exhumation would provide further evidence to support my story."

"And what about your mother," I said. "You told me how hard your father's illness has been on her. What do you think it would do to her to find out that the man she's been married to for forty years is a murderer?"

Nathaniel Bonner was no longer defiant. We let him think for a few minutes. "And if I do confess," he said, "then nothing about my father comes out?"

Whitaker and I both promised we would reveal nothing about what happened in 1869.

His head low, Bonner nodded. "I'll make a statement."

○ ○ ○

We'd all moved to a larger room in the station, and had been joined by Detective Forsch, two patrolmen, an assistant district attorney, and a stenographer.

Bonner began by confessing to the murder of Oliver Perriman, giving the same account he had in Adela Whitaker's office. His objective, he admitted, was to find the Red Stockings accounting ledger so that he could use it to blackmail the Whitakers.

He continued, "So Perriman was dead, and I still didn't have the ledger. That's when I thought up the idea of presenting a bat like my father did and getting involved with the exhibit—that way I'd have a chance to look around some more.

"But Lloyd Tinsley caught me going through Perriman's desk. I swear he could read on my face what I'd done. I'm not ashamed to admit that I'm no cold-blooded killer. I was angry at Perriman . . . frustrated . . . that's why I shot him. It wasn't something I planned."

"Yes, you mentioned that before," Forsch said. The detective was unmoved by Bonner's attempts to diminish the severity of his crime. "Go on."

"Tinsley got me to tell him what I was looking for. But he didn't want to turn me in. He said Perriman was going to stay dead no matter what, so there was no point worrying about it. The question was what to do next—and that was to find the ledger. He didn't say so, but I think Tinsley was expecting a pretty good cut for himself. He told me that Perriman had given some things to Rawlings and that I should check it out. I didn't have it in me to go through that again myself, though. So Tinsley told me he knew somebody who could help: Rufus Yates. I gave Yates the money to get out of jail, and he broke into Rawlings's house."

Forsch raised the question I'd asked him to. "How did Tinsley know Yates?"

"Yates played for Wichita when Tinsley ran that club. Then in 1919, Yates was here in Cincinnati. When New York gamblers were looking for locals to lay down bets on the Reds for them, Yates convinced Tinsley to put down twenty grand. Tinsley got ten percent for doing it."

"Tinsley told you this?" Forsch asked.

Bonner shook his head no. The assistant district attorney instructed him to avoid answering with gestures. "No," Bonner said. "Yates told me."

"After you had Yates search Rawlings's house, then what?" Forsch asked.

"Then it was out of my hands. At first, I was glad to listen to Tinsley. He had a clear head, and I was pretty nervous about things. But then he kept calling the shots, and there was no way I could refuse him—he could have turned me in at any time.

"Anyway, with the Sox trial going on, Tinsley's main interest became protecting himself. If it came out that he'd fronted for gamblers in '19, he'd be out of baseball for sure, and probably in jail. One of the things he worried about was Rawlings poking around—thought he might have found something on that World Series. So he had Yates and me set him up. I took the picture of the two of them and sent it to Garry Herrmann.

"Then Yates caught on to how worried Tinsley was about being found out and he started blackmailing Tinsley. So Tinsley had me ..." Bonner's voice faded and he looked away.

"Had you what?" Forsch prompted.

"Lloyd Tinsley had me kill Rufus Yates."

"Thought you weren't a cold-blooded killer," Forsch said. "How'd he get you to do that?"

"He told me that Yates already knew about me killing Perriman. I asked him how he found out, and Tinsley said he told him. Tinsley set it up so I *had* to kill him."

"Rawlings had nothing to do with it?" Forsch asked.

"No. Tinsley paid that Knucksie goon to say that Rawlings tried to hire him to kill Yates. He figured that way both Yates and Rawlings were taken care of, and nobody would find out about him taking Arnold Rothstein's money."

Forsch and the assistant district attorney asked a few more questions, Nathaniel Bonner answered every one of them, and the stenographer got it all on paper. But I'd already heard enough to know I'd be able to make the case I needed to Judge Landis.

ooo

The train ride to Chicago Sunday morning was one I actually enjoyed. I was confident with the knowledge that Lloyd Tinsley and Nathaniel Bonner were both behind bars and that a copy of Bonner's statement had been sent by special messenger to Judge Landis. Only one development was disappointing: because of all the negative publicity surrounding the collection, Garry Herrmann had decided to postpone indefinitely the exhibit to honor the 1869 Red Stockings.

The return trip Monday was even better. Landis had cleared me, and even said a few words that came about as close as I expected he ever got to apologizing. And I'd be back in time for the Tuesday game in Redland Field against the New York Giants.

ooo

Ambrose Whitaker came to the game as my guest, and afterward the two of us took a trolley to Eden Park.

We walked along a lane north of the reservoir. Soft, warm

breezes rippled through the trees. A number of picnickers were in the park taking advantage of the mild weather and late sunshine. Two small boys were flying a kite, and several other children were playing a game of tag.

As we neared the water tower, Whitaker drew to a stop. With his cane, he pointed to a grassy area where a young couple were eating a basket dinner in the shade of a magnificent oak tree. "That's where Sarah Devlin is buried," he said.

"By the tree?"

"Directly under it. I planted that oak as a seedling a few months after we buried her. My intention was to hide the crime; I thought nobody would dig underneath a tree. I've come here often since then, seen it grow over the years. As time passed, I stopped worrying about anyone finding her body. I got to thinking of that oak as a monument—a living headstone."

"It's prettier than any headstone I've ever seen," I said.

We stared at the burial spot for a while, then resumed strolling. "I've made another confession," Whitaker said. "Went to see Charlotte Ashby in the Work House. I explained everything that happened."

"How'd she take it?"

"Not too badly. I asked her if Sarah Devlin left any family that she knew of; I wanted to tell them what happened, too. Mrs. Ashby says the family's all gone by now; there's no one to tell. And she didn't seem to hold it against me that I've never come forward before now. She says it's probably best to keep it a secret at this point. Poor woman's feeling like a fool herself for shooting that Dick Hurley impostor. Letting something fester for years like that can certainly warp your judgment."

"She's probably going to spend the rest of her life in jail for it," I said.

"Perhaps not. Mrs. Ashby said she will talk to the police now, and tell them that she thought the man she shot was somebody else—won't mention anything about Sarah or Hurley, though. She'll try to make them think she's just a dotty old woman and hope for mercy. The fellow didn't die, so maybe she has a chance."

"He won't be testifying against her, either," I said. "He's left town." John Cogan had decided to end his Dick Hurley impersonation; he'd sent me a note, telling me he was going back home to Indiana, and thanking me for not exposing his charade.

"Well, then she might only receive a light sentence."

"I hope she does get out again."

"So do I," said Whitaker. "When she does, I'm going to bring her here to see the tree."

His pace picked up, and I asked him something I'd wondered about for some time. "I understand you retired from business for health reasons," I said. "If you don't mind me asking, what's wrong with you?"

"Not a thing." He smiled wryly. "When Josiah Bonner became ill a few years ago, it started me thinking. One thing I thought about was the past; that's when I decided to leave some record of what happened in 1869, so I put that note in the baseball. And I also thought about the future. Nathaniel Bonner, I knew, had a great deal of difficulty when he replaced his father as head of the lumber company. Josiah had left it in poor financial shape and had never taught his son the skills necessary to run a business. By the time Nathaniel had to assume control, Josiah was no longer capable of helping him learn the ropes. I didn't want that to happen with my children. So I decided to let Aaron and Adela think I was too ill to continue working, and let them take charge of the business. In the event anything went wrong, I could still step back in and help them out."

"Maybe it would be a good idea to tell them what really happened," I said. "They're probably imagining some pretty bad things right now, after all they heard from Nathaniel Bonner. Might be better that they know the truth. I think they can take it."

"I suppose you're right. It has been good to be getting things out in the open."

He turned to me. "Now I've got a question for you."

"Yes?"

"I realize my memory isn't what it used to be, but I've been trying hard as I can, and I don't remember Dick Hurley giving Josiah Bonner a red-stocking pin at the banquet."

"That was a bluff," I said. "I thought something in print might help convince Nathaniel Bonner of your story. Looks more like solid evidence." I'd torn a blank page from one of the old guides Perriman had given me, Karl Landfors wrote a revised report on the banquet, and his friend printed it up to look like a genuine newspaper clipping.

I reached into my jacket pocket, and handed Whitaker the pages from the accounting ledger. "These are for you." I could see no reason why his embezzlement from the Red Stockings should ever be revealed. "Might want to make a little fire when you get home," I suggested.

○ ○ ○

After leaving Ambrose Whitaker at Eden Park, I walked home. In front of our house, Erin Kelly was jumping rope while her brother and several playmates watched from the stoop. Margie twirled one end of the rope, and Karl Landfors, looking as animated as a hitching post, held the other. From his expression, I had the feeling he was wishing that he was already back in Boston.

The game stopped when I arrived. The children all ran off to play elsewhere, and Margie, Karl, and I went into the parlor.

Over a round of lemonades, I told them about my talk with Whitaker.

Karl said, "There's something I don't understand. How did Nathaniel Bonner get the idea to try blackmailing Adela Whitaker?"

That was something Ambrose and I had asked him. "Soon after he took over Queen City Lumber," I said, "he checked the accounts and found that his father had been getting regular 'consulting fees' from the Whitakers' company. He asked his father about it. Never got a single coherent answer, but he kept trying until he had enough bits and pieces to put it together. He understood that his father had blackmailed Ambrose Whitaker for embezzling from the old Red Stockings and that the Bonners had the accounting ledger to prove it. Nathaniel decided it should continue to the next generation, and went to Adela Whitaker. It wasn't until Adela told him to show her proof that he looked for it. What he didn't know was that his father hadn't kept the whole ledger. Josiah had put the account pages in the back of the score book—that way if the Whitakers ever tried to find the ledger, they'd come up empty." Bonner hadn't included this in his official statement because he would say nothing to incriminate his father.

"Was it because the lumber company was in financial straits that he needed the money?" Karl asked.

"That's what I assumed," I said. "From seeing the lumberyard, I could tell that business was way down from earlier years. But Bonner said even if he didn't need the money, he'd have done it because it was 'his due.' "

Margie asked, "How did Ollie Perriman end up with the accounting pages in the first place? If Josiah Bonner had been using them to blackmail Ambrose over the years, how did Perriman get them? And how did Nathaniel Bonner know Perriman had them?"

"Bonner told me his mother was the baseball fan of the family," I answered. "When Perriman started putting his collection together, Mrs. Bonner donated a box of material that her husband had from the old Red Stockings. Josiah was in a home, and Nathaniel had no interest in baseball, so she decided to give everything to Perriman for the exhibit. She didn't know what was in the score book."

I smiled, remembering two months ago when Patrick Kelly uttered the lament so many boys have spoken over the years: my mother threw out my baseball cards. Then I imagined Nathaniel Bonner in prison, and wondered if he would be voicing a similar complaint to his fellow inmates.

In 1934, Powel Crosley, Jr. purchased the Cincinnati Reds, and Redland Field was renamed Crosley Field.

The final game in the historic ballpark was played on June 24, 1970. At the time, the former brickyard at Findlay and Western was the longest continuous site of major league baseball, dating back to 1884.

Crosley Field was torn down in 1972, but has been partially reconstructed in Blue Ash, northeast of Cincinnati. The scoreboard appears exactly as it did at the moment of the last pitch of the final game.

Please turn the page for an exciting sneak preview of

Hanging Curve by Troy Soos—

a Fall, 1999, hardcover release from
Kensington Publishing Corp.

Chapter One

○○○

Springtime. The enchanted season of rebirth and hope, when every wishful dream seems destined to become reality. The exhilarating time of year when career .200 hitters imagine winning the batting championship, dead-armed pitchers feel strong enough to win thirty games, and St. Louis baseball fans believe that this will be the year the Browns finally capture an American League pennant.

The post-game crowd straggling out of Sportsman's Park certainly had the seasonal fever. As I lingered near the Dodier Street gate, I overheard confident predictions of a championship. According to some, the Browns would be powered to success by the bats of George Sisler and Ken Williams. Others put their faith in the pitching arms of Urban Shocker and Dixie Davis. Not one mentioned the name "Mickey Rawlings," but since pennant hopes rarely ride on a team's utility players, I was accustomed to being overlooked.

A few fans claimed that the city's National League Cardinals, managed by Branch Rickey and sparked by the hitting of Rogers Hornsby, would also win their first title. If so, the entire 1922 World Series would be played right here in North St. Louis, in the classic ballpark that both teams called home.

I began to drift along with the crowd toward Grand Boulevard, where packed trolleys slowly shuttled fans home. I sidled close to a group of men near me, eavesdropping on their optimistic discussions, and hoping their fever would prove contagious. Because, so far, I didn't have it. Spring was arriving late for me this year.

The traditional signs of early April were abundant. Robins sang in the elms and sycamores that lined the street, and daffodils bloomed in the city parks. Mild weather had relegated winter overcoats to the closet, and most of the automobiles crawling by were open-topped touring cars and roadsters.

But of course the true harbinger of sping is the start of a new baseball season. Here, too, the outward signs were all positive. With the Browns' opener four days away, the roster was the strongest in the club's history, and the team was already on a winning roll. Today's 6–3 win over the Cards, before a record crowd of almost 30,000 in the final game of the city series, gave us the championship of St. Louis and a 20–1 record for the preseason.

By any objective criteria, everything looked promising. However, the *feeling* of springtime—the internal buoyancy that lightens every step—eluded me.

So in my mind's eye, I jumped six months ahead, imagining that today's game had indeed been a preview of the World Series, and trying to envision myself playing in my first Fall Classic. I could see the packed stands draped with bunting and streamers, and hear the cheers, and smell fresh-roasted peanuts. But I couldn't conjure up an image that included me in any part of the *action*. All I could imagine for myself was watching the Series from the bench. Well, at least that would be an improvement over the way any of my previous seasons had ended.

Could that be the problem? Perhaps it was the experience of seasons past that kept me from getting my hopes up about this one. After ten years of big-league ball, with six different teams, I'd been through enough Aprils and enough Septembers to know that the promise of spring is a hollow one. I wasn't going to win a batting championship—hell, I'd be lucky to end up within a hundred points of the champion. And if I managed to last the entire season with my new team, would I end up playing in my first World Series? Unlikely. I'd already played for some of the best clubs in baseball history, and never got to fulfill that dream.

So here I was, a thirty-year-old utility infielder, in a new city, with a new team, but no reason to believe that the new season would bring a change of fortune.

Stepping more quickly, I was about to hop a streetcar for home when a gruff voice behind me called, "Hey, Rawlings! They don't even let you play in a game that don't mean nuthin'?"

I turned to see a hulking, bareheaded man of about forty approaching. His homely face was familiar, but I couldn't quite place him. "I know you?"

He smiled, exposing several scattered brown teeth and a great deal of barren gum. "Chicago. 1918."

It took me another moment, then I pictured him in a Cubs uniform. "Wicket Greene," I said. "I'll be damned." His hands remained jammed in the pockets of his ill-fitting Norfolk jacket, and I didn't offer mine. Our acquaintance wasn't one that I'd ever hoped to renew.

Greene's dark eyes seemed to withdraw deeper into their sockets. "Nobody calls me that no more."

"Oh, sorry." When we were teammates on the Cubs, Greene had picked up the 'Wicket' tag because of his knack for letting ground balls through his legs at third base. His real name didn't come to mind.

"It's 'Tater' now," he said, sounding proud of the new nickname. He probably got it because his balding, lumpy head resembled a spud, but at least it was no slur on his playing skills.

"What are you doing now?" I asked. Greene had remained on the Cubs roster during the Great War primarily because he was too old to be drafted. As far as I knew, his baseball career had ended when the Armistice allowed younger players to leave the battlefields for a return to the ballfields.

"I'm in the automobile business," he answered. "Monday to Friday, anyhow. Weekends, I still play ball." He gestured to a row of curbside pushcarts, where vendors were aggressively hawking their last sausages and pretzels to the dwindling passersby. "You want a dog?"

I was tempted, but shook my head no. Margie would have dinner waiting at home.

"I'm gettin' one." As we walked over to the cart, he said, "I play in East St. Louis. It's only semipro, but the club's a good one—better than a lot of minor league teams I seen." Greene flipped the vendor a dime for a sausage with kraut. "That's what I want to talk to you about."

I couldn't see where he was going with this conversation —and it wasn't one that I wanted to prolong. "What you mean?"

Greene hooked one of his remaining teeth into the frank-furter and tore off a bite. As he chewed, he spit out the answer. "Want you to play for us."

I fought back a chuckle. "Why would I want to go from the St. Louis Browns to a semipro outfit?"

"We'll give you ten bucks to play in one game. Tomorrow afternoon."

"Sorry, can't do it. Fohl wants us rested for Opening Day." Browns manager Lee Fohl would fine me a lot more than ten dollars if he learned that I'd hired myself out to another team.

Greene snorted, and a piece of bread fell from his lip. "Browns give you any more rest, you might as well trade in your mitt for a pillow."

His comment hit me like a kick in the stomach. It was an accurate assessment, and it probably explained why I couldn't catch the spirit of the season: It's hard to dream of batting .400 when they won't even let you in the batter's box. The Brown's weren't giving me enough of a taste of the game to be teased into hope.

"Besides," Greene coaxed, "the Browns won't find out. You'll be wearing our uniform, and you won't be using your real name."

"You mean—"

"What the other team don't know won't—" His mouth gaped open in an ugly grin. "Come to think of it, if you play good, it *will* hurt them."

I was flattered that they wanted to bring me in as a ringer, and mulled it over for a moment. I could use the practice, after all, and maybe playing would give me that spark of spring fever I so badly needed. But I wasn't convinced that it was a wise idea; if Fohl got wind of it, I might not get into a Browns game for a very long time. "Sorry. Wish I could help you, Wick—uh, Tater."

"We could really use you," Greene persisted. "We're going up against a helluva club, and need to field the best players we can find. Got a lot riding on this game."

As much as I liked being counted among "the best play-ers," I again declined.

"Might be something a little different for you, too. Team we're playin' is colored. You ever play against coloreds?"

"No. Always wanted to, though." I'd wished for years that I could get in a game with Negro players. Since it didn't appear that such a game would ever be played on a major league diamond, this might be my best chance.

"Them boys can sure play ball," Greene said.

"Yeah, I know. I've been to their games." I'd seen some of the Negro League's best teams—Kansas City Monarchs, Chicago Giants, Indianapolis ABCs, Detroit Stars—and I was impressed by their talent and their style. "I'd like to," I admit-ted. "But I'm not sure . . ."

Greene pulled a pencil and a scrap of paper from his pocket and scribbled a number. "Gimme a call tonight." He sounded confident that he had me.

Remembering some of the colored pitchers I'd seen, like Bullet Joe Rogan and Dizzy Dismukes, I imagined myself stepping to the plate against them. And I knew he had me, too. "You sure nobody'll find out?" I asked.

"Hell, you think we want 'em to know we had to bring in ringers?" He handed me the paper. "By the way, it ain't just your bat and glove we need. You still know how to use your dukes?" Greene had had some experience with my fists when we were on the Cubs; his and mine hadn't been a friendly relationship.

"Can fight if I have to," I said. "But if I go, it's only to play ball."

"There's been some bad blood between the teams the last few years." He gave me a playful punch to the shoulder. "Expect to be doing both."